MW01473137

“Just when I thoug d me with a plot twist. I enjoy unforeseen villains, and *Lake of the Cross* delivers the unexpected.”

—Stacey Weeks
Author of *In Too Deep* (2017), *The Builder's Reluctant Bride* (winner of Best Christian Romance 2016), *Glorious Surrender* (winner of the Women's Journey of Faith 2016) and *Unexpected Love* (Finalist in Best Inspirational/Devotional of 2016)
www.staceyweeks.com

“L.D. Stauth has done it again! Suspense, intrigue, romance and humour, with a tasteful sprinkling of faith, compel the reader toward the very last page. *Lake of the Cross* is an excellent read.”

—Lisa Elliott
Inspirational Speaker and award-winning author of *The Ben Ripple* and *Dancing in the Rain*

“In her second book, *Lake of the Cross*, L.D. Stauth not only offers another good, clean read, she weaves lessons on wilderness survival, she interlaces the importance of friendship, the joy of relationship and she also manages to gently assure the reader that God loves us despite our imperfections.

Lest one thinks that *Lake of the Cross* is a tame, predictable book, it is far from that designation. Intrigue, romance, faith, high-adventure and mystery are only some of the labels I would gladly add to this title. Linda has a way with marvellous metaphors and she has a wonderful ability to create believable, stubborn, compassionate, tender characters; a charming gift that she shares with her readers.

Lake of the Cross is a work of fiction but because of Linda's love of the lake and her stunning descriptions I found myself being transported and wishing I could experience firsthand, some of the magnificence.

I highly recommend this book to anyone who enjoys a page-turner with a twist."

—Glynis M. Belec
writer@glynisbelec.com
www.glynisbelec.com
Angel Hope Publishing
angelhopepublishing@glynisbelec.com

A Campground Mystery #2

LAKE OF THE CROSS

L.D. STAUTH

LAKE OF THE CROSS
Copyright © 2018 by L.D. Stauth

All rights reserved. Neither this publication nor any part of this publication may be reproduced or transmitted in any form or by any means, electronic or mechanical, including photocopying, recording or any information storage and retrieval system, without permission in writing from the author.

This book is a work of fiction. Names, characters, incidents and setting (with the exception of a few named cities or towns) are fictitious and are a product of the author's imagination. Any similarity between persons (living or dead), places or events is purely coincidental.

Printed in Canada

ISBN: 978-1-4866-1582-7

Word Alive Press
119 De Baets Street, Winnipeg, MB R2J 3R9
www.wordalivepress.ca

Cataloguing in Publication may be obtained through Library and Archives Canada

"For since the creation of the world God's invisible qualities—his eternal power and divine nature—have been clearly seen, being understood from what has been made, so that people are without excuse."
—Romans 1:20 (NIV version, Zondervan 2011)

ACKNOWLEDGEMENTS

And so, this unbelievable journey continues.

Lake of the Cross would not have been possible without the encouragement and support of so many wonderful people. It's almost impossible to thank each one individually, but there are a few that have stood out over the course of the launch, many book signings, and sales for *Stormy Lake*.

My sister Gloria Richmond, promoted my first novel with zealous fervour among her co-workers and friends in Colchester and Kingsville, Ontario. Thank you, sis, for your continual support and love. A shout out also to Dagmar Ray and her book club ladies in Colchester. You spoiled me rotten.

Dr. Malcolm Carlson, pathologist at Stratford General Hospital, provided the wonderful opportunity for a book signing in the hospital lobby. Considering there was a demented pathologist in *Stormy Lake*, it was incredibly big of him. Of course, no similarity at all.

The continued support of family, friends, and co-workers always blows my mind.

Glynis Belec, your kind words fuel my desire to keep writing, even though I often feel inadequate for the task.

My editor, Sara Davison, keeps my head on straight. Humour is not appropriate in the climax of a suspense novel. Who knew? Just kidding. She is an amazing editor.

Ann Brent, my lifelong BFF, I couldn't have walked the 'author road' without you.

To all my readers and fans out there—your reviews and comments amaze and humble me. Keep them coming. They go a long way.

I've saved the best for last. Thank you, God, for not only opening doors, but blowing them right off their hinges (Ann Brent's apt description).

Stay tuned for book #3—*Starry Lake*.

PROLOGUE

"I don't know why Maya agreed to get married like this." Karly leaned toward Blake and whispered in his ear, careful not to tip her lawn chair. "I'm an outdoor enthusiast, but this is a bit much."

"Shush!" Blake waved a hand at her. "They're in the middle of their vows. I can't hear what they're saying."

Karly snorted. "I'm not surprised. With the waves crashing against the sides of the dock, seagulls squawking overhead, and the booming thunder from that approaching storm, I'm amazed we can hear anything at all. Who in their right minds would get married in fluorescent orange lifejackets, in a bobbing canoe, no less, while their guests undulate in lawn chairs on a floating dock?"

Blake nudged her gently in the upper arm with his elbow. "It's unique and very romantic. Now could you please stop talking for one second, so I can listen?"

Karly sighed, crossed her long legs, and attempted to focus her attention on the ceremony.

Maya smiled longingly into her groom's face and soaked in every word as Kerrick promised to love, honour, and cherish her until death parted them.

Did her best friend really know what she was doing? After all, it had been only eleven months since Maya first met the handsome park superintendent. Wasn't she rushing things a little? What was the hurry?

Of course, Karly had no one to blame but herself. If she hadn't suggested camping none of this would have ever happened. But she had, and it did. In fact, it seemed that from the moment Maya and Kerrick had laid eyes on each other, right on this very dock, it was game over. Which was slightly different than the way she and Blake had started out.

Karly would never have guessed, from their first few encounters, that they would end up dating. If that's what they were doing. With her in Kitchener and Blake still living in North Beaver Falls, they'd only seen each other a handful of times over the last several months. Long distance dating was extremely hard. And their relationship seemed stalled or in some sort of holding pattern.

"I now pronounce you husband and wife. You may kiss your bride."

A lump the size of a tennis ball lodged itself in Karly's throat as Kerrick leaned forward, making a valiant effort to claim Maya's lips in a rocking canoe.

When his first try resulted in a miss, his lips brushing her chin, Maya giggled, triggering a rolling wave of snickers across the handful of guests.

Karly pressed both hands to her cheeks. "If that was me, I'd be so embarrassed, I'd probably dive overboard."

"It's not you."

Was that annoyance in Blake's voice?

The happy couple now stood, wobbling precariously, arms wrapped around each other and lips locked, while the dock rang out with applause from the guests.

Kerrick and Maya had arranged for a barbecue under a pavilion, close to the lake. After the cake cutting and wedding dance, Karly slipped from the picnic table to stretch her legs. Where was Blake? He'd disappeared just before the dance.

A beautiful sunset cast a pink glow over the now tranquil water. Thankfully, the storm they'd heard off in the distance earlier had taken a different route. Spotting Blake on the dock, staring out over the water, she stole up quietly behind him and wrapped her arms around his waist. His body stiffened. When he removed her arms, she felt leprous.

She moved to his side to study his face. "What's wrong?"

His silence sent a tsunami of fear bolting through her.

"Okay, spit it out. You've been acting weird around me all day."

Blake turned to face her, his expression in turmoil. "I ... um ... I ... phew."

He wiped his brow with the back of his hand. "It's really warm for June, isn't it?"

A knot formed in Karly's stomach. That delicious strawberry cake wasn't sitting so well. *He's going to break up with me.* She knew it down deep inside. He didn't like this long-distance thing. And neither did she. But she endured it because she had strong feelings for the handsome man in front of her.

"I don't know how to tell you this."

"I'll spare you the torment." Karly's jaw tightened. "You want to end things between us? Fine. They're ended." She whirled around and stalked back toward land.

When she was halfway down the dock, a strong hand gripped her arm and turned her around. "Blondie, wait. Let me explain."

No. She knew exactly what was happening and it was humiliating. Karly Foster had never been dumped in her whole life and she wasn't about to give Blake the opportunity. She yanked her arm free.

"Karly. What's wrong with you today?"

An odd impulse came over her. She grabbed him by the lapels of his tux and pressed her lips against his. For a few seconds, the world grew dim around her. Nothing existed but the two of them.

Her spontaneous act seemed to confuse and throw him off balance. Blake teetered on the edge of the dock like a one-legged, well-dressed stork. "Good-bye, Blake Fenton." The pain in her chest was so unbearable that it quickly turned to anger. Cruella couldn't resist. She gave him ... just a little nudge.

And over the edge he went.

Karly's eyes filled with fluid. As she was unable to corral them, tears spilled down her cheeks. Blake's head popped up above the surface of the water. She should feel guilty, but she didn't. Not in the least.

She had to get away. She turned and fled back up the dock as fast as her four-inch, hot-pink heels could take her.

"Stop, Karly! You've got it all wrong." Blake's urgent voice echoed across the waterfront and under the pavilion where the music had suddenly stopped.

The entire wedding party, Maya and Kerrick's guests, and some nearby campers all stared in her direction.

Karly removed her heels and raced toward her car, wincing as sharp stones cut her feet. And she never looked back.

CHAPTER ONE

Three years later

Her binoculars aimed at the isolated barren rock, Karly stood deathly still as sweat dripped off her brow, threatening to obscure her view. A quick swipe with the back of her sleeve absorbed the droplets just in time.

"Here she comes," her co-worker whispered.

Hours of waiting in the bush had finally paid off. Karly's heart raced as she watched the stocky white bird circle the bare, low-lying island and land on the pebble-lined nest. Soon several others joined her, alighting nearby.

"You were right," squealed Karly. "That island in the middle of White Bird Lake is home to a colony of *Pelecanus erythrorhynchos*.

"I told you." There was a hint of pride in her supervisor's voice. "Why do you think it's called 'White Bird Lake'?"

"Really? Because of the pelicans? I never made that connection before. I should have trusted you right from the start. But I was so sure you were wrong." Karly turned her head sideways to look at him.

"What do you say now?"

"I admit it. Your observations were right on the money."

Harrison chuckled. "Don't take it too hard. You are the new one on board. I've been a park naturalist a lot longer than you."

"Still ..."

The giant man laughed deeply. "Karly Foster doesn't like being wrong."

She pulled the binoculars away from her face. Her eyes narrowed. "That's not true." *How did he know that about her?*

"Keep your voice down." Harrison put a finger to his lips. "You're startling the colony."

"Me? I realize the birds are extremely sensitive to disturbances of any kind, but you're making more noise than I am."

"I am not." Harrison poked her playfully in the shoulder. "However, I am very impressed with your knowledge of the white pelican."

"Thank you. And I just can't believe it. I'm so excited." She shivered in delight.

"Why are you so surprised? Like I told you before, the colonies like to stay extremely isolated from human activity and White Bird Lake in No Trace Campground definitely falls into that category."

"True, but don't they prefer Lake of the Woods and Lake Nipigon?"

"And where do you think we're located? In this area, west of Thunder Bay, we're practically sandwiched between those two lakes. Occasionally they have been known to nest as far away as the Great Lakes shoreline, so wouldn't it be logical to expect that they could be here?"

"Okay, I get your point. I just never thought I'd get to view an actual colony."

Harrison tucked his binoculars into their case and stepped closer. "Have you had your fill for the day? How about I take you out to celebrate our discovery?"

Karly could feel his breath on the side of her face. She quickly removed her binoculars and busied herself getting everything ready for the long hike and canoe ride back. "I don't think so, Harrison. I'm tired. The heat and humidity are too much for me today. But, thank you. How about a rain check?"

"Fine."

Did she detect disappointment in his voice? Maybe she was imagining things. She reached in her backpack and grabbed her bottle, downing the last few drops of lukewarm water before slinging the pack over her shoulder. Her partner was quiet as she followed him on the dense, meandering trail through the bush, heading toward their canoe. As she trudged wearily behind, the hot sun bearing down on her, she thought about the enormous, broad-shouldered man ahead of her. Harrison Somerville was one of the nicest men she had ever met. He was a true gentleman in every sense of the word. Although uncertain of his age, she wouldn't be surprised if he was pushing forty. With the build of a football tackle, Harrison was the strongest and largest man she knew. And the only hint of his creeping age was the occasional sprinkle of silver on his face when he missed a day of shaving.

"Are you keeping up back there or have you melted into a puddle?"

Karly sighed as she added 'considerate' and 'kind' to his list of character traits. "I'm fine."

But his eyes held a touch of sadness and she wondered if he'd been hurt deeply in the past and maybe even today when she declined his offer. Harrison was a great guy. In the last few months she'd gotten to know him quite well and what she knew she really liked. He was like a big teddy bear—large and furry on the outside but his insides were soft and mushy like a gooey marshmallow. She sensed that he was sort of attracted to her, but she didn't feel anything other than respect for her supervisor. What if she got to know him better? Should she give him a chance? That idea didn't really hold any appeal to her. At least, not yet.

Karly gazed around her contentedly. It had taken a huge career change, but it was worth it. At thirty-one years of age, she finally discovered what she had been missing all her life. This was it. She had arrived. The bush was where she was meant to be, studying and enjoying the wonders of nature. It was just too bad it had taken her so long to figure that out.

For four years, she had worked as a medical lab technologist in a Kitchener hospital. Although she was competent, she felt unfulfilled. Then, a few years ago, after a serious brush with death, she began to re-evaluate her life. She'd always loved camping—a summer tradition started by her father after the loss of her mother to cancer when she was quite young. Each year, she had grown more in love with the great outdoors and became skilled at hiking, canoeing, and even rock climbing. Somehow, it had never occurred to her to make it a career. Instead, she allowed her well-meaning aunt to steer her into the medical field.

Another deciding factor to swing Karly to this recent decision had been a day spent job-shadowing Blake Fenton at Williwaw Lake Campground. It had started out as a precaution to keep her safe when suspicious occurrences had led Kerrick Kendall, the park superintendent, to believe her life was in danger. Not only had his hunch proven correct, it played a contributing role in her major decision to change careers. Even though she never would have admitted it to Blake at the time, she had absolutely loved her day as a campground employee. Deep in thought, she suddenly realized they had reached the lake where Harrison's green Kevlar canoe sat at the water's edge.

"Let me help you with that." Her co-worker pulled the heavy pack from her shoulders.

Karly pressed a hand to her stomach. The heat had truly been too much for her today and, foolishly, she hadn't packed enough water. She dropped down on a bulky log near the shoreline.

"You don't look well." Harrison's forehead wrinkled with concern.

She looked up sheepishly. "Would you have any extra water?"

He reached in his backpack and produced a surprisingly cool bottle.

"How did you manage this?"

"I have a large freezer pack in my lunch bag. It helps." He smiled down at her.

"Take small sips. Don't gulp."

Despite his instructions, she indulged greedily and wiped away water trickling down her chin and onto her tan-coloured uniform.

"I guess there are a few things I could teach you about survival," he goaded.

"I know everything there is to know. I just overslept this morning and I was running late and that's why I wasn't prepared." She handed his water bottle back.

He shook his head. "You can keep it."

"Oh no, I couldn't take all your water."

"I'm fine. Besides, I have another one tucked away."

She re-capped the half-empty bottle, jammed it into her bag, and headed for the canoe, ignoring the inner critical voice nagging her for being unprepared and ill-equipped for their day in the bush. Thankfully, Harrison didn't feel the need to berate her for it. Not like someone else she knew. Blake wouldn't have let her off so easy. But why was she making mental comparisons to her old boyfriend? They had called it quits a little over three years ago, just after the wedding of her friend Maya to Blake's brother-in-law, Kerrick.

Why am I thinking about him now?

Perhaps because Harrison was the first man she even felt slightly attracted to since Blake? No. That wasn't it. She didn't have any feelings for Harrison other than friendship and respect. Being with the giant fur-ball made her feel comfortable. Yes, that was all it was.

"Stern or bow?" Harrison picked up a paddle. "You are a little over-heated, perhaps taking the stern and steering us would be advisable to the bow."

Karly parked her hands on her hips. She didn't like people telling her what to do. And yes, maybe she was a little bit tired, but she certainly had the energy needed to get them home. Didn't she?

Karly flapped a hand in the air. "I'm fine. I'll take the bow."

"Stubborn." Harrison chuckled and steadied the canoe while she climbed into the front and plunked down her bag.

In a few minutes, with the relentless sun burning down on her, Karly's stomach pitched and rolled. Why had she agreed to an exploring expedition today of all days? It was just so hot. But the long paddle across Samson Lake, down White Bird Creek, into White Bird Lake, and then hiking through the bush to the small secluded patch of land had been worth it. A wave of dizziness caused her vision to cloud. She swayed momentarily. Painful cramps shot up and down her arms so that she could barely paddle.

"Harrison?" Even to her, her voice sounded weak.

"Yes?"

His voice sounded so far away. "I don't feel very ..."

The words had barely left her mouth when she wretched over the side of the canoe.

"Just as I suspected."

Her eyes shot open as cool water splashed onto her face, arms, and feet. "What are you doing?" When she tried to sit up her head pounded so forcefully she thought she would vomit again.

"Lie still, Karly."

"What happened?"

"I think you're suffering from heat exhaustion. You fainted in the canoe. Thankfully, we weren't very far from shore, so I turned us around."

Propping herself up on her elbows, Karly stared at her wet shirt and bare toes.

"Why am I wet?"

"I needed to get you cooled down as quickly as possible."

"I feel so foolish. I'm sorry. I should have taken stern and you the bow." She attempted to stand. "I think we should get going. We have a long way to go."

Harrison helped her to a standing position. Her legs felt like sloppy, over-cooked spaghetti noodles. His strong arms wrapped around her waist for support.

"Are you sure you're up to it?"

"It's now or never. I don't want to get stuck out here overnight and be eaten alive by mosquitoes. Or meet a rogue bear. Who knows what lurks in the wilds of No Trace Campground?"

Harrison chuckled. "Aren't we being a bit dramatic?" He pulled his ball cap off, exposing a mop of thick, black, short-cropped hair, and plunked it on her head. "This will help. And you sit still. No paddling."

"You won't get any argument from me." Although Karly wasn't fond of bossy men, she truly appreciated Harrison's take-charge attitude. "I couldn't paddle if my life depended on it. I'm exhausted."

The bushes rustled nearby, and her body tensed. "What's that?"

"I'm not sure. Stay put." He led her to an over-sized rotting log and eased her down onto it. "I'll check it out."

"Be careful. What if it's a bear?"

Karly watched him sidestep the dead and decaying branches of a large fallen tree. Suddenly he was slapping a man on the back. "Josh Rutherford. What are you doing out here in the bush?"

The young summer student, whom Karly vaguely remembered meeting once before, looked in her direction. The short, wiry man removed his hat and wiped the sweat from his forehead, revealing a balding scalp with, sparse, reddish-blonde hair. "I was checking out a complaint from an interior camper."

"I wasn't aware of any complaints."

"It, uh, it came in after you guys left this morning," Josh stuttered.

"Oh?" Harrison's bushy eyebrows drew together. "What was it concerning?"

"Just a bear causing chaos, disturbing some campers in the night, hanging around their campsite, keeping them hostage in their tent."

"But he didn't attack them or cause any harm?"

"No. Some campers are such wimps. Why bother interior camping if you're afraid of the bears?"

An odd silence permeated the air momentarily.

Then Josh shrugged. "Anyway, nothing seems amiss and the campers are long gone. What's wrong with Karly? She doesn't look well."

"A little too much sun, she'll be okay." Harrison glanced in her direction. "Will you be following us back then? Where's your canoe?"

"It's down the lake a bit. Meet up with you later."

Karly watched the top of Josh's hat disappear around a dense stand of trees. Harrison crossed his arms and stared down at her. "I've stressed that employees should never enter the bush alone, always in pairs. I'll need to talk with him about that."

Something felt off. She couldn't put her finger on it. Maybe it was the heat exhaustion or maybe it was the fact that Josh, whom she barely remembered, knew her name. No matter. All she cared about was getting back and dropping into her bed.

Now at the stern, Karly managed to stay awake long enough to view the shoreline ahead. And that's the last thing she remembered.

CHAPTER TWO

Karly struggled to keep awake. Just as she began to drift off, she felt her body being jostled. She opened her eyes and found herself in the arms of her supervisor as he sloshed through the shallow lake.

"Hang in there, Karly," Harrison urged. "You'll feel better once you're out of the heat and in the cool of the air-conditioned building."

Harrison's face blurred and she slumped against his chest. When she opened her eyes again, she lay on a couch in the library of the main registration and information center. Her supervisor was on his knees and had a hand under her neck. "Lean forward, Karly and take some sips of ..."

His words were jumbled and didn't make any sense. Karly's heart pounded rapidly, as if it were trying to climb out of her chest. She blinked at the horrifying scene before her. Large, furry black spiders crawled over books on the shelves and scurried across the carpet in all directions. Karly screamed. "Why are there so many spiders inside?"

She drifted off again until her flaming cheeks were assuaged with a refreshing coolness. She awoke to find Harrison wiping her face with a wet cloth.

"Heather!"

Why did her supervisor sound worried? Maybe he wanted Heather to get a fly swatter and kill all the spiders. The out-of-focus face of a middle-aged woman suddenly stared down at her. When it morphed into a mystical-looking creature with a human body and the face of a white pelican, Karly pointed at it with a trembling hand. "Get that thing away from me."

Harrison looked back over his shoulder at the pelican-woman. "Call *Wilderness Bush Adventures* for me, Heather. We need to get Karly to the Aspen Ridge Hospital for medical attention immediately."

Karly's forehead wrinkled, and she struggled to sit up. "Hospital? Me?"

"Relax, Karly. Everything will be okay." His hand on her shoulder gently steered her back down to the cushion.

Male voices roused her.

"Hi, I'm Harrison. You must be new around here. We need to get this woman to the hospital in Aspen Ridge as quickly as possible."

"What seems to be the problem?" A second male voice asked.

"I think she's suffering from heat stroke. She has all the symptoms."

Karly's body floated effortlessly. A seagull squawked. Am I outdoors? Harrison fastened her into the back seat of a floatplane and climbed in beside her. The pilot stopped on the dock and peered in the open doorway. Why was he staring at her? Karly squinted, struggling to make out his features. Was that—? No, it couldn't be. The heat had really messed with her head. He leaned in closer, until she was able to make out the look of disbelief on his face that no doubt mirrored her own. Blake? He was the last person on earth she wanted to see. She couldn't help herself. Her arms swung wildly out at him.

The pilot grasped both her wrists gently but firmly.

Harrison rested a hand on her upper arm. "I'm really sorry. She's not herself."

A wry grin crossed Blake's face. "Actually, she's behaving exactly like the Karly I remember."

Karly glared at him. "Let me go."

"Believe me, lady, I did. Years ago."

Harrison's eyes narrowed. "You know this woman?"

Blake let go of her wrists, shut the door, and climbed into the front seat. "Regrettably, yes, I do."

CHAPTER THREE

Karly woke with a start. Where was she? What was that horrible noise? The room spun around her, and she blinked to get it to stop. It slowed a little, and she lifted her head off the pillow. When a crimson-faced nurse poked her grey head up at the side of her bed, she was even more confused.

"I'm so sorry." The nurse held up a metal bedpan. "I've got butter-fingers lately."

"Where am I?"

"You're in the Aspen Ridge emergency. Are you feeling better now, dear?" The woman gently touched her arm, but didn't wait for an answer. "If you're up to it, there's a tall, good-looking man waiting to see you."

"Oh?" Karly frowned.

"His name is Harrison."

Her neck felt as though it was trying to support a fifteen-pound bowling ball. Succumbing to the weight, she flopped back onto the pillow. *Harrison?* When the face of her supervisor came to mind, she nodded. "Okay, send him in."

"I'll just run and get him, dear. Don't go anywhere. I'll be right back."

"As if that's going to happen," Karly muttered. In her present condition, she couldn't leave if her life depended on it. Her thoughts were muddled, and she tried to recall what must have happened to bring her to emergency. Was she injured? An I.V. dangled from her arm and the hammering in her head was excruciating. What time of day was it? Her eyes searched the cold, antiseptic room for a clock just as the door opened and Harrison entered. His brow wrinkled in concern.

"How are you feeling?"

"Like a wrung-out dish rag." She sighed. "I'm trying to remember what happened, but I'm a bit fuzzy. Can you fill me in? Did I have an accident? Why do I have this I.V.?"

Harrison pulled up a chair and plunked down heavily beside her. "You didn't have an accident. You're suffering from heat stroke."

"Heat stroke?"

"Don't you remember? We spent the day in the bush. It was very hot and humid. I think it was a little too much for you."

As Karly stared at him, images began flitting through her mind. "Did we see a colony of white pelicans today?"

"No."

"No?"

"Technically that was yesterday. It's four in the morning." He tapped his wristwatch and smiled.

"It's coming back to me. I remember the island of white pelicans, walking back to the canoe, and ..." She pressed the back of her hand to her head. "Oh no. I totally humiliated myself by vomiting over the side, didn't I?"

Harrison offered her a small smile. "I've seen worse."

Karly dropped her hand. "I remember it being almost dark when we reached the dock. After that things are really fuzzy."

"Probably because after that you fainted, fell into the water, and began hallucinating. That's when I realized you needed medical help immediately and I brought you here."

"That's strange. Why did I suffer from heat stroke?"

"I'm not sure. Everyone's body reacts differently to extreme temperatures."

"But I've never experienced it my entire life and I'm outdoors all the time."

Harrison shrugged.

"You are too kind, Harrison. This was your chance to reprimand me for not being prepared. I didn't bring enough water and I should have worn a hat."

"Both very good suggestions. We all make mistakes."

"Maybe I was dehydrated beforehand. That was it. I did take an antihistamine the night before because my allergies were acting up. They always make me extra thirsty."

"There you go." He touched her hand briefly. "It wasn't your fault after all."

"How did we get here?"

Harrison cleared his throat. "I called *Wilderness Bush Adventures* for a seaplane. You needed help quickly. I thought it was the best option at the time."

"Is there something else I'm forgetting?"

Harrison stood. "That just about sums it up. Look, Karly, they're keeping you a few more hours for observation, but the doctor said you'll probably be released around nine o'clock in the morning. I'll let you get some sleep and pick you up then. Does that sound okay?"

She yawned as Harrison walked toward the door. "Okay, I'll see you then."

"Rest. I'll be back before you know it."

Karly watched her supervisor disappear out the door. Harrison was so kind. Did people like him really exist? She'd never met anyone like him before. Her eyelids grew heavy and she felt herself drifting to sleep. A sudden image startled her awake. Blake Fenton? What had made her think of her old boyfriend? That was weird. Heat stroke sure did a number on a person's brain.

✤

"Thanks for coming to get me." Karly yawned as she mumbled to her co-worker and roommate, Madison, in a sleepy voice from the backseat of the park truck. "Sorry, I just can't seem to stay awake."

"That's okay," Harrison patted her leg. "Yesterday took a lot out of you. As soon as we get back, you head directly to bed. I don't want to see you until tomorrow morning when you report in for work."

Karly tilted her head back. When she realized she was leaning on his shoulder, she sat up quickly. "Sorry, I didn't realize I was using you for a pillow."

"I've got broad shoulders." Harrison grinned. "Besides, I feel partly responsible. I noticed the heat exhaustion signs earlier, but didn't act on them quickly enough. I'm sorry."

"Don't blame yourself. It was my stupidity coupled with the antihistamine. It happens."

"Do I get the day off too, boss?" the young, purple-haired driver asked.

"Unless you're suffering from heat stroke Madison, I think not. Nice try."

"Hey, Karly?" Madison yelled over her shoulder as she drove. "Guess what I heard. There's a hot new pilot in the area. He works for *Wilderness Bush Adventures*. I forget his name. Brian or Bentley or something like that."

Harrison cleared his throat. "Who needs a good-looking pilot when you've got me?"

Madison giggled.

"What's so funny?" the large man asked.

"No offense, sir, but like … how old are you?"

"Madison!" Karly tapped the back of the driver's seat with her fist. "That's not very nice."

"I call it as I see it. No sense beating around the bush."

As Madison yammered on incessantly about the pilot's good looks, Harrison stiffened. "Just ignore her," Karly whispered. "You don't look old at all to me. She's only twenty-two after all. Everyone over thirty looks old to her. Including me."

"Really?" A smile lit up his face.

"Most definitely." Karly's head slumped back against the seat. "Besides, she suffers from logorrhea."

"What is that?" Harrison's brow wrinkled.

"Diarrhea of the mouth."

"Gross." Harrison grimaced. "Thanks for that nasty word picture."

"You're welcome." Karly giggled.

Half an hour later, Madison dropped Harrison at the main building.

"Don't forget we have a meeting at noon and I expect you to be there." Harrison climbed from the truck.

"Aye, aye, Captain." Madison saluted.

"You're sassy. It's good we have a laid-back supervisor." Karly unbuckled her seatbelt as Madison pulled into the small dirt driveway in front of the cabin they shared together.

Karly climbed from the vehicle and trudged wearily toward home. Madison held her arm and guided her inside and to her bedroom. Karly flopped onto the bed, clothes and all.

Her co-worker pulled off Karly's boots and threw a light sheet over her. "Can I get you anything before I leave?"

"No, I'm fine. Just pull down the shade." Karly shielded her eyes with a hand.

"Okay, but I have one thing to say before I go. You better watch yourself."

"What do you mean?" Karly's eyelids desperately fought to stay open.

"Just be careful. I've heard rumours." Madison's voice took on an eerie tone.

"I'm confused. What are we talking about?"

"Karly Foster, sometimes I think you are denser than a block of concrete."

"Huh?"

"I'm talking about Harrison."

"What about him?" Karly stifled a yawn with one hand.

"Things are not as they seem."

"You're speaking in riddles. Can we discuss this another time? I'm dead tired."

"Okay, but don't say I didn't warn you."

Madison's voice grew hazy, but her last words replayed in Karly's head. *Don't say I didn't warn you.* Her roommate couldn't be talking about Harrison. Karly must be hallucinating again.

CHAPTER FOUR

Blake Fenton sat in the diner, sipping his morning coffee, unable to believe what had transpired last night. Was that really Karly Foster he'd flown to the hospital? If he hadn't had another call directly after he would have stayed long enough to see how she was doing. What was Karly doing in No Trace Campground?

It had been a little over three years since he had seen her last and obviously a lot of things had changed. But maybe not everything. If her violent reaction at seeing him was any indication of how she truly felt, she obviously still harbored deep-seated hostility towards him. Even in her hallucinatory state, she had taken a swing at him. Not that she'd remember any of that today, she'd been so out of it. Blake shook his head.

Judging by her uniform, she was now employed at No Trace. What had caused such a significant career change? From blood-sucking vampire to nature-loving enthusiast?

Maybe ... just maybe ... he'd played a role, even indirectly. He'd really like to find out. But they'd parted on not-so-good grounds. With frustration, he thought of the last time he'd seen her at Maya and Kerrick's wedding. If only she'd given him a chance to explain.

"Would you like some more coffee, Blake?"

He looked up into the striking indigo eyes of the waitress. "You've twisted my arm." Blake held up his cup.

Scalding coffee poured over his hand and down onto his leg. "What the ..." A mountain of curse words came to his lips, but he managed to squelch them. His cup crashed to the table, spilling even the small amount of coffee that had managed to make it inside.

Swiftly he stood, avoiding the trail of racing hot liquid streaming over the edge of the table.

A look of horror crossed the waitress's face. She set down the pot and grabbed a pile of napkins. "I'm so sorry, Blake." She dabbed at the front of his shirt. "I'm just so clumsy sometimes. Let me get a cold cloth."

"No, I'll be all right."

She ignored his remark and hurried off towards the kitchen. Blake couldn't help but watch the exaggerated sway of her hips. With her midnight-black hair, and curves in all the right places, she was very attractive. Although she was petite in stature, she emitted an eye-catching appeal that was hard to deny. Or resist. He had a lot of trouble not following her every move. Since he'd moved to the Aspen Ridge area a month ago, he'd visited the diner frequently and lately they'd moved to a first name basis.

"Here you go. Again, I'm so sorry." The cool cloth refreshed his red, stinging palm. As she wiped gently with one hand, she held his fingers with the other.

"Raven!" An angry male voice boomed from somewhere in the kitchen.

"I have to go." She hurried away so quickly, she left the coffeepot sitting on his table.

Blake moved to the counter and, paid his bill. Even though he kept his eyes riveted on the kitchen door, he never caught another glimpse of the pretty waitress. Making his way to his aging Ford pickup, he headed to work. As he drove, he couldn't help but marvel at the amazing wilderness around him.

Had it only been four weeks since he'd started his own business? And to think he owed all of this to his ex-brother-in-law. Many years ago, his sister Katie had been briefly married to Kerrick, but the marriage fell apart quickly. Blake would never understand in a million years why she wanted out of that marriage. What had possessed her to be unfaithful? Although he loved his sister, Kerrick was a great guy and Katie needed her head examined. To this day, he rarely saw his sister.

On the other hand, Kerrick and Blake kept in touch. But they were more than former relatives. Kerrick was a good friend. Although they lived several hours apart, they managed to keep their friendship going. Blake choked back emotion as he thought about all that man had done for him, steering him from a life filled with rebellion, anger, and even a juvenile police record, to what he was today—a bush pilot with his own business in remote Northwestern Ontario, near the town of Aspen Ridge.

While Blake was deep in thought, the metallic green roof of the small wooden building that housed his business and his home came into view, causing a surge of surreal emotions to course through him. Sometimes, he still had to pinch himself to believe this was real. He turned into the gravel parking lot in front of a large sign advertising his business, Wilderness Bush Adventures, and headed inside, turning the 'OPEN' sign around on the way in.

A quick check of his answering machine revealed no new messages, which was fine with him. He ran a one-man operation, at least for now. If his business took off, then he'd see about hiring more help. At present, he was busy enough and couldn't afford to pay another person's wage. Maybe next year if all went well.

The door creaked open and in walked the well-built outdoor survival guide he'd recently become affiliated with. "Good morning, Henry."

"Good morning, Mr. White Pelican." He laughed deeply, slapping Blake on the shoulder.

"I don't know why you insist on calling me by that name." Blake rubbed his shoulder. The middle-aged guide carried a powerful punch.

"It's easy. You resemble the bird: white-blonde hair, beak burnt yellow, a love of fishing, and you fly in the clouds all day."

Instinctively, Blake's hand reached up to touch his nose. *Did Henry think he had a big nose?* "I've never been told I have a beak before and yellow at that."

Ear-splitting laughter belted from his bronze-skinned friend. "Just kidding, my friend."

"That's good ... I guess." Blake tried to see the humour. "Do you have more business for me?"

"Yes, I do. I need you to fly me back to Shadow Lake. I'm taking more canoeists to the interiors of No Trace Wilderness."

"No problem, Henry, follow me. But I think I'll charge you extra for calling my nose a beak."

Again, the man hooted in amusement as they followed the meandering dirt trail to the Cessna float plane, bobbing in the lake.

"Where are your guests? Don't I have to fly the canoeists in too?"

"Not this time. These guys are crazier than most. They insist on driving the eighty kilometers on long Shadow Road. They don't realize it is so much cheaper and faster to fly with the White Pelican Man."

"Oh, I see. Just keep telling everyone that and my business will boom."

Within a few minutes, Blake brought the Cessna down into Shadow Lake, much to the delight of Henry. "I never tire of this. You're a good pilot. You probably fly as good as the white pelican."

"What is it with the White Pelican? You seem obsessed with the bird."

Henry only chuckled at Blake's remark.

Shutting off the engine, Blake followed Henry ashore, blinking at the gruesome sight that welcomed them. Directly in front of him a young buck, hanging from a nearby tree, had been gutted down the middle. It had obviously been shot in the head. As much as Blake loved it up here, there were some things he didn't think he'd ever get used to.

His eyes travelled to the tranquil azure lake surrounded by pines; the smell and the sight were incredible. About fifty people lived in this remote town of Shadow Lake; many of the inhabitants could trace their ancestry back to European or Indigenous roots. Blake had learned much from his friend Henry over the last few weeks. He discovered the people of Shadow Lake were a strong, united community that existed simply. They lived off the land as much as possible, and took care of each other. Many survived by being outdoor survival guides just like his friend.

"Come." Henry motioned to Blake. "My wife will feed you lunch."

"Oh no, I couldn't impose."

Henry stared into his eyes, a fiercely determined look on his face. "You are insulting me. Besides, my *better half* will be annoyed."

"I can stay only briefly, but yes, I'll come."

"Good, good, massive white bird. Come and enjoy the hospitality of my teeny, weeny wife."

Blake was amused at Henry's description as he followed behind him. He couldn't wait to see what the bride of the muscular survival guide looked like. And Blake had a strict policy of never turning down a free lunch. Life was good.

They passed by the buck, which swayed in a sudden breeze. The movement played tricks with Blake's mind, making him think, for a split second, that the animal was still alive. He shuddered, trying to shake off the eerie feeling that something bad was about to happen. What was wrong with him? It was a beautiful day and he was in the company of friends. He had nothing to worry about.

Blake pushed back his shoulders and hurried to catch up with his friend. Everything was fine. The sight of the bloody dead buck had spooked him. That's all it was.

CHAPTER FIVE

The sound of rock music dragged Karly from her much-needed sleep. Glimpses of purple-spiked hair whipped in and out of view as Madison flitted across the kitchen floor, dancing with a frying pan. She certainly had a colorful roommate. The whole thing would be funny except that her head still hurt too much to laugh. Maybe she should get up and have something to eat.

"Look who's risen from the dead. You've slept the day away. It's almost ten o'clock at night." Madison set the pan down on the stove and parked her hands on her hips. "I've been so bored. I'm making grilled cheese. Would you like one?"

"Sure. Food might help me get rid of this headache." Karly stumbled toward the can of coffee on the counter. "A good stiff brew couldn't hurt either. I think I'm suffering from caffeine withdrawal."

"Add enough for me. I'll join you." Madison buttered a piece of bread and set it in the pan. "It's actually good you slept all day. The meeting was boring, and Harrison was miserable, snapping at everyone."

"Harrison?" Karly's eyebrows shot up in surprise as she turned on the coffee maker and sank down on a kitchen chair. "I've never known him to be like that. He's always so cheerful and composed."

"I told you he's not what he seems." Madison laid a slice of cheese on the bread in the pan.

"You did? When?"

"This morning."

"I don't remember."

"You were out of it, but I've heard stuff ..." Madison's voice had gone all mysterious. She stopped buttering the second slice of bread and, knife in hand, leaned over the table, staring into Karly's face.

"What kind of stuff?"

"It's really creepy."

Karly held up her hands. "Is what you are about to tell me truth or gossip?"

"It's truth, of course." Madison grabbed a spatula. "Anyway, as the story goes, years ago Harrison had a thing for one of his new, young, female employees. I heard she was stunning—tall and blonde with a supermodel-type body. Now that I think about it, kind of like you." Madison froze with the sandwich in mid-flip. "Oh. That's not good."

"Stop it, Madison. Just tell the story."

"Unfortunately for him, the feelings weren't reciprocated. He pursued her relentlessly, bringing her flowers and dropping off unsigned love notes."

"Let me stop you right there." Karly held up both palms. "If they were unsigned, how did anyone know they were from him?"

"Minor technicalities, Karly. Will you let me tell the story? Apparently, his affection for her grew to the point of obsession. Then one day, she didn't report for work. They never found her body, Karly."

"Oh, I'm scared." Karly snorted. "If we were sitting around a campfire in the dark, this would be spine-chilling and spooky."

Madison slapped the sandwich back into the frying pan a little harder than necessary. "Mock me all you wish, but you might be sorry if you don't take me seriously. Everyone can see that Harrison has a thing for you."

"They can?"

"How do you feel about him? Please tell me you haven't fallen for him."

"And if I had?" Karly's lips twisted in a sideways smirk.

"Have you not been listening?"

Karly rose from the kitchen chair and poured herself a coffee. "As far as I'm concerned, it's all gossip. If the police suspected Harrison, he would have been charged."

"They can't charge him if they never found the body."

"I suppose. By the way, when did all this happen? I never heard anything on the news about it."

"A few years ago, from what Raven told me."

"Who's Raven?"

"She's a waitress at *Moe's Diner* in Aspen Ridge. She grew up in the area, so she would know."

Karly tapped a finger against her chin. "I may have met her. Does she have jet-black hair, dark-blue eyes, and a small build?"

"Yes, that would be her."

"She waited on us one day when we stopped at the diner for lunch."

"You and Harrison again? You guys are together a lot. That has tongues wagging, you know."

Madison dropped the steaming sandwich on a plate and grabbed the bottle of ketchup. "You have feelings for him, don't you?"

"You're being ridiculous. It's just that the Harrison I know is one of the kindest, gentlest men I have ever met. He wouldn't hurt a fly. What you told me doesn't fit with what I know about him."

"Things aren't always as they seem. As your friend, I'm warning you to watch your back. You better take me seriously."

Karly rubbed her temples. "Warning noted, but I don't think you could be more wrong. Don't fall prey to every little bit of gossip you hear floating around out there."

A sound at the door caused them both to jump. "Now look what you've gone and done. You've spooked us both." Karly let out a nervous chuckle as she padded to the front door.

"Don't open it!" Madison warned from behind her.

"Why not?"

"It's dark out there."

"So? It's probably the wind banging branches against the front of the house. It happens all the time when it blows from the north. We really need to get some tree trimming done." She opened the door to a large gust of wind that whipped her hair around her face. A dark shadow shifted suddenly. Karly swallowed. Was that a man ducking into the bushes a few feet from the cabin?

Madison let out a screech beside her and Karly's heart sprinted erratically. She whirled toward her roommate. What was she screaming about? Madison bent down and picked up something from the front step.

"Flowers!" The bouquet shook in her friend's hands.

Karly took a deep, steadying breath. "Calm down. It's a beautiful bunch of wild flowers, that's all. See? You're worried for nothing. It's one of those weird coincidences. They happen all the time."

Karly closed the door and locked it, although she'd never felt the need to do that before.

"Then who sent you flowers?"

"I don't know. Maybe they want to remain mysterious. Either that or they forgot to send a card. Come to think of it, since there is no name, they could be meant for you."

"Get real, Karly, I've never been sent flowers in my entire life. And in a case like this, I hope they're not for me."

"What do you mean, a case like this? You're letting your imagination get carried away.

Madison shook her head and walked back to the kitchen. "Just be careful, Karly. If I were you, I wouldn't allow myself to be alone with him anymore. Why not err on the side of caution, just in case?"

"Because you are being ridiculous, allowing a rumour from years ago get to you. As far as I'm concerned, I never heard any of this. I'll continue to treat Harrison the same way I always have, as my knowledgeable supervisor and friend. There's nothing else between us."

Karly took the bouquet to the kitchen, snipped the stems on an angle, immersed them in an empty juice jug, and filled it with water. "They are really pretty. Wouldn't you agree?"

Her roommate shook her head and crossed her arms. "You are one stubborn woman. I just hope it doesn't kill you in the end."

CHAPTER SIX

Blake's stomach growled, reminding him he was overdue for breakfast. Which would make sense, since he hadn't eaten a thing since his lunch feast yesterday at Shadow Lake with his friends. Henry's wife, Shawna sure knew how to cook. In the past, his weight had never been a problem but if he continued to eat like that, his floatplane would never get off the ground.

Blake stared out the window of his Cessna. The view was out of this world and Blake hoped it never became mundane. For miles and miles, as far as the eye could see, the earth was a blanket of dense green forests, innumerable deep clear cerulean lakes, meandering rivers, and foamy white waterfalls. As he banked his plane to the west, a sense of wonder and awe filled him.

Soaring effortlessly, he loved flight and everything about it. Apparently, he was good at it too. Who knew that Blake, the high-school dropout, juvenile delinquent and troubled teen, would obtain his bush pilot's license and go on to graduate at the top of his class in flight school?

Then, wonders of all wonders, the opportunity to own *Wilderness Bush Adventures,* complete with the sea-plane, presented itself like a dream. If Blake's maternal grandmother hadn't left him a substantial amount of money in her will, the schooling and purchase wouldn't have been possible. He couldn't believe how different life was now. The last few years had brought about immense changes.

Blake fought his emotions. Finally, after many tough years, life was good. There was only one thing missing. Until last night, he thought he had moved on. But seeing Karly lying all helpless and vulnerable caused a mountain of old memories to re-surface ... and just when he was beginning to feel something for another woman. Or was he? He really didn't even know Raven. She was beautiful and mysterious, but she was still a stranger. Although he'd been hoping to change that. Maybe he still would. But should he contact Karly? Or visit her in the hospital? Would she even want to see him? He doubted it.

Judging by the protective nature of her supervisor, maybe she had moved on. Harrison had seemed smitten with her. But then, who wasn't? Almost every man who met Karly was starry-eyed within minutes. That was just surface attraction, though. Blake had gotten to know her on a much deeper level. And he had let it all slip away.

He circled the floatplane and came in low for his landing on Beaver Lake. His pontoons hit smoothly, and he gradually brought the Cessna near the dock and cut the engine.

Blake climbed in his truck and drove to the diner. A few minutes later, he was seated in his favourite booth by the window at *Moe's*. Raven had clearly spotted him the moment he came in the door as she rushed over to serve him.

"Good morning, Blake, you're a little later than usual. It's ten o'clock. I thought you'd stood me up today." Raven flipped her hair off her shoulder.

"I had an early-morning flight to drop off three American fishermen to an inland resort and it took a little longer than expected. I'd like your lumberjack special, please."

"Coming right up." She smiled and turned to leave.

"Raven?" Blake grabbed her arm. When she winced, he let go. "I'm sorry; I didn't mean to hurt you."

"You didn't."

Blake narrowed his eyes at the finger-sized bruises on her arms. "What happened the other day? I heard Moe yelling at you. Was he mad because you spilled the coffee?"

"Yelling? When? What do you mean?"

"Raven, you're not being honest with me. Did he cause these bruises?"

She spun on her heels. "I have to go. I'm very busy."

Something didn't sit right with Blake. What or who had caused the bruising, and why was she being so evasive? Hopefully, he'd have a chance to find out. Maybe he should ask her out after all, get to know her better. It was something he'd been seriously mulling over until ...

A movement in the parking lot caught his peripheral vision. Several people were exiting a white truck with the No Trace Campground logo on the side. Harrison climbed out the driver's door and a young man of slighter build jumped out from the front passenger seat. A funky-looking, purple-haired young woman exited one of the back doors. The other back door opened, and Blake nearly choked on a swig of his coffee. A sense of panic raced through him, sending his heart rate into overdrive. If he wasn't so hungry, he'd make a mad dash for the bathroom and climb out the window. He shook his head at the cowardly thought. What kind of a man was he?

The last three years had done nothing but improve Karly Foster's stunning looks. She was more breath-taking than ever. Before the bell over the door even had a chance to jingle, Blake swiftly scooted over to the opposite side of his booth, so he was sitting with his back to the entrance. He couldn't take the chance the two of them might make eye contact. He was certain she wouldn't remember that it had been him the other night who transported her to the hospital.

Only a few seats remained between him and the restroom. He was safe for now. It's not that he was running; he just wasn't ready to face her again.

But when he heard the campground quartet directly behind him, a nervous sweat tickled his brow. In the next minute, being the efficient hostess that she was, Raven hurried to take their orders. Blake listened intently for the sound of Karly's voice. When she ordered yogurt and fruit, he smiled. That would be the health-conscious woman he remembered.

Pushing back a niggle of guilt, he listened in on their conversation. Maybe the awkwardness of their proximity had its advantages after all. Were Harrison and Karly an item? He had to find out.

"Weren't you facing the other direction a minute ago?"

Blake jumped at Raven's observation. "You must be mistaken. That was yesterday."

Raven's forehead wrinkled. "I could have sworn ... and why are you whispering?"

"I'm not whispering. Your ears must be plugged."

When she put the palm of her hand against one ear and slapped it, he couldn't help himself and laughed aloud at her gullible-ness. Was that even a word? It did describe her well; he had the idea that he could tell her just about anything and she would believe it.

"More coffee?" She held up the pot.

Blake was relieved when the hot brew hit the cup this time. "Bulls-eye!"

'What does that mean?" Her eyes narrowed in confusion.

"You hit the cup."

"Oh. Now I get it. You're so funny. Be back shortly with your breakfast." She scurried away.

Not the sharpest tool in the shed. Blake immediately felt bad for that nasty thought. After all, he had started the whole thing by insisting he hadn't been facing the other direction. He gave himself a mental reprimand to be kinder. And to tell the truth.

He took a sip of the tasty beverage, his ears keenly tuned to the talk behind him. Thankfully, the conversation at the next table was loud enough to have drowned out his voice a moment ago.

"Just ask him," a female voice suggested. Blake's grip on the white mug tightened. Were they talking about him? Had he been spotted?

"No, Madison." Karly's voice was firm.

"Ask who, what?" the younger male, his voice higher-pitched than Harrison's, asked.

"As if it's any of your business, Josh, but Karly received a surprise bouquet of flowers last night. And she was wondering if they were from you, Harrison." Madison blurted out. "Ouch! That hurt, Karly. I can't believe you just kicked me under the table."

Blake suppressed a chuckle as his mind flashed back to the last time he'd seen Karly—besides the other night. She'd sent him flying into a frigid lake, suit and all. And that wasn't the first time she'd taken her frustrations out on him in a physical way. He flexed the fingers on his right hand. On rainy days, the middle digit still ached. Of course, she'd sworn it was an accident when she slammed his hand in the car door.

"Well? Were they?" Despite the kick, Madison clearly wasn't prepared to give up.

"No comment," Harrison answered.

Interesting response. Blake drummed the fingers of his free hand on the table. If Harrison had feelings for her, he was keeping them hidden.

"They could have been from me," Josh piped up again. "Why do you just assume that Harrison sent them? I'm a full-blooded male."

"That's absurd, Josh. Flowers? From you to Karly? You're not even in the same league. Get your head out of the clouds," Madison replied saucily.

Ouch. The purple-haired woman didn't mince words.

"Lumberjack special." Raven plunked the plate down in front of him. "Enjoy, Blake."

Silence followed. Had the table behind heard his name? Had Karly?

Raven lingered a moment longer. "Is something wrong today? You're acting strange."

"No, I'm just hungry." He picked up his fork and dug heartily into his syrupy pancakes to prove his point.

"Then I'll let you eat." Raven whirled around and scurried away.

Was she annoyed? Oh well, it couldn't be helped. He needed to speak as little as possible. As he shovelled in his Canadian bacon, he listened attentively again.

Soon, Raven returned with food for the table behind him. A sharp clanging and crashing caused him to stop chewing in mid-bite.

"Of all the idiotic things to do," the high-pitched voice snapped loudly. "Stupid, clumsy waitress."

Blake gritted his teeth. It didn't matter what had happened, he couldn't tolerate that kind of treatment of another human being. Should he turn and confront Josh? Raven might appreciate his support, but his identity would be revealed.

"I'm sorry." Raven's voice was pleading. "I shouldn't have tried to juggle all four plates at one time. I usually have no problem. That one just slipped."

"Apologize, Josh, that was unkind. It was an accident." The firmness in Karly's voice made the words sound more like a command than a suggestion.

Blake heard shuffling, as if Josh was getting up. "I'd like to see how you'd react if you had hot scrambled eggs and greasy hash browns in your lap."

"Looks good on you," Madison goaded him.

Harrison's voice was firm, but gentle. "I agree with Karly, Josh. You owe this woman an apology, and I'd expect nothing less from one of my employees, student or not."

Blake was impressed. Harrison seemed to be a decent guy. Before any more words were uttered, though, footsteps thundered from the back. "What seems to be the problem, Harrison? Did Raven cause this mess?"

Blake frowned. Moe was upset again. It didn't seem to take much, and the object of his wrath always seemed to be Raven. What did he have against her?

A moment of silence followed before Harrison spoke. "There's no problem, Moe. I think I may have accidentally bumped her arm as she reached across with Josh's plate. No harm done. In fact, I'll pay for the lost meal."

"Is that the truth? Because if Raven is responsible, I'll see to it that she's docked. She'll pay handsomely for her mistake."

Given the bruises he'd seen on Raven's arms, Blake could just imagine how he would make her pay. He shook his head in disgust. Thankfully, Harrison appeared to have defused the situation. That spoke highly of the man, and raised Blake's opinion of him another notch. If he and Karly were involved, maybe he should leave well enough alone.

"Is that what happened?" Moe sounded considerably more subdued.

"That's how it happened." Josh's reply sounded forced.

"Fine, what were you having again? I'll have another plate sent out directly."

Moe's footsteps grew quieter and Blake heard the kitchen door swing shut.

"You'll pay for this." Blake's eyes widened at Josh's muttered threat. He watched as the man hurried past his booth and into the men's room, hash browns and scrambled eggs littering the floor behind him.

"You really shouldn't have stuck your neck out for me." Raven sounded irritated with Harrison after she returned with a cloth. "I didn't ask for your help. I could have handled it myself."

Blake's eyebrows drew together. If he were Harrison, he would have been annoyed by her lack of appreciation. To his surprise, the man didn't offer a response.

"Excuse me, but there's one more place you need to clean." Blake's chest tightened at the sound of Karly's voice. He'd missed it, even if she was mostly making fun of him or being difficult, when he'd heard it in the past.

Raven giggled, and Karly and Madison joined in. "I don't think the gentleman will find it very funny." Harrison replied, a touch of humour in his voice.

Who were they talking about? What had happened? Blake desperately wanted to turn around. A firm hand patted him on the shoulder. He looked up to see Harrison standing in the aisle beside his booth. "Sir, I hate to tell you this, but you have a hash brown sitting on your ball cap." He took a step back. "Hey, don't I know you?"

Alarm raced through his veins as he reached up to brush off the runaway potato. Oddly he hadn't felt it land on his head.

I guess it was time to stop hiding, whether he wanted it to be or not. Blake stood up and shook Harrison's hand. "We met the other night. I'm Blake Fenton and I'm the owner of Wilderness Bush Adventures."

When he heard a gasp behind him, Blake turned, staring directly into a pair of brilliant blue eyes. "Hi, Karly, you're looking much better today."

The colour drained from his ex-girlfriend's face as her spoon clanged to her plate. Madison smiled flirtatiously. Raven's eyes narrowed in suspicion and Harrison shifted from one foot to the other.

"Blake?" Karly's eyes were enormous. "What are you doing here?"

"Having breakfast. What are you doing here?"

"I'm an employee at No Trace Campground now."

"I know. I flew you to the hospital the other day."

"You did? You're a pilot? How? When?"

"It's a long story."

Josh walked up behind him to stand beside Harrison, and Madison began to giggle hysterically. Blake turned to look. The scrawny man had stuffed a large sheet of paper towel into his belt so that it hung down over the front of his pants.

"Stop laughing." Josh threw his hands in the air. "I tried to rinse the grease out of my pants and it made things worse."

Karly bit her lip. Blake had to turn away from the spectacle himself to avoid a hilarious outburst.

"It looks like I wet myself and I had to cover it up somehow." Josh shrugged. "The restaurant is packed. How would I get to the truck unnoticed?"

Madison snorted. "And hanging a paper towel in front of your crotch doesn't warrant attention? You're crazy."

Blake covered his mouth and coughed to hide the chuckle he couldn't hold in any longer.

"Time to get back to work." Harrison tossed a set of keys to Josh. "You go ahead. We'll settle the bill and join you shortly."

Again, Blake was impressed with Harrison's kindness. As the girls slid off the bench, Blake's eyes met Karly's and held them. He had to see her again. To get closure from the past. That was the only reason. Wasn't it? "Um ... Karly?"

"Yes?"

"I was wondering ..."

Madison parked herself against the table, crossed her arms, and stared directly at the two of them while Harrison stepped around the group and headed for the cash register. Blake was suddenly tongue-tied. This was awkward enough without Madison gawking at him.

"Can you give us a moment please, Madison?" Karly asked her friend.

"Fine." Madison snatched her purse from the bench and joined Harrison in line at the front register.

Blake's heart hammered against his ribcage as he faced Karly. "I'd really like to catch up? Do you think we could ...?"

"How about here, tonight, six o'clock?"

Her swift answer startled him and left him a little ... flustered. "Sure, that would work, I guess," Blake stuttered.

Karly spun on her heel and strode for the front door, her long, silky blonde hair flying behind her. Blake watched her until she opened the door and climbed into the park truck. Why hadn't she joined the others in line to pay her bill? Was Harrison paying for her meal? Or did she feel as shaken as he did and just forgot?

He heard a noise behind him and turned to see Raven clearing away his breakfast dishes. He pressed a palm to his abdomen. His lumberjack special burned like a forest fire in his stomach. What had he gone and done? Maybe he should have left the past where it belonged.

Too late now. The fire had already been ignited.

CHAPTER SEVEN

"Totally cool. You used to date that hot pilot? Whatever happened? Never mind. Not my business. That means he's free though, right? I mean, you wouldn't object if I gave it a whirl?" Madison sat beside her in the back seat and plied her with questions.

Karly didn't know how to answer her friend. And wasn't she a little young for Blake?

Unfortunately, Josh wasn't as tongue-tied. "Breathe, Madison, for heaven's sake. He's just an average male. I don't understand what all the excitement is about. Why would you be interested in that gangly dude when you have Harrison or me to choose from?"

Madison snorted. "If you can't see it, I'm not going to explain it. I see nothing wrong with that good-looking guy whatsoever."

Karly half-heard the exchange. Blake was a pilot. Imagine that. He'd really made something of himself. She couldn't wait to meet him tonight and get the whole scoop. Her stomach flipped just thinking about it. A million emotions rushed through her: shock, curiosity, anger, hurt, and excitement. Which one truly reflected her feelings for him?

"You didn't answer my question Karly."

"Huh?"

"So ... you'd be okay if Blake and I were to ..."

Karly batted a hand through the air. "I don't have any hold on him. It's a free world. Do what you want."

"Are you ticked?" Madison cocked her head. "That means one thing. You're still hung up on him."

"After three years? Get real. I was totally surprised to see him, that's all."

"Did I hear that you guys are having supper together tonight?" Josh rested his arm on the back of the front seat as he turned to face her.

Karly gripped the door handle. Was her past relationship with Blake seriously the top news around here? Couldn't they talk about anything else? And why was Josh so interested? Ignoring his question, she turned to Harrison. "What's on the agenda for today, boss?"

Her supervisor remained silent. Harrison had been oddly quiet the whole drive. Come to think of it, he was the only one not bombarding her with questions.

"Harrison?" Josh stared at him from the passenger seat.

"Yes?"

"You didn't answer Karly's question."

"Oh, I'm sorry. My mind was elsewhere. What was it?"

"She wants to know if you're going to drag her back into that hot bush and cause her to suffer another bout of heat stroke. In my opinion, that was really an unwise decision. The weather was unsuitable for that kind of expedition."

Karly sucked in a sharp breath. "I said nothing of the sort." Josh was really over-stepping his bounds. After all, he was only a summer student. He had a lot of nerve speaking to Harrison that way. She glanced at her supervisor. The veins in his neck bulged. She bit her lip. What was he going to do? Thankfully, the next words out of his mouth were calm, cool, and collected.

"Josh, let me remind you of your position with No Trace this summer. You are here to learn and observe. Your thoughts and opinions are always welcome if they are accurate and informed. If you have a concern, then you are encouraged to talk with Brian Wolf, the park superintendent. Otherwise, you need to respect those in authority over you."

"In other words, shut-up, you moron," Madison snapped.

Karly elbowed her roommate. "Madison, that wasn't very nice."

Josh glared at Madison, his face beet red.

Harrison brought his palm down on the steering wheel. "Enough. You're acting like children. Grow up."

"Sorry." Madison grunted a half-hearted apology.

Josh didn't respond. The final few minutes of the drive were silent until they pulled into the campground. Harrison turned off the engine. "I'll see everyone in fifteen minutes in the conference room. Don't be late."

"I can't make it in fifteen minutes. My cabin is on the far side of the campground and I need time to change my pants." Josh sounded panicked as he opened the truck door.

"Fine, you can arrive late if necessary. But I would hurry if I were you. I have an announcement to make that you won't want to miss."

Josh sprinted down the road, his paper towel flapping as he ran.

CHAPTER EIGHT

Karly rested her elbow on the table and supported her throbbing head on her palm. She tried desperately to focus on the poem Harrison was reciting.

"If you go out in the woods today,
Be sure to study the ground.
If you go out in the woods today,
Ancient plants will abound."

"Have you ever wondered at the odd-looking foliage that carpets the forest floor? Quite likely they are part of the Lycopodiaceae, a class of vascular, flowerless, epiphytic plants in the family of clubmosses. Does anyone know what an epiphyte is?" Harrison looked around the room. Karly avoided eye contact, hoping he wouldn't call on her. "Jeff?"

A tall, thin student straightened in his seat and cleared his throat. "Uh, plants that grow on other plants?"

Harrison nodded. "That's right. An epiphyte is a plant that grows on another plant, deriving nutrients from the atmosphere and accumulated plant debris. It doesn't however, harm the host. No Trace has four species of clubmosses, but oddly, none are epiphytes."

"I can't seem to focus today. My head hurts." Karly whispered to her friend.

"Is it Blake?" Madison's loud reply caused Harrison to look their direction.

Karly's cheeks warmed as she shrugged.

Harrison frowned, but addressed the entire group. "While we're out on the trails today, observe the clubmosses at your feet. There are four species we might encounter. They are not to be disturbed, only observed. The first person to identify one gets a free dinner on me."

Josh raised his hand. "Is this the announcement you didn't want me to miss?"

Harrison's frown deepened. He held up a sheet of paper. "Here is the information you'll need to help you with identification. The four are as follows: Wolf's Paw Lycopodium, Stiff Clubmoss, Ground Pine, and Ground Cedar."

"Is the one called Wolf's Paw named after Brian Wolf, the park superintendent?" Josh's comment echoed boldly through the conference room.

An odd snort of a laugh flew out of Madison's mouth beside her and giggles and snickers rippled across the room.

"I've never thought about that correlation before, but somehow I don't think so. Glad to see you're paying attention anyway, Josh." Harrison threw an annoyed glance at Madison before pointing at the sheet in his hand and proceeding to explain the different variety of clubmosses.

After a couple of minutes, he set the paper down on his desk. "Don't forget to pair up on the trail. No loners."

The class filed out slowly, everyone grabbing a sheet of paper as they walked past the desk. Karly stood as Harrison approached.

"Do you have a partner?" he asked.

"Hello? Who am I?" Madison's eyes were bright with mischief.

"I thought you might want to go with Josh. After all, you're both about the same age." A lopsided grin broke out on Harrison's face.

"That better be a joke, because there isn't a chance in ..."

"I'll go with you, Madison; I need a partner." Josh suddenly joined the group.

That guy is a sucker for punishment. He knew Madison disliked him. Why would he subject himself to more of her cruel taunts?

"You may come with the three of us, but I'll warn you, it may not be to your advantage. I've been known to lead in the opposite direction. I can't let others think my group gets special attention."

Lake of the Cross

"In other words, if you're coming along, hoping to win that free dinner because you're with the boss, forget it." Madison elbowed Josh in the ribs.

Soon the four were ambling along the Sawmill Trail, searching for the elusive plants. Madison really went out of her way to irritate Josh. Karly had to admit that it was mighty tempting to join her. There was just something about the guy that invited it. Eventually both seemed to have had enough, and wandered off in opposite directions, despite Harrison's warning to stay in pairs, leaving Karly alone with Harrison.

"Are you feeling okay?" He stopped walking and turned to face her, both hands on his hips. "You look tired. Are you still suffering the effects of that horrible day in the bush your dumb supervisor subjected you to?"

"I'm a little tired, but I'm fine." She wiped her forehead with the back of her hand. "Like I said before, I wasn't prepared, so quit blaming yourself. Josh was out of line to suggest that."

Harrison sighed. "But I can see that you still aren't feeling well, and it bothers me."

"Just between me and you, did you send those flowers?"

"Would you like it if I did?" His lips twitched just a little.

"Maybe"

"Then, yes, I did."

"Thank you. They were beautiful and that was very sweet." Karly's cheeks grew warm as Harrison held her gaze.

"Guess what I've got. I believe this is none other than Wolf's Paw Lycopodium." A plant suddenly dangled in their faces, scattering dirt down their clothing and breaking the mood.

"What have you done?" Harrison's voice rose. He brushed dirt from his shirt. "You dug it up?"

Josh's eyes grew large. "Um ... well ..."

"You were supposed to lead us to it, not kill it." Harrison pulled the sheet of paper from his pocket and jabbed a dirt-stained finger at the sentence. "What does this say? These plants are classified as endangered, exploitable, and vulnerable. In Northwestern Ontario, we're lucky to be able to see them." Harrison glared at Josh. "You obviously didn't take the time to read the information or heed my earlier advice.

If you are serious in your quest to become a park naturalist, you'll have to understand our goal—to preserve the world's ecology by observing plant and animal life, and participating in projects to protect our forests, parks, rivers, and wetlands. It is not to destroy it." Harrison's voice bellowed through the bush, followed by an eerie silence.

Josh let the plant dangle at his side. "Does this mean I don't get a free supper?"

CHAPTER NINE

Dressed in her white shorts, flip flops, and double-layered tank tops of navy and fuchsia, Karly entered the diner. When she spotted Blake in a booth with his eyes glued to her, her stomach somersaulted. What was it that he did to her? After all this time, old feelings surfaced like no time had passed between them. Taking a calming breath, she ambled forward.

The first words out of his mouth were delivered with a smirk. "You owe me a new suit."

Somehow, she knew he'd bring that up. "Not my fault. You lost your balance." She tossed her bag onto the bench and plunked herself in the booth across from him.

"But it was that unexpected passionate kiss that knocked me off kilter."

Karly's heart pounded wildly at the memory of that moment. The fact that he had brought it up confused yet pleased her. "I guess I should say I'm sorry, but you deserved it. You were dumping me." Her hands trembled as she turned the pages of the menu, pretending to deliberate on the choices.

When she looked up, Blake's penetrating gaze took her breath away. "I need to tell you something very important. You never even gave me a chance to explain what was bothering me that day. I wasn't dumping you."

"You weren't?"

"No."

"What were you going to tell me?"

"Does it matter now?"

"Tremendously." Karly set down the menu and clasped her hands together tightly in her lap.

"Hi, Blake." The same waitress who had dropped the plates the other day stood at the end of their booth. "You're looking extra handsome tonight. What can I get for you?"

"The fish and chips special." Blake closed the plastic folder.

"Coming right up." She snatched both menus off the table and turned to leave.

"Excuse me, Raven." Blake held up a hand. "I think you forgot something."

She stopped and turned around slowly. "What? Oh, I know. I'll bring you tartar sauce." She flipped her long black hair off her shoulder and laughed.

"No. You didn't take my friend's order."

Raven pivoted toward Karly, finally making eye contact with her. "What can I get for you?" Her words were as cold as the air-conditioning unit shooting air directly on the back of Karly's neck.

Karly forced her voice to remain steady. "I'll take the special too, but with a garden salad and diet cola. No fries, please."

Raven flounced away, but not before sending Blake a flirtatious smile.

Karly folded her hands on the table and waited for his gaze to come back to her. When it did, she lifted one hand in the air.

"What?" Blake asked, an innocent look on his face.

Karly frowned. "What was that all about? She acted like I was a ghost. What kind of a waitress does that?"

Blake shrugged. "Don't take it personally. She's just a little forgetful."

"Oh please. That wasn't forgetful; she knew exactly what she was doing. She wanted me to feel like I wasn't worth her noticing. Is she mad that I'm here with you? Is that it? Does she like you?"

"That's ridiculous. I barely know her."

"Well, she looks like she wants to get to know you a lot—" She froze when Blake reached across the table and clasped her arm. Tingles of electricity shot across her skin. Really? After all this time?

"I don't want to talk about Raven, Karly. I want to talk about us."

She gulped. "Okay. How about we get back to what you were saying. So, you weren't going to dump me that day?"

Blake pulled back his hand. "No, I just wanted to tell you about my plans—plans to go to Confederation College in Thunder Bay, get my pilot's license, and operate my own bush plane operation. I knew it would mean that we would have to move even farther apart, and we were already having trouble with the long-distance thing. I didn't know how to break the news without you thinking that I wanted space. Because that wasn't it at all."

A weight settled in Karly's gut like a rock. What had she done? She pressed a hand to her abdomen, her appetite suddenly gone. "And before you even had a chance, I jumped to the wrong conclusion. But why didn't you clear up the misunderstanding?"

"I tried, but you went incommunicado and disappeared off the face of the planet."

Karly snorted. "That's a slight exaggeration."

"Karly Foster!" Blake's voice grew loud enough to attract stares from nearby patrons. He dropped it a decibel or two. "You are so exasperating. How was I supposed to find you when you changed your cell phone number, quit your job, and moved out of your apartment? I even contacted Maya who hadn't heard from you since the wedding. And your father, no matter how hard I begged, respected your need for solitude and refused to tell me where you were."

Raven appeared at the end of their booth and dropped Karly's salad plate in front of her with a heavy clunk, then scurried away. Karly pushed the tomato slice around the edge of the plate for the next few minutes. An awkward silence followed until the waitress approached again. "Are you finished with that yet?"

Before Karly had a chance to answer, her plate was lifted away.

Her eyebrows shot upward as the waitress stalked off. "What's her problem?"

Blake waved a hand through the air as if to dismiss Raven. "Why did you leave your job?"

"I didn't at first. I had a lot of time for some soul-searching when my boyfriend dumped me ... or so I thought ... and Maya was off setting up house with Kerrick. I realized then that I didn't like my job anymore. I felt like I'd reached a turning point in my life."

"You weren't happy with your job? I never knew that. Why didn't you ever tell me?"

Karly shrugged. "When I took the time to think about it, I realized I felt unfulfilled. As though I had chosen the wrong career path. Missed the mark, so to speak."

"And your job as a park naturalist is the result of all that."

"Yes. I went back to school to get my Bachelor of Science. Then I apprenticed here late last summer before graduating and being hired."

"It had nothing to do with the day spent job-shadowing me at Williwaw Lake?" Blake grinned roguishly.

That smile of his still created chaos with her emotions. Her palms grew sweaty and she wiped them on her shorts.

"Don't flatter yourself. I've always had a love of the outdoors and it started the summer after my mother died of cancer when I was eight years old. My father began an annual family camping trip that year and I fell in love with nature. Maybe it was a sort of healing thing, I'm not sure, but those wonderful memories are what brought about the change, not you."

Blake winced. "That was rather harsh. I see you haven't changed much, Cruella."

Raven appeared again and dropped their dinners in front of them. She grabbed the ketchup bottle from the next table over and set it in front of Karly with a thud before moving to the next booth.

Karly poked at her fish with her fork and Blake practically inhaled his fries at warp speed.

"What made you become a pilot?" Karly sipped her diet drink.

"I've always had a love of flying."

"You have? How come I didn't know that?"

"I can answer that. You didn't know because you never asked. What *do* you know about me, Karly?"

His words stung. She opened her mouth to reply, but his raised hand cut her off.

"Wait, I'll tell you. Blake Fenton was a troubled youth and juvenile delinquent with a police record. That's all you saw, so you became disgruntled with our relationship."

"I what?" Karly placed her tall glass of pop back on the table.

"You couldn't see past the loser that I was, and you wanted out."

Karly stood to her feet, placed her hands on the table and glared down at him. "You're crazy. Where did you ever get that idea? I never said anything of the sort."

"You didn't have to. Sit down, Karly. You're making a scene." Blake pointed at the bench.

Karly glanced around the restaurant. Many eyes were fixed in her direction. Her cheeks grew warm. She slithered down onto the bench, wishing she had a hole to crawl into. Blake still had the capacity to push her buttons.

With impeccable timing, the pretty, dark-haired waitress appeared again. Her attention was entirely focused on Blake however. "Are you interested in dessert?"

Blake shook his head. "No, thanks."

Karly knew him well enough to know he was upset. Why did she always have to over-react to everything Blake said?

"I can't tempt you?" The woman ran her hands down her hips in a seductive manner, in the guise of smoothing her apron. Blake squirmed in his seat as Raven smiled at him. Karly looked back and forth between the two of them. Was something going on here?

"Fine. I'll take a piece of Moe's coconut cream pie." Blake's voice croaked like a frog in the marsh after sunset.

The waitress giggled and ran a finger down his arm. "You're so dumb. That isn't what I meant. And I just served up the last piece. But you're welcome, to come back after we close. I'll have a scrumptious dessert waiting just for you."

Blake's eyes bulged and his face reddened. Karly's cola went down her throat the wrong way and she began to cough.

"Are you choking?" Blake jumped up, a panicked look on his face. Raven took a step backwards.

"I'm fine." She grabbed her napkin and wiped at her nose and mouth.

"You scared the life out of me, Karly." Blake eased his tall frame back into the booth and swiped a palm across his forehead. "What did you choke on?"

"The look on your face. If you could have seen yourself." Karly bit her bottom lip to squelch any more outbursts.

The waitress practically ran toward the kitchen and disappeared through a swinging door.

Blake slouched down in the booth. When one of his knees bumped hers, warmth spread through her leg. He must have felt it too as their eyes connected and held for a brief second.

Blake pulled back his knee as if he'd just been zapped, sat up straight, and stared out into the parking lot. Then he scrunched a napkin between his fingers. He seemed agitated and uncomfortable, but Karly couldn't let it rest. She had to know.

"That was pretty bold of Raven. I assume she doesn't offer free dessert after closing to all her customers. Is there something I should know?"

"Concerning what?"

"Not what ... who. Raven. Is there something going on with you and that waitress?"

"No comment. What about you and Harrison?"

Karly's forehead wrinkled. "Why would you ask that?"

"His feelings for you were written all over his face the night I flew you to the hospital."

"Frankly, I don't know what you see in that woman. She's so tiny she could fit in your tackle box. She'd make great bait for the fish."

"Who said I saw anything in her?"

"Your 'no comment' says it all."

"There you go again, jumping to conclusions. And you didn't answer *my* question."

"What question?"

"You know, the one you're avoiding about you and Harrison." Blake tapped the table with his thumbs in rapid succession as if playing the drums. It was a nervous habit she remembered from when they were dating.

"No comment."

"Ah ha! Just as I suspected." Blake slapped his palms on the table.

"What do you mean? If my 'no comment' means what you think it does, then I guess your 'no comment' does too."

Blake pursed his lips. "I'm not sure I got that. You lost me there somewhere with all those comments about *comments*."

Karly reached in her purse, threw some money on the table, and clambered to her feet. She couldn't see the humour in his *comment*, or in any part of the time they'd just spent together. "I don't think there's anything else to say. I guess I'll let you go home and get freshened up."

He threw the money back at her. "I've got it covered. Freshened up?"

"For your scrumptious dessert, later tonight."

Blake leaned back against the leather fabric of the booth, crossed his arms, and smirked. "Your eyes are green with envy. It doesn't flatter you. I prefer your natural, crystal-blue ones."

Karly's emotions swirled in a jumbled, conflicted maze. Was Blake flirting with her? She clutched her bag to her chest. *I need to get out of here.* She felt a sudden need to go for a run. If it wasn't so far, she'd jog all the way back to No Trace Campground.

Karly whirled away from the booth and took long strides toward the door. She'd only made it a few steps when she heard a loud crash. She glanced back to see a metal napkin holder on the restaurant floor near Blake's feet and Raven glaring at her, with her arms crossed.

Did I do that? Oops!

She barged out the glass doors into the warm evening air without looking back again.

CHAPTER TEN

Blake watched Karly go, feeling as tense as a loaded spring. After all this time, how could they both still get to each other that easily?

"She's crazy!" Raven stooped to pick up the dented container. "I think she needs an angry madam course."

He squelched the irritation that sprang up. None of this was Raven's fault. Was it? "I think you mean an anger management course. And it was an accident, Raven. Her purse knocked it off the table when she left."

She shrugged. "Who is she, anyway?"

"My old girlfriend."

"Oh." She paused, but only briefly. "I see no problem if she's old."

Blake was speechless. Her seductive smile troubled him. Things were moving way too fast for his liking. He hadn't even made up his mind about Raven and she was already acting like they were a couple.

"Are you coming back for dessert?"

Blake's mouth went dry. She was serious? He had assumed she was flirting to upset Karly. "No, Raven, I have a flight at five tomorrow morning. I'm turning in early tonight."

Raven stuck out her lower lip. "Another time then."

As he made his way home he was terribly confused. Karly was more beautiful than ever. But even after all this time, a tangible tension existed between them.

Despite his troubling thoughts, he had to laugh at the reaction on Raven's face when the airborne napkin dispenser dropped at her feet. Karly's occasional impulsive acts aside, she really wasn't dangerous. Fiery, that's what she was. And if you played with fire, well …

And what was he to do with Raven? Although he found her attractive, he really hadn't decided if he wanted to pursue any kind of relationship with her. Had he been overly attentive towards her lately and led her to think they were more than they were? By her actions tonight, it appeared so. Her ignorant and rude treatment of Karly had shown him another side of her. When he added in the unappreciative, ungrateful attitude towards Harrison earlier today when he lied to protect her from an angry boss, Blake realized he didn't really know Raven at all.

Blake shook his head. Her forward mannerisms also had him on edge. Although he was confused by the whole situation, one thing was clear. He wasn't going to rush into anything. He'd give it time. Which had nothing to do with the fact that Karly had shocked him by suddenly re-entering his life.

Nothing whatsoever.

CHAPTER ELEVEN

Her hands shook so badly, she could barely hold the steering wheel. *Calm down, Karly.* Was she the one that had knocked that napkin dispenser to the floor? Why didn't she go back and pick it up? And how would she ever show her face in Moe's Diner again after causing such a scene?

After all this time, Blake could still make her blood boil. What did it mean? Did she still have feelings for him? No, that was impossible. She'd gotten over him long ago.

Then why had her insides flip-flopped both times she had seen him today? Just because he was the most handsome man on the planet, didn't mean they were meant for each other. Looks were important, but there was more to a relationship than that. Karly bit her lip. Her head knew that, but did her heart?

And what about Harrison? He was handsome too. She couldn't deny that he was kind, caring, and even-tempered. Not like someone else she knew. Karly tried to imagine herself with Harrison, but came up blank. Why was that? Maybe she needed to give it more time. But a relationship with her supervisor would be inappropriate. Wouldn't it? She didn't know the campground's policy for dating a co-worker. Maybe she should find out.

She turned into the campground, her headlights illuminating the dirt road to her cabin. Throwing her Kia Sportage into park, she shut off the engine, locked the doors, and headed inside.

Judging by the dark interior, Madison was out. Groping around, Karly found the switch for the small table lamp near the door and pressed it. Something moved on the sofa and Karly jumped.

Madison cried out and bolted upright, her fleecy throw landing on the floor. "What's going on?"

"You scared me half to death." Karly pressed a hand to her heart.

"The feeling's mutual." Her friend's face was pale.

"I'm sorry. I thought you were out."

"And just where would I be?" Her roommate's spiky hair stood up at weird angles.

"With Josh, maybe?" Karly teased.

Madison yawned and rubbed her eyes. "What would ever make you think that? I can't stand the guy. They don't come any nerdier."

"I think you protest a little too much." Karly plunked herself down in the large, well-worn recliner and kicked off her flip-flops.

"You've got to be kidding. Am I the only one who thinks he's weird?"

"He is a little different, I have to agree."

"That's putting it mildly. He gives me the creeps."

"Josh and Harrison both? Do you have a thing against men?"

Madison stood and stretched her arms towards the ceiling. "Of course not. That new pilot, Benton, is pretty darn hot and not the least bit creepy."

Warmth rushed into Karly's cheeks. "His name is Blake."

"Oh. How was tonight?"

Karly jumped up, ran to the closet, and pulled out her running shoes. "I'd rather not talk about it."

"Where are you going?" Madison trailed behind her. "You just got in. I want all the juicy details."

"I suddenly feel the need for a little air. I'm going for a run."

"Alone? In the dark?"

"I'll be fine. I won't follow a trail into the woods, if that's what you're thinking. What could go wrong?"

"That's probably what that other girl thought." Madison pointed a finger at her. "You know, the one who went missing."

"Are you trying to freak me out? If so, it's not working." Karly grabbed a water bottle from the fridge.

"If you're not back within the hour, I'm calling park security."

Karly shook her head. "You are such a worrier. I'll be fine." She went out into the black night and closed the door behind her.

Following the lights of the Visitor Centre, she made her way toward the main building. Perhaps a walk with Harrison would clear her mind. When she stepped inside, a warm feeling came over her. She loved this place. Off to the left a family of five searched a campground map, likely looking for their site. Directly ahead of her, a realistic exhibit behind glass depicted life in No Trace a few centuries ago. The wax figure of a woman with long dark braids sat at a fire in front of a backdrop of woods and several stuffed birds, stitching an animal hide.

After circling around behind the display, Karly descended the winding staircase to the research library. She knew she'd find Harrison here. He was slumped in a large stuffed chair with his eyes closed and headphones on. He often spent hours listening to recordings of a former park naturalist who had spent the last forty years accumulating data on the area.

Karly stopped on the bottom step. Since the opportunity presented itself, she took a moment to observe him. His rich, mocha-coloured hair, styled in a short crew cut, suited him. Overdue for a shave, the bottom half of his face appeared to have been dipped in milk chocolate with the occasional sprinkle of coconut. Long, muscular, hairy legs and arms spilled awkwardly from the chair.

A smile came over his face. Something he heard must have been funny. Karly frowned. Suddenly, she felt extremely awkward spying on her supervisor. *Why was she here?* Conflicted, she turned to leave just as an overwhelming urge to sneeze came over her. When Karly Foster sneezed, she was almost certain the Richter scale registered a tremor. Try as she might, she could never manage to diminish the excruciatingly loud sound. Before she could make her escape, an ear-shattering achoo ricocheted off the walls.

Harrison sat up suddenly, and his headphones fell from his ears. His large eyes met hers and he tilted his head. "What happened?"

"I sneezed." Karly had covered her mouth and nose with one hand and the words came out all muffled.

"Is that what that was? I thought someone was being attacked."

Unbidden, Madison's warnings about the missing girl echoed in her head. "I'm sorry. I shouldn't have come." Karly spun around and stumbled up the next few steps.

"What's wrong? Did you come to talk to me about something?" Harrison caught up with her halfway up the staircase and grabbed her arm.

"Um ...yes ... no ... I can't remember."

Harrison gently turned her to face him. "Did that sneeze jar your memory loose?"

Karly shrugged. Why had she let Madison's tall tale affect her? "Actually, I came by to see if you wanted to go for a walk. But I'll go. You're busy."

"I'm never too busy for you, Karly." He smiled. "Just let me put away this recording and I'll be right with you."

A few minutes later, as they ambled along the dirt trail that led to Samson Lake, the tightness in her chest eased. What on earth had she been so paranoid about earlier?

"How did your dinner with Blake go?"

Karly sighed. "Not well."

"I wish I could say I'm sorry and mean it, but that would be untruthful."

She swallowed the large lump that formed in her throat. Maybe this wasn't a clever idea after all. Being alone with her supervisor, when she was feeling vulnerable and confused, was risky. What had made her want to talk to Harrison? She should have unloaded her concerns on her friend, Madison. But she couldn't have done that since Madison seemed infatuated with Blake.

They stepped onto the beach and were met by a half-moon peering above the tree-line and casting a beam of light across the tranquil lake. When a loon called in the distance, Karly inhaled deeply. "I love it here. I'm so happy I decided to change careers."

"I'm happy too. For you, that is," he stammered.

Despite her reservations, her heart warmed to his shyness.

A loud splash in the lake not far down the shoreline brought Karly's head up sharply. "What was that?"

Harrison leaned in close and whispered, his breath tickling her ear. "If we're quiet, we'll hear it swimming."

"Hear what swimming?"

"Let's go find out."

A thrill of anticipation raced through her as she followed him in the dark. "This is so exciting. What could it be?"

"Careful on the rocks. Watch your footing." A few steps ahead of her, Harrison stopped and pointed. "There it is."

Karly reached his side. At first, she couldn't see a thing. Then a head moved through the moonlight on the lake. "Is that a moose?"

"Yes."

"It's beautiful."

"So are you."

Karly's stomach knotted. What had she gone and done? Why did she seek out her supervisor tonight when she was so confused about Blake? It all felt wrong.

A bright light shone directly into her face and she squinted. A hand flew up to shield her eyes.

"Park security. Who's there?"

Saved by a flashlight. Karly's heart pounded as she stepped back from her supervisor.

"Put away your flashlight, Rob; it's Harrison and Karly."

"Ah. The subject of our missing person investigation. Not missing after all, I see."

"Missing person?" Harrison's voice rose in concern.

Karly sighed. "That crazy Madison. She said if I wasn't back in an hour she'd notify security."

"Ah." Harrison waved a hand through the air. "Thanks for checking, but you can run along now. Everything is fine here."

"It definitely appears that way." Rob's chuckles trailed off into the bush.

Karly could just imagine the smirk on the security man's face. Great. All she needed was for rumours to start.

"Where were we?" Harrison reached for her.

Karly took another step back. "We were leaving."

He frowned. "What's wrong?"

"I shouldn't have sought you out tonight. I just needed a friend to talk to."

"I'm a good listener."

"I know, but I don't think you can help me, or if it's even fair of me to ask you to."

He contemplated her for a moment before nodding curtly. "You still have feelings for him."

Karly gaped at him. "Who?"

He folded his arms over his massive chest. "You know who."

"How ... did you know I was going to talk to you about Blake?"

"You've been distracted since he arrived."

Karly drew in a slow, steadying breath. "You're very observant." She began picking her way back over the rocks. She heard the skittering of rocks beneath his shoes as he followed her, but she didn't look back.

"I have a confession to make." Harrison touched her elbow as they arrived at the main road leading back to Karly's cabin.

Karly's mind raced. Was he going to admit to the murder?

"I didn't tell you that Blake was in the area. That he flew you to the hospital that night."

So, he isn't confessing to murder?

Harrison froze in his tracks. "What did you just say?"

Karly clapped a hand over her mouth. *Did she say that out loud?* "That Madison and her stupid stories. It's all her fault."

"Let me guess. You've heard the rumours about Jessica Wakely."

"Was that her name?" Karly's voice rasped, and she cleared her throat.

"Will I ever be free of that murderous accusation?" Harrison sounded weary. "Where did Madison get her information?"

"Raven." A porcupine waddled across the road in front of them and Karly jumped.

"That figures."

"Speaking of Madison, I should probably get back before she calls out the Canadian army to find me." Karly checked to make sure the porcupine had disappeared into the bushes, then started walking. "Do you want to talk about it?"

Harrison fell into step beside her. "Jessica was hired here as a park naturalist two years ago. To say she was attractive was an understatement. We hit it off from the start. We were great friends, but that's all it ever was. Jessica had a longtime boyfriend, Adam, who lived in Kenora. One morning she didn't report for work. A search of her cabin showed no signs of a struggle or break-in. She just disappeared. No trace of her has ever been found."

"Why would you be a suspect?"

"Everyone knew we were friends and spent time together on the job and off. So naturally, when she went missing I was a suspect."

By now the pair had arrived in front of Karly's cabin. They stopped outside the front door.

Harrison raked a hand through his hair. "The whole thing might have been put to rest by now if it wasn't for Raven."

"Why would she spread such nasty rumours if you were innocent?"

He grimaced. "There's something else you should know."

Karly tensed. What was she about to hear?

"Raven and I were engaged. I broke it off shortly after Jessica came along. When I realized that I preferred to spend most of my leisure time with Jessica over Raven, I knew something was off in our relationship. Marrying Raven would have been so wrong. Besides, we had other problems. My friendship with Jessica just forced them all to the surface."

"Let me get this straight. After two years, Raven continues to spread these deadly accusations, out of spite towards you?"

"You know what they say about a woman scorned."

"That explains her rude treatment of you today when you tried to protect her from that angry chef."

Harrison's shoulders sagged. "She's never forgiven me for ending our engagement. And why she allows Moe to treat her the way he does is beyond me. I can't comprehend how he gets away with his abusive behaviour."

Her heart ached for Harrison. No wonder she detected sadness behind those dark- brown eyes. The cabin door flew open, spilling light onto the yard. "There you are. I sent security looking for you." Madison parked her hands on her hips. "Do you know what time it is?"

Karly glared at her friend. "I appreciate your concern, but I'm a big girl, Madison. I can take care of myself. I'll be in shortly."

Madison eyed the two of them suspiciously before closing the door.

"I guess I'd better go before another rumour starts—one about you and me." Harrison kicked at a pine cone. "I'm sorry if my actions were inappropriate on the beach." He took a step back. "I guess I got my signals crossed and got caught up in the moment. It won't happen again."

"It's fine. Thanks for being a good friend. Good-night." Karly grasped the doorknob just as the outdoor cabin light flickered off and on several times.

"Your roommate is very protective. And a little annoying." Harrison shook his head.

"Life with her is never dull. But she's really the sweetest thing when you get to know her."

"I'll have to trust you on that one." Harrison waved, then headed down the dark trail.

For a long moment Karly stared through the trees where Harrison had disappeared. Was he telling the truth? Could she really trust him? She'd trusted another man and been deeply hurt. She wasn't sure her heart would be able to take that again. With a heavy sigh, Karly pushed open the door of the cabin and slipped inside.

CHAPTER TWELVE

"Are you still mad at me?" Madison asked, her breath ragged as she and Karly jogged along a park trail.

Karly frowned. How did she answer her friend truthfully without hurting her feelings? "I'm not mad, Madison. Wild dogs get mad. I'm annoyed."

When the dirt trail changed to a narrow wooden boardwalk over a swampy area, Karly picked up her pace and moved ahead of her friend. She stopped in the middle of the low bridge and stared out at the large beaver lodge ahead and to their right. She'd always liked this spot. And a beaver sighting was such a treat.

"I only did it out of concern. I care about you. Is that such a crime?" Madison stopped behind her, planted her hands on the wooden rail and lowered her head, breathing heavily.

Karly uncapped her water bottle. "No, it's not a crime to care about someone. But, honestly, Madison, I'm thirty-one years old. I don't need a curfew."

"You've got a point. But I've had this uneasy feeling lately that I can't put my finger on. It feels ... like something bad is going to happen."

Karly took a swallow and re-capped her bottle. "You've got yourself all worked up lately with Raven's unfounded accusation of murder. In fact, Harrison and I talked about that very thing last night."

Madison straightened. "You did? What did he say? Wait!" She held her water bottle in the air. "Of course, he'd say he was innocent. What man would confess to murdering someone if he'd gotten away with it so far? He may as well tie a noose around his neck."

Karly sighed. "You don't know the whole story. Did Raven tell you that she and Harrison were engaged?"

Madison's eyes grew large. "No, she didn't mention that. But what does that have to do with anything?"

"He broke off the engagement."

"Why? Was it because of that woman?"

"Her name was Jessica and they were just friends. Harrison mentioned that he and Raven had been having problems before Jessica came along. The fact that he would rather spend his free time with another woman while engaged set off alarm bells for him and he felt it was best to end things."

"No wonder Raven's bitter. I don't blame her."

"Two years is a long time to be bitter." Karly propped a foot on the railing and reached out to grab the toe of her running shoes with both hands, stretching her tired muscles. Then she alternated with the other foot. "She needs to let it go and stop spreading horrible rumours. She and Harrison just weren't meant to be."

"Someone I know needs to listen to her own advice."

Before she could respond, Karly heard a splash and straightened. Mesmerized, she watched a beaver swimming toward his lodge. When the animal slid out of sight, she turned to her friend. "I'm not bitter. And it's been three years." Karly broke into a run.

Madison's laughter echoed across the water behind her. "Keeping count, are we? Judging by what I saw last night, it appears that you have moved on. It's just too bad it's with Harrison."

"Are we back to that again? I can't understand why you don't trust him, even after what I just told you."

Madison caught up with her and ran at her side. "Actually, what you just told me makes me even more suspicious of him. Think about it, Karly. The guy admitted he spent a lot of time with Jessica. Maybe he was secretly in love with her and when he found out he couldn't have her, he snapped."

"You're being unfair. I know him far better than you. Harrison is kind, gentle, and caring. He could never hurt someone, let alone kill them. If you could see how tormented he is about this whole murderous rumour, you'd believe that he was innocent, like I do."

"Whatever. Let's pick up the pace." Madison glanced back over her shoulder. "I think someone is following us."

"Oh, Madison, you really are spooked, aren't you?"

"I told you I have this awful feeling."

Karly pointed to the trees on their left. "Let's put your fears to rest, once and for all." She brushed back branches with both arms as she made her way into the bush about a dozen feet before stopping behind a large boulder. "Let's hide here and see if someone comes. But, I'm telling you right now, you're wrong. No one is following us."

After a few minutes had passed, Madison brushed a twig from her shorts and started to stand. "I guess I was wrong. Let's get going."

Something caught Karly's eye and she grabbed her friend's hand, pulling her back down beside her. "Hold on. Don't get up. I saw a flash of colour."

From her knees, Karly poked her head above the rock. Someone was approaching, very slowly, on a bicycle.

"It's just a camper out for a bike ride," Madison hissed. "Boy, do I feel stupid."

"Duck!" Karly pushed Madison's head down below the top of the rock.

"Who is it?" Madison asked as the pair crouched as low to the ground as possible.

Karly pressed a finger to her lips. Her chest tightened at the sound of someone crashing through the trees, moving toward them.

"Busted! What are you guys doing behind that rock?" Josh peered down at the pair.

"Madison lost an earring and I'm helping her find it," Karly lied. The speed at which she came up with that fabrication surprised even her.

Josh's eyes narrowed.

"It's true." Madison went along with her story, patting the ground around her with one hand.

Josh crossed his arms, his feet spread widely apart. "Either you made up the story, or you've lost both your earrings at the same time, since you aren't wearing any. What are the odds of that happening?"

Karly stood up. When her friend rose too, Karly patted her on the back. "Actually, the truth is that Madison isn't feeling well. She didn't want to admit that to you just now, because it's embarrassing when you eat tacos the night before and you get caught in the bush." Karly started back toward the trail. "Let's give her a minute on her own." Deep inside, she was rattled at how quickly she had come up with another untruth. But the fact that Josh may have been following them gave her lies justification. Didn't they?

"Good point. If she's so sick, why are you back here with her? Didn't she want some privacy?"

Karly spun around and jammed both fists into her hips. "Not that it's any of your business, but I was helping Madison find a safe spot away from poison ivy. She's terribly allergic to the plant, you know."

Moaning and groaning came from behind the rock. Karly resisted the urge to roll her eyes. Madison was really playing the part.

Josh backed into a thorny bush. "Ouch." He rubbed the back of his arm. "I guess I deserved that. I'm sorry." He followed her back to the trail and stopped by the bike he'd dropped at the edge of the trees.

Karly levelled a cold look at him. "Why were you following us?"

Josh swiped a jittery hand across his forehead and bent down to lift his bike. "I was just out for a ride." He started to wheel it down the path, then he stopped abruptly and whirled to face Karly. "I hope you remember how to dispose of waste properly. You need to remove the top layer of vegetation and dig a proper hole about six inches deep. Make sure to bury the ... um ... excrement, and then mark the area with a rock or two crossed sticks."

Karly did roll her eyes this time. "We know, Josh, but thanks for the reminder. You'd better be on your way now as this is really embarrassing for Madison. You won't mention this to anyone, will you?"

Moans grew louder and more pitiful from behind the boulder. "Oh, the pain."

Karly bit her lip. Madison had missed her calling in life. She could win an Academy Award for that performance.

Josh broke into a full-out sprint. Hopping on his seat, he pedalled away as though a nest of hornets were on his tail.

Karly took one look at Madison—who had popped up from behind the rock—and lost it.

"We're bad together, aren't we?" Madison giggled, holding her sides.

"Oh yes." Karly swiped at a tear that had started down her cheek. "We certainly are."

As the girls jogged back to their cabin, a heaviness settled over Karly. Something didn't feel right. Was it the fact that she had so easily lied, not once but twice? Or was it Josh's behaviour that had shaken her? Was Madison, right? Had Josh been following them? A chill travelled the length of her body, but she pushed back her shoulders and did her best to ignore the scary tingle. Madison's fears were getting to her. That's all it was.

CHAPTER THIRTEEN

"What kind of lure do I need for smallmouth bass?" Blake asked Henry as they stood in front of a fishing display in the Wagami Outfitter's store.

"Ah, my friend." The guide clapped him on the shoulder. "You've asked the right guy. There are many lures to tempt you, but I like the method my grandfather used."

"And what was that?"

"A hook and large worm." His laugh came from deep within his belly. "But when all else fails, you can use spinnerbaits, diving crankbaits, jerkbaits, tube jigs, and bomber jigs."

Blake smiled. "I think I'll try the old-fashioned way. For one thing, it costs less."

"I like the way you think. Do you know which reel to use? What pound test?"

"Spinning reel with a light line ... four to six-pound test?"

Henry nodded. "Not bad. Tell me what you know about smallmouth bass."

Blake crossed his arms. "Is this a quiz or something?"

"Maybe." The guide grinned. "I'll let you know if you pass."

Blake drummed his fingers on one arm. "Let's see, what do I know about smallmouth bass." He smirked. "They've got small mouths?"

Henry shook his head slowly. "You've got to do better than that if you expect me to let you loose on the waters of No Trace."

Blake sobered. "All right. They feed mostly on minnows and crayfish, I believe. Their skin secretes a chemical that smells like a crayfish and draws crustaceans out from their hiding spaces, so they can gobble them up. Is that correct?"

Henry stared at him. "Where did you hear such foolishness?"

Blake stiffened. "Um ... I always thought ... I mean, I can't remember ..."

Boisterous guffawing echoed throughout the store. "Got you! You're very smart. It's possible that you'll make a great fisherman, but I'm not finished yet. Where's the best place to find the fish?"

Blake's forehead broke out in a sweat. "Rock shoals and rocky points?"

"Do you use weights?"

"No, they'll only get caught on the rocks."

"What time of day?"

"Early morning or evening."

"Tell me how you will catch the smallmouth bass."

Blake's eyebrows drew together. "With patience, luck, and a big fat worm?"

"Wrong."

"Do you mean the procedure? Like casting and stuff?"

Henry nodded, a serious look on his face.

"Using a lightweight line, cast as far as you can. Let the worm sink a couple of feet, then pull it gently towards you until it hits the surface. Then drop it again and repeat the procedure until the bronzehead bites." Blake stuttered through his answer.

A powerful smack of Henry's hand across Blake's upper back caused him to cough. "I'm impressed. You even knew another name for the fish. You pass."

"You don't know how happy that makes me." Blake swiped at the beads of sweat on his brow with the sleeve of his T-shirt. "You are one tough teacher. I felt like a kid back in school."

"No, only the fish are in schools." Henry chuckled. "Get it, Mr. White Pelican? That was a good joke."

"Yeah, that's very funny, Henry. You need to perform at a comedy club."

Henry's brow wrinkled.

"You'd be really entertaining." Blake headed towards the checkout with some lightweight fishing line.

After Blake paid the cashier, the pair walked toward Blake's truck. "That was quite the test, Henry. You've got me all stressed out now." Blake blew out a long breath as he climbed inside.

"I can't let you upset the balance of nature, big bird."

"I don't want to do that either. So, I guess you're forgiven." Blake fastened his seatbelt and inserted the key in the ignition. "Do you want to go fishing with me in the morning?"

"I'd be honoured, but the little wife wouldn't be happy. She thinks I'm gone too much. You know how it is."

"No, I don't know how it is."

"Maybe someday?"

"Maybe someday."

"I'm known to be a good matchmaker. I'll find you Mrs. White Pelican."

Not sure how to respond to that, Blake reached for the paper cup in the holder.

"You'll be married by the next full moon."

Blake choked on a swig of his cold takeout coffee. "You're joking, right?"

"I'm as serious as a bull moose in heat."

Blake offered him a salute before pulling out of the parking lot. Henry had to be the funniest man he'd ever met in his entire life. And he was going to find Blake a wife within the month. Good luck with that. The way things had gone with him and women the last few years, climbing Mount Everest would be easier.

CHAPTER FOURTEEN

The early morning mist hanging over the tranquil cobalt lake added to the surreal moment. Blake felt like dropping to his knees in worship as he stared in awe at the magnificent sunrise. Cloaked in hues of magenta, fuchsia, stormy grey, and sapphire, the mesh of colours screamed of a master artist, unrivalled by any mortal that had ever picked up a paintbrush. If the only thing he took away from the pre-dawn fishing trip was this view, it would be worth it.

As he stood on the rocky shore and cast across the serene waters of Potter's Lake, Blake found himself growing emotional. He had changed so much in the past three years, and although his former brother-in-law, Kerrick, was a key factor, Blake owed his transformation ultimately to God's love. He would never have believed that life could be this good. Not good the way most people judged but good inside, with an indwelling sense of peace and love that was beyond words. If only everyone could know this peace, especially those he cared about. Karly's face flashed in his mind and he shoved it away. He couldn't go there. It hurt too much.

He pulled in his line without the chubby night-crawler. Those sneaky bronzebacks. How did they do it? Re-baiting his hook, he cast again. While he waited for a nibble, Blake's eyes soaked in the beauty of the area he had discovered totally by accident. One day, he had taken a wrong turn and found himself driving down an old ski and trapping trail that led to this tiny, remote body of water. It was a jewel, tucked into the bush just a few short minutes from the main highway.

After reeling in an empty line for the third time, Blake set down his rod, opened his thermos, and poured himself a steaming cup of coffee. Ah! There was nothing comparable to sipping the hot beverage in the wilds of northwestern Ontario while enjoying God's incredible handiwork.

Blake's mind wandered back to one of the most amazing days of his life—the day he held Maya and Kerrick's newborn son—the day that changed his life forever. It didn't matter how many times he recalled that moment, the emotions were as strong as if it happened yesterday. Of course, it had only been a few months ago.

As he stood in the hospital room, holding the miraculous bundle of marital love, his life flashed before him. An overwhelming sorrow compelled him to pass the precious baby back into the mother's arms and flee.

In the dark waiting room down the hall, Blake had dropped onto a worn stuffed chair, as painful memories bombarded him against his will. His whole horrible life ran through his mind like a demented family video. Why? He didn't want to remember, then or ever. The harder he fought, though, the clearer they became.

Heart-wrenching images of verbal abuse and physical neglect from not one, but two, drug abuse parents assaulted him. Remembering the ensuing rebellion in his teenage years, his brush with the law for spraying graffiti on the side of City Hall, and even the devastating breakup with Karly, the only woman he had ever cared about, filled him with such despair, he wanted to die.

He buried his head in his hands and jumped when a hand touched his shoulder. Without looking, Blake knew it was his friend Kerrick, who had taken time on the day of his son's birth to search him out. The love of his ex-brother-in-law still amazed Blake.

Coffee in hand, Blake ambled slowly along the rocky shoreline. Although it had been difficult, it was the most joyous day he had ever experienced. As Kerrick knelt beside him, his hand still on Blake's shoulder, he uttered a prayer Blake would never forget, *Please, God, reveal your love to Blake.*

With his eyes closed, a vision of Jesus flashed in his mind. What he experienced hit him like a ton of bricks. A lump formed in his throat as he remembered his Saviour's nail-scarred hands and feet. Whether it was truly a vision, or just a remembrance of Kerrick's description of the death of Jesus on the cross, he wasn't sure. But it seemed so real. At the same time, he heard Kerrick's words, *God sent his son Jesus to die for your sins, Blake. He died to set you free. And He did it because he loves you.*

Deep inside, he finally understood. The love that flooded through him was not of this world. He'd never felt anything like it before.

A loud obtrusive squawk brought Blake back to reality. Glancing upwards, he observed a jet-black bird on the branch of a fir tree, feathers glistening in the sunlight. As he stepped over exposed tree roots and continued along the shoreline, he noticed several other crows alight nearby.

Life was good but not perfect. Situations and relationships still caused pain and anguish. He had no contact with his parents; he didn't even know if they were alive. He hadn't spoken to his sister, Katie, in a little over a year. Suddenly, he felt convicted. Maybe he should make more of an effort to re-connect with them. After all, he knew the truth—the truth his family so desperately needed.

Henry's words about finding Blake a wife floated through his mind and he laughed out loud. He had to admit he longed to fall in love, settle down, and have children one day. Although he wrestled from time to time with patience, he was learning to wait and trust God for his timing. Besides, God knew the perfect match for him. Who knew what kind of marital candidate Henry would pick? To his credit, Henry did appear to be happily married. Blake had sensed that the other day when he stayed for lunch at their modest home in Shadow Lake.

Raven's face flashed into his mind. Blake wasn't shallow enough to think good looks would make a great marriage. The longer he read his Bible, the more he realized that spouses needed to be like-minded. Before he made any moves in that direction, he'd pray and make sure that the next person he dated loved God as much as he did.

Deep in thought, he stumbled over a piece of driftwood that had washed up on the shore. Absently, he picked it up. He was about to toss it into the lake when he realized it wasn't driftwood at all but the long bone of an animal. Blake studied it. What kind of animal had it belonged to?

As he perused the area, his eye caught something between piles of jagged rocks at the water's edge. Stepping closer, he peered into the crevice. Bile climbed up his throat. He dropped the bone as he stared at what appeared to be human skeletal remains.

His legs collapsed beneath him and he fell to his knees on the shore, the cup of coffee clattering onto the rocks. The grisly discovery sucked the beauty from the magnificent sunrise. Shock and sadness coursed through him at the life that had been lost. This was someone's loved one and a creation of God.

The murder of crows sang a merciless, haunting chorus. Anger charged through him. Lumbering to his feet, he hurried toward the mocking birds, flapping his arms and yelling like a lunatic. "Get out of here, heartless scavengers."

His outburst only elevated their taunting several decibels. Blake stumbled back toward the body. He was no forensic pathologist or crime scene investigator, but judging by the condition of the skeleton, the body had to have been in the water for a long time.

The sun glistened on a piece of partially-tarnished jewellry hanging around the neck of the skeleton. Did he have the courage to look? Should he touch the body? Or what was left of it? Cautiously, he peered down at the chain. It was a heart pendant. Did that mean the remains were female? With a shaking hand, he reached for the locket, but thought better of it and quickly pulled away.

Blake reached into his pocket for his cell phone, hoping he'd get a signal since he wasn't that far from the main highway. Relief coursed through him when he heard an operator ask him the cause of his emergency.

"Please come quickly." Blake's voice rasped, and he pressed a fist to his mouth and cleared his throat. "I've just found human remains at the end of the old logging trail leading to Potter's Lake.

CHAPTER FIFTEEN

Blake ran a hand through his already dishevelled hair as he contemplated the scene before him. Yellow police caution tape marked a large perimeter around the gruesome find. Two OPP (Ontario Provincial Police) officers sat on rocks, sipping coffee and whispering quietly among themselves while another spoke on his cell phone a few feet away.

From what he had learned, the body would not be moved until a crime scene investigator flew in from Toronto. Until then, two officers would be left to guard the remains.

It had been three full hours since Blake gave his story and he still felt numb. When one of the officers mentioned that he wondered if the body belonged to a No Trace Campground employee that had gone missing a few years ago, Blake's ears perked up. He had no idea what they were talking about, but if it were true, some family might be receiving closure. That would be the only positive slant he could think of to this situation.

Since he was free to go, he gathered his fishing gear and trudged toward his pickup truck. How had such an incredible day turned so horrendously morose?

It was only ten in the morning and he was exhausted, the heaviness of his discovery weighing down on him. He couldn't imagine what it would feel like to be on the receiving end of such heart-wrenching news.

He climbed in his truck, and whispered a prayer for the family of the deceased—for God's strength and comfort in their time of need.

A few minutes later he saw the entrance to the campground and turned into the parking lot. *What am I doing here?* He'd intended to go back to his office, but must have turned the wrong direction after leaving Potter's Lake. Blake was not directionally-challenged but he chalked up his mistake to nerves.

As he sat in his truck, which idled in the middle of the parking lot, his brain couldn't seem to erase the shocking discovery from his mind. He probably shouldn't be behind the wheel in his present state.

A thunderous jolt shook his truck suddenly, catapulting his thoughts to the present while jerking his head forward and back. Blake stared in his rearview mirror to see the back of a white park truck slammed against his rear fender.

For a few seconds, he sat in stunned silence. Then he shifted the truck into park, unfastened his seatbelt, and climbed out, just as the driver of the wayward vehicle opened the door and stalked toward him.

"Karly Foster. I should have known."

"What should you have known?" Karly stopped and slammed her palm down on the bed of the truck. "Why was your truck sitting in the middle of the parking lot?"

"I um ... just arrived and was debating where to park. You're supposed to look before you back up." One hand reached up to rub the back of his neck. "I think you gave me whiplash."

"Oh please! You always exaggerate everything." Karly waved a hand through the air. "I didn't hit you that hard."

Blake stepped to the rear of his vehicle and studied their bumpers. "Can you please move this thing forward, so I can see what damage you've done? And by the way, don't you have a back-up beeper?"

"I disabled it."

"Why?"

Karly shrugged. "It seemed to be malfunctioning. It was going off every few seconds and I couldn't hear the birds. And I thought I heard a pileated woodpecker just now. That's why I didn't see your truck."

Blake blew out a breath. "So, you were looking up into the trees instead of where you were going. Wait until the insurance company hears that one. You'll be laughed right out of the office."

Karly's lower lip quivered slightly. Blake repressed a sigh. Maybe he'd been too hard on her. She didn't say anything though, just climbed back into her truck and parked it under a tree before walking back to him.

"Aw gee, Karly!" He ran his hand across the left fender. "Look at this huge dent and smashed taillight."

"Oh. Do we need to call the police?"

"We really shouldn't bother them with something so petty. They're tied up in a situation way more serious." Blake's stomach knotted.

"Petty? But you just said ..."

Time to confess.

He grinned. "You didn't damage my truck. It was already in this shape before you hit it."

Karly pointed a shaking finger at him. "You are still the same despicable jerk you were before." She poked him in the chest.

"Forgive me." His smile faded as he grabbed her hand. "I was out of line to tease you like that. I'm not myself today."

His apology appeared to stymie her briefly, then she cocked her head. "The Blake I remember would have acted just like this and never said he was sorry. Something is *different* about you."

He didn't want to let go of her hand. He clasped it tightly.

She didn't pull away. "Why did you say the police were busy with more serious issues? Has something happened?"

"Unfortunately, yes." Blake forced himself to let her go, then removed his hat and wiped his brow with the sleeve of his T-shirt. "Do you have a moment?"

She reached in her shirt pocket, pulled out her cell phone, and glanced at the screen. "As a matter of fact, it's time for my break. Let's go inside."

After Blake backed his aging truck under the tree beside her vehicle, Karly led him inside the main building and downstairs to the empty lunch room where a pot of coffee sat ready for the taking.

"Help yourself." She pointed toward the mugs.

Blake's hand trembled as he poured himself a drink. He desperately needed a strong cup of the beverage right now to calm his nerves. The pot clanged loudly as he placed it back on the burner.

Karly reached across him for the coffeepot. "Are you okay? Did that little fender bender shake you up that badly?"

"I found a body."

Karly's hand froze on the handle. "Are you serious?"

"Dead serious." He winced at the unintended pun. "I was fishing at Potter's Lake early this morning, and when the fish weren't biting, I took a walk along the shore. That's when I happened upon the ..."

Karly planted her palm between his shoulder blades and steered him toward the chair. "You don't look so well. Sit down while I get my drink."

"You don't have to tell me twice." Blake eased himself down and gazed into his coffee mug. His stomach lurched, and he couldn't bring the cup to his lips.

Karly sat down across from him and wrapped her fingers around her mug. "I thought you looked pale, but I figured that was because of the accident."

Blake rubbed the back of his neck again. "It has been a rough day. And now that you mention it, I am a little sore."

To Blake's surprise, she jumped up and came around behind him. "Maybe I can help. It's the least I can do after all you've been through."

Blake closed his eyes as her thumbs not only kneaded sore muscles, but miraculously reached deep inside to stroke tender, achy cords around his heart. Until this moment, he hadn't realized how much he'd missed her.

"What did the police say about your discovery?"

"They didn't say much to me, but I overheard one of them mention a possible connection to the unsolved case of a missing campground employee. Have you heard anything about that?"

"Blake? What are you doing here?" At the sound of a man's deep voice, Karly's fingers disappeared from his shoulders—so quickly he felt a slight breeze on the back of his neck. Harrison's enormous frame loomed in the doorway.

"Blake was in the area and he decided to stop in." Karly offered, a slight hitch in her voice.

Harrison didn't move. Did his shoulders just droop a little? He appeared shaken and ... hurt? *Yep, he's got it bad for Karly.* A knot formed in Blake's already upset stomach.

With a flash of purple, Madison appeared from behind her supervisor and hurried to Blake's side. "Hi, I'm Madison." She extended a hand toward him.

Blake nodded as he shook her hand. "I know. I met you at the diner the other day. Don't you remember?"

Madison giggled. "I remember. It's hard not to notice the new good-looking pilot. I just wasn't sure you even knew I existed. You seemed ... distracted." Madison glanced at Karly before sitting in the chair beside Blake and opening her water bottle.

Harrison lumbered to the fridge and pulled out the coffee cream. "What brings you out this way?" The words were friendly, but the look he levelled at Blake was decidedly heated.

"Whatever it was, I'm sure he forgot after the trauma I put him through this morning when I crashed into his vehicle." Karly's words tumbled over each other.

She's nervous. Interesting.

Harrison's eyebrows shot upward.

Karly held up both hands, palms out. "Before you freak out, the truck is fine. I backed up and hit Blake's back fender. I didn't see him sitting there. I think I gave him a little case of whiplash."

"Yes, I think she did." Blake rolled his head, testing the muscles.

"That's why you caught me giving him a massage." Karly blurted, her cheeks flushed.

"Are you okay, Karly? Were you hurt?" Harrison asked.

"I'm fine." Karly replied.

Madison batted her eyelashes at Blake. "I'm glad nothing happened to you. It would have been such a loss." Then her eyes darted quickly to Karly's. "And you too, of course.

Awkward. Blake gulped the last few mouthfuls of his coffee and stood. "I guess I'd better be going and let all of you get back to work."

"No need to rush out on our account." Madison touched his elbow. "But if you must leave, we're all going to the Cedar Canoe tonight. Why don't you join us?"

"I'm new around here. What's the Cedar Canoe?"

"It's a coffee house on the main street in Aspen Ridge. A local band, Moosemeat, is playing. They're really good."

"If I don't get any last-minute calls, I might come."

"Great!" Madison clapped her hands together.

"Okay, then." Karly shot a look at her friend that Blake couldn't quite decipher. "I'll walk you out and double-check both our vehicles for damage. I want to make sure we didn't miss anything."

She headed for the door and Blake followed her.

"What's up?" he asked as they walked side by side through the parking lot.

"What do you mean?"

"I'm surprised you didn't mention my discovery."

"It's a little awkward to explain."

"Try me."

"I didn't want Harrison to get wind of the news."

"Why?"

"Because a few years ago, a No Trace employee named Jessica Wakely went missing."

Blake's forehead wrinkled. Was that the employee the police officer had mentioned? "And?"

"There are rumours."

He circled his hand through the air. "Go on."

"That Harrison had something to do with her disappearance."

Blake stopped at the side of his truck. "Ah. And what do you think of these so-called rumours?"

"He's innocent, of course."

"Are you sure?"

Karly sighed. "Harrison told me all about his relationship with Jessica. They were good friends and he was devastated when she went missing. But that's all. He's heartsick that this gossip about him is still circulating."

"If it's still circulating, maybe there's some truth to it."

Karly shook her head so vehemently her long blonde tresses whipped back and forth.

A sudden urge to run his fingers through her silky hair, almost overwhelmed him and he crossed his arms, tucking his fingers out of temptation's way.

"If you knew the source you wouldn't say that."

"Who's the source?"

"Raven."

"Why would she spread such horrible lies?"

"Harrison and Raven were engaged until Jessica came along."

Blake stiffened. Clearly, he knew very little about Raven. "You are just a wealth of knowledge. Are you sure about all of this?"

Karly paced back and forth in front of him. "I thought I was, but Madison, with her gossip, has me second guessing everything I know, or thought I knew about Harrison. It's just that, when I spend time with him, he seems so genuine, kind, and thoughtful. I can't imagine him ever doing anything like that in a million years."

Blake's mouth went completely dry as he remembered the heart-sick look on Harrison's face. "You sound like you know him pretty well. Are you sure you guys aren't more than friends?"

She stopped pacing and faced him. "No comment."

"So, we're going to play this game again." Blake leaned back against his truck.

"I have no idea what you are talking about; I don't play games."

"Yeah, okay." He smirked.

Karly pursed her lips. "Will I see you tonight at the Cedar Canoe?"

"Maybe."

"You'd better not bring her." Her finger poked him in the chest again. She seemed to like doing that. And honestly, he didn't mind. Not one little bit.

"Her who? Madison or Raven?" Blake couldn't help himself.

"You know who I mean." Karly scrunched up her nose.

"Oh really? Then you'd better not bring him." He poked her shoulder, then couldn't seem to pull his hand away. A breeze blew her silky hair across his hand, and this time he couldn't resist temptation. He reached out to gently sift the golden tresses through his fingers. His heart ricocheted against his rib cage.

Karly swallowed. "I'd better get to work." She took a step backwards.

Blake watched her turn and sprint to her vehicle. He took a deep breath and willed his breathing to return to normal.

"For the record, you owe me a new taillight," he yelled after her.

Karly whirled toward him. "What? I thought you said ..."

Blake chuckled, opened his door, and climbed in. The engine rumbled to life and he drove toward the parking lot exit. As he stopped to wait for traffic, he glanced in his rearview mirror. Karly stood by her truck with the door open, staring after him. Blake shook his head. He was a messed-up bundle of emotions. First the dead body and then ... what was happening between him and Karly? Was there something there after all these years?

Get a grip, Blake. It was over long ago. Do you seriously want to go there again?

CHAPTER SIXTEEN

As Karly savoured her extra-creamy vanilla latte, she sighed contentedly, relaxing into the leather sofa. Being with friends and listening to the band play renditions of their latest hits was relaxing. The Cedar Canoe was a cool place.

According to Harrison, who had grown up in the area, it had once been the town's hardware store. When a large chain store opened only a few hour's drive away in Kenora, the local shop slowly went out of business. After the building had sat vacant for several years, an entrepreneur and local business man fulfilled their dream of creating an establishment to cater to the town's young people. Remote northwestern Ontario towns usually had very little to offer for entertainment. As a result, the enterprise was an enormous success.

Canoes, fishing nets, and outdoor survival gear hung from the walls. A woodstove in the corner recreated a campfire experience. Thankfully, with the summer they'd been experiencing, it wasn't pumping out heat. A life-sized bear, family of raccoons, and birds in simulated flight added to the entire nature-filled experience.

"I give the owner of this establishment credit." Karly leaned close and yelled in Harrison's ear. "What a great idea. It's like he brought the outside indoors."

Harrison shouted in return. "Yes, I agree. The only problem is the sound. It's deafening. The band is good, but can't they turn the volume down a notch?"

"You're just getting old." Karly elbowed him in the side.

"Madison said the same thing recently." Harrison's brows drew together. "I'm starting to notice a theme. Maybe I should be concerned."

"Did I hear my name?" Madison stood in front of the couch and stared down at them. She wore a glittery lavender tank top that complemented the colour of her hair. "Anyway, it doesn't matter." Madison waved a hand through the air. "Have you heard the news? It's all over Aspen Ridge."

Karly bit her lip. Had the news of Blake's discovery been leaked?

"What news?" Harrison shifted on the couch to face Madison.

"A local fisherman found a body and there are rumours circulating that it could belong to that missing No Trace woman."

Karly studied Harrison's face for his reaction. His features remained even although something flickered in his eyes.

"Where did you hear that?" Karly asked.

"Raven."

Karly sighed. "Raven again. And you believe her?"

"Of course. Besides, it's all over Twitter and Facebook. So, it must be true."

Harrison bolted to his feet and hurried toward the exit. Karly jumped up to follow, but Madison blocked her way. "Don't go."

"Why?"

"Like I said, I have this terrible feeling."

"Oh, you and your feelings." Karly gripped her friend's shoulder and gently steered her away. "He's upset. I want to see if he's okay. After all, how would you like to receive news that a good friend's body might just have been discovered?"

"I'd feel horrible if I was innocent, but panicked if I was guilty."

"Stop it." Karly scowled. "I don't want to hear any more." She darted across the room.

"Please be careful." Madison's warning trailed after her, barely discernible above the din of the restaurant.

Karly shoved against the heavy metal door, and flew into the black night, slamming into a brick wall. At least, that's what it felt like. When it gasped and grabbed her arms, she knew it was human.

The man held her tightly as they stumbled together and crashed into a large wooden object. It was all a horrifying, perplexing blur. Snapping and cracking sounds filled the air as Karly hit the unforgiving sidewalk.

What had just happened? Stunned, she fought for a breath as she lay flat on her back. Her chest felt so heavy. Was she having a heart attack?

"Henry! Are you okay?"

Karly blinked. Was that Blake's voice she'd just heard in her foggy brain? Who was Henry? The man she'd run into? She squinted into the darkness. It *was* Blake. She recognized his features in the dim glow of the streetlight nearby.

"Wait one minute. Is that you, Karly?" Blake dropped to his knees at her side. "Are you okay?"

"It hurts to breathe," Karly whispered.

"Wait." Blake grunted as though he was exerting an enormous amount of energy. "Is that better?" he asked. "I removed the head."

Head? What head? Horror charged through her. Just how hard had she hit the man? Then she heard groaning beside her. *Phew! If he could groan, he mustn't be ...*

"Are you okay, Mister?" Karly turned her head sideways.

"Lady, you hit me harder than a flying Muskie."

Karly propped herself up on her elbows and contemplated the man sprawled awkwardly on the ground, the splintered torso of what appeared to be some sort of animal draped across his legs. From the corner of her eye she caught a glimpse of a wooden head with one mangled antler on the ground beside Blake. *That* was the head Blake referred to. Things were starting to make sense—a little.

"Did I cause all this? I'm so sorry. I didn't see you standing there in the dark."

Blake extended a hand toward the man who was attempting to get up. "Let me help you."

The middle-aged man, his ball cap askew, grasped Blake's hand and stood, unburying himself from the wooden catastrophe in the process. "I think Flying Muskie Lady needs help."

"No, I don't." There was no way she was going to accept Blake's assistance. Not under these circumstances. He'd never let her live it down. She moaned as she scrambled to her feet. "Muskie Lady is ... I'm fine." She dusted herself off and put a consoling hand on Henry's arm. "My name is Karly Foster and again I'm really sorry. Are you sure you're okay?"

The man rubbed his backside. "I'll live, but I think the moose left a hoof print on my behind. Time to call it a night."

"But Henry, we just got here," Blake protested. "Besides, how will you get back home to Shadow Lake?"

"I'll crash at my brother-in-law's for tonight." Henry clapped Blake on the shoulder. "Get the 'crash' pun? I am quite funny, aren't I?"

Blake shook his head and chuckled. "I see you've managed to retain your sense of humour."

"You enjoy yourself. *Miss White Pelican Lady* will help. Henry winked before hobbling away, one hand still on his right buttock.

"I feel so horrible. Do you think he'll be okay?"

"I think so." Blake turned to her. "He's made of tough stuff. But what were you thinking? You flew out that door like a—"

"Flying Muskie?" Karly supplied.

Blake grinned. "Exactly."

"Who's Miss White Pelican Lady? Was Henry referring to me? Because he just called me Flying Muskie Lady, so I'm confused."

"Just ignore him." Blake planted a hand between her shoulder blades and steered her toward the door.

Karly pursed her lips. *Odd. He almost seems uneasy.* What was that about?

"He has this thing with calling people animal names." Blake reached around her to grasp the handle of the door. "Do you want to tell me what happened?"

"Not really."

"Your knee is all scraped up." Blake stared down at her leg in the open doorway as light spilled onto them.

Karly glanced down. A dark red trail made its way down her shin. "I hope it leaves a scar. I can tell everyone I was attacked by a moose."

Blake snorted. "I'm pretty sure it was you who attacked the moose, not the other way around. And I didn't realize women liked to brag about scars."

"This one does." Karly stepped into the restaurant. "After I clean up this bloody knee, I'll find the owner and see if there's anything I can do to make up for destroying his statue."

Blake walked her to the ladies' room. "See you in a few minutes."

Karly cleaned herself up as well as she could. After washing her hands, she drew in a deep breath and exited the washroom. Blake was nowhere in sight, so she headed toward the snack bar. It was now or never.

A young female server stood behind the counter. Karly stopped in front of her and pressed both palms to the cool wooden surface. "Excuse me? May I please speak to the owner?"

"Sure. I'll get him." The waitress tossed her towel onto the counter and disappeared into the back through a swinging door. While Karly waited, she scanned the crowd for Blake. *Where did he go?* He wouldn't have just left, would he? The disappointment she felt at the thought surprised her almost as much as it scared her. When she spied him on a loveseat next to Raven, a knot formed in her stomach. Had he planned to meet the pretty, dark-haired woman all along?

"Can I help you, lady? My name is Moe Lalonde and I'm the owner."

Karly spun back around. A heavily tattooed, obese man with an apron tied around his bulging middle, crossed his arms and glared at her. She tilted her head. "Aren't you the chef at Moe's Diner?"

"That's me, in the flesh. I own both establishments." His speech was abrupt and businesslike. "What do you want?"

"I like what you've done with this place." Despite her attempts not to stare, Karly couldn't tear her eyes from the hideous skulls on his arms that seemed to bore holes right into her.

When her compliment summoned only a glare, Karly bit her bottom lip. How would he accept the news of his broken display animal?

"I'm a busy man. Spit it out."

"Um ... I'll pay for the damages."

The owner tilted his head and folded his arms across his chest. "Damages?"

"I'm not sure what it was. It's now all in pieces." Her mouth was suddenly drier than a desert sandstorm. "It had antlers, so I assume it was a deer or moose."

Beads of sweat dotted the heavy man's forehead. "Just what are you trying to tell me?"

The threatening look in his eyes sent a shudder rippling through her. How did Raven ever work for him? If she were a betting woman, she'd wager this was the missing No Trace woman's murderer.

"I accidentally fell into your display animal moose thingy and busted it."

Silence followed for what seemed like an eternity. Then, if possible, his face grew darker. "Clumsy woman. Five hundred dollars by a week from today or you'll pay the consequences."

Karly's nostrils flared. "Is that a threat?"

"Take it any way you like, but that moose was a one-of-a-kind work of art from a friend of mine who is now deceased. So, as you can imagine, if your little blonde brain will let you, it cannot be easily replaced."

Karly bristled. "You have a right to be upset, but it was an accident. I said I was sorry. There's no need to treat me in such a condescending manner."

"And just what do you propose to do about it? Attack me with your nail file?"

Everything in Karly longed to wipe that sarcastic smug right off his face. She pressed her lips tightly together. "I'll pay what you requested as soon as I can come up with the money. A week is not a long time, but I'll do my best. And after that, I hope to never have to deal with you again."

Karly spun on her heels, but before she could walk away strong fingers dug into her arm and she winced. "A week from today or else."

"Let her go, Moe." Harrison towered over the bar, his voice like iron.

Relief flooded through her. *Where did he come from?* No matter, she was glad for the intervention.

Instantly Moe let go of her.

Harrison stepped closer to the bar and leaned over it, stopping inches from Moe's face. "I'm warning you, Moe, don't ever touch this woman, or any woman, again or you'll have me to answer to."

The two men glared at each other and, for a moment, Karly wondered if there was going to be an all-out brawl in the coffee shop. Deep inside, she wished Harrison would sock him hard in the chops. When Moe stomped away and disappeared behind the kitchen door, Karly rubbed her left arm.

"Are you okay, Karly?" Harrison rested both hands on her shoulders and stared down at her, his voice as gentle now as it had been tough before. His fingers slipped from her shoulders and ran down her arms.

"I'm fine. He's just a bit rough."

Harrison touched the spot on her arm where a bruise was already forming. His jaw tightened. "Do you want to press charges? That man has been getting away with this abusive behaviour far too long. It's about time someone put a stop to it."

"No, I think I'll just avoid him from now on."

"Why was he threatening you?" Harrison let go of her arms and brushed a stray strand of hair off her face.

"I destroyed some of his property."

"What do you mean?" His eyes widened. "Wait one minute. Are you in any way responsible for that pile of wood that used to be a moose outside the main entrance?"

Karly bit her lip to squelch the pout that was trying to form. "Yes. It was an accident. I think I'd like to go home now."

"No problem." Harrison took her elbow and steered her through the coffee shop and across the dance floor.

When Karly bumped shoulders with a couple, she apologized. But when that couple turned out to be none other than Blake and Raven, anger stampeded through her like a herd of wild elephants.

"I've changed my mind, Harrison. I'd like a dance before you take me home." Karly didn't wait for his answer, but grabbed his hand, pulled him close, and began swaying to the soft music. When she turned and caught Blake's gaze, his eyes narrowed.

Blake tapped Harrison on the shoulder before the song had ended. "May I?"

Harrison didn't look very happy, but he nodded and let her go. As Blake put both hands on her waist, Raven stormed from the dance floor.

"What's going on?" Blake snarled.

Karly wrapped her hands around his neck. "What do you mean?"

"Don't play innocent with me. The way you were draped all over that guy was disgusting," he hissed.

"Me draped all over Harrison? What about you and Raven?

"If you must know, Raven dragged *me* to the dance floor. And after what I witnessed by the bar, with Harrison's paws all over you, I really didn't think you'd care."

"Do you have any idea what just happened back there?" Karly pulled his hands off her waist and stepped back.

"You're playing with fire, Karly Foster. You can't toy with a guy's emotions like that and not expect fallout. Take it from another guy who knows what he's talking about."

"That's just it. You have no idea what you're talking about. The owner was not at all pleased about my accident and he turned nasty." Karly's voice hitched. "Harrison came to my rescue. Where were you a few minutes ago when I needed help? Wait, I know the answer to that question. You were snuggled next to Raven on the loveseat."

The music suddenly stopped.

"I wasn't *snuggled*," he whispered between gritted teeth. "It was the only vacant spot in the place. She found me. I didn't even know she was here. You took so long in the washroom and the place was filling up, so I decided to grab us the last available seat."

"If you cared enough, you would have supported me. That man was threatening and physically abusive. I have bruise marks on my arm to prove it. Do you want to see them?" Karly flipped her arm around.

"How was I to know the owner was going to act inappropriately?" Blake stared at her arm, then raked a hand through his hair.

"You must have your suspicions about Moe by now."

"Moe's the owner of the Cedar Canoe? I didn't know he owned both establishments. It's not fair to hold that against me."

"Flying White Muskie Pelican Woman ... or whatever your friend called me ... is leaving. Harrison?" She waved at her supervisor who had just finished a dance with Madison. "Can you take me home please?"

"I hope you know what you're doing." Blake threw a heated look in her direction as Harrison and Madison approached. Karly couldn't recall ever seeing him quite that angry.

"Where are you going, Karly? I don't want to leave just yet." Madison pouted.

"I don't ... um ... feel so well," Karly stammered as she rubbed the back of her sore arm. "Harrison is taking me home. Will you be okay getting a ride back?" Karly asked.

Madison smiled. "Don't worry about me. I'll bum a ride from someone or stay with Raven." She pulled on Blake's arm. "Come dance with me."

What are you doing, Madison? Why would her friend betray her like that? Of course, Madison was all about fun. After all, she had just danced with Harrison whom she deemed old. Perhaps her flirtation with Blake was innocent? As well as her friendship with Raven?

Blake paused briefly, then a wide sassy grin spread over his face as he caught Karly's gaze and Madison's hand at the same time. "Don't mind if I do. That's the best offer I've had all night."

A flash of heat coursed through her. Linking her arm through Harrison's, Karly couldn't resist one final dig as they passed the smiling Blake and Madison. "He's not who he seems, Madison."

Blake wrapped an arm around Madison's waist. "If I were you, Harrison, I'd run. I've got the battle scars to prove what a relationship with Karly will get you. By the way, don't trip on the carnage she left just outside the door."

Karly fought tears as she followed Harrison from the coffee bar into the dark night, stepping cautiously over the ... carnage she had created. What a horrible night! She didn't know what she was more upset about, her humiliating accident, Madison's behaviour, or Blake's cutting words. A few tears spilled over before she could stop them, but she swiped at them before Harrison could see. This time she was thankful for the darkness outside the restaurant.

She stooped down, picked up broken moose fragments, and tossed them in a pile by the side of the building. Harrison joined her.

"Tell you what." He grabbed the odd-looking moose head and added it to the pile. "I know just the thing to get your mind off an abusive chef and an irritating pilot."

"You do?" Karly chucked a hoof toward the building. It was kind of Harrison to think of her when he was dealing with some possibly traumatic news of his own. Sometimes she could be so selfish.

"By the way, how are you doing? I tried to find you earlier and this is the result." Karly pointed at the haphazard pile of wood.

"The news hit me hard. I had to get away and think. In one way, I hope the body is Jessica's so there can be closure for her loved ones. And if there was foul play involved in her disappearance, maybe forensic testing will help find her killer." He took a deep breath. "Let's change the subject, okay?"

"What did you have in mind?"

"A wolf-howl."

"Excuse me?"

"At ten o'clock every Friday night through the month of August, hundreds line up at Percy's Ridge and howl collectively over the bog into the dark night."

Karly lifted a finger. "Come to think of it, I've heard of those. But I've never attended one."

"You joined us just after the howls concluded last year."

"So how do they work?"

"Basically, we just howl and then wait for the wolf pups to howl in return. It's an unforgettable experience."

"Sounds like the perfect thing for both of us after the evening we've had. Let's go." Karly trailed behind Harrison to the park truck. This was just what she needed. A distraction. She couldn't get Blake's hurtful remarks from her head. Battle scars? He may have physical ones from unintentional accidents she had caused, but hers were deeper and caused far more pain. Had she been crazy to think that maybe, just maybe, there was still something between them?

As she well knew, scars of the heart didn't heal as easily as those of the flesh.

CHAPTER SEVENTEEN

Shielding her eyes from daylight, Karly threw her pillow over her face. It couldn't be time to get up already. Wait a minute. Wasn't it Saturday morning? With relief, she rolled over and drifted back to sleep.

A booming crack of thunder jolted her awake. Karly's eyelids fluttered open. Through blurred vision, she focused on the clock on her nightstand. When the numbers registered in her foggy brain, her eyes widened. In fifteen minutes, it would be noon. She really should get out of bed.

As she listened to rain pelt her bedroom window, she yawned deeply and flopped back onto the pillow. She'd always loved the raw power of a thunderstorm. It added excitement to everyday life.

She frowned as yesterday's upsetting events flooded back into her mind. That was why she'd slept so late. She had tossed and turned most of the night as she wrestled with her jumbled emotions.

There was the humiliation of running down a man and breaking an outdoor business display. Not to mention her aching, scraped knee. Then being threatened by that nasty business owner. And now she owed him five hundred dollars and had no idea how she was going to come up with that kind of money, in a week, no less. Would he harm her if she didn't?

And what was up with Madison? Karly's chest tightened. Should she be worried about her friend moving in on Blake? She shook her head. Madison might be infatuated with Karly's former boyfriend, but to make a move on him would cross the line. Although Madison was a little immature and somewhat flirty, underneath it all she had good morals and values. Karly recalled a deep conversation only a few weeks ago, where Madison told her she had professed faith in God as a little girl in Sunday School. Karly hadn't really been interested in hearing anything more, though, and had cut her friend off.

Even if Madison did make a move, Karly had no hold on Blake. There was nothing between them. She flopped her arm over her forehead. Then why did the memory of Blake with his hands around Madison's waist, or seeing him snuggled next to Raven on the loveseat make her chest feel heavy? As if the cumbersome moose head still sat on it.

Truly, her confrontation with Blake had been the worst part of the whole evening. That man still had the ability to make her want to shove a fishhook in his mouth and cast him into the lake. She didn't know another person who could rile her like he could.

Then there was Harrison. The pressure in her chest lifted slightly. What a thoughtful man. The wolf howl had been a unique and nature-filled experience. Goosebumps had risen on her arms when the pups howled back.

The topic of the gruesome discovery never came up again. He apologized about the bruising she'd taken on her arm, as if it were somehow his fault. Did they come any nicer than Harrison? There was no tension between them. No fiery emotions whatsoever.

Karly rolled over, sat up on the edge of the bed, and lowered her feet to the floor. The house was oddly quiet. Had Madison slept in too? Still groggy, she padded to the kitchen in her pyjamas, filled the coffee pot with the required amount of grounds and water, and flipped the switch.

Glancing toward Madison's bedroom, she noticed the door was open and the bed was made. *Odd.* Come to think of it, when she had turned in for the night, Madison wasn't home. Perhaps her roommate had borrowed a park truck and gotten up early and headed into town for groceries, which were sorely needed.

But as Karly poured her beverage, an unsettled feeling came over her. Maybe Madison had stayed at Raven's. She slipped the glass pot onto the heating element. That was another thing that bothered her. Madison and Raven's growing friendship, especially with the gnawing suspicion that Blake and Raven had something simmering just below the surface. *Don't go there, Karly.*

Karly reached for her phone and checked her messages. Nothing. Madison usually sent Karly a text message to let her know of her plans. Should she be worried?

The last she'd seen of Madison, she was in Blake's arms. What if she had asked Blake for a ride? Worse yet—what if he had given it to her? All the way to his place? She didn't think Blake was that kind of guy, but after last night she'd realized she didn't really know him at all. Her coffee suddenly tasted like mud in her mouth. She poured the remainder down the sink and reached for her cell phone. A quick text ought to sort things out.

She sent the message and waited a few minutes. When Madison didn't return her message, Karly decided to call her. After several rings, it went to her voice mail.

Should she call Blake? No. Yes. Karly bit the inside of her lip. What could it hurt? If Madison was with him, it would settle things on two accounts. She'd know Madison's whereabouts and find out exactly where things stood between her and her ex-boyfriend.

She took a deep breath and punched in Blake's number. He answered on the first ring, but she could barely hear him over a loud humming noise and crackling sounds. Karly cupped her hand over the mouthpiece. "Where are you? I can barely hear you."

"Remote island ... bad connection ... can't talk now."

Karly ended the call and began to pace. What if Madison was up there in his Cessna with him? *Get a grip, Karly.* This was ridiculous. Maybe a trip into town to get groceries was a good plan. At least it would distract her. And if Madison was shopping, she'd bump into her or pass her on the way. The town only had one grocery store and one main road in and out. And if she didn't see her, Madison would probably be home by the time she got back.

Evening came and went. By nine pm, Karly still hadn't heard from Madison. She paced back and forth until she couldn't stand it any longer. Was she worried about Madison's whereabouts because something sinister could have happened to her, or because she could be having a fantastic time with Blake? Karly shook her head. She was worried about her friend, of course.

She called her again, even though the last dozen calls had gone unanswered. Karly chewed on her thumb nail. Madison had warned her that something bad was about to happen. Had her fears come true?

She'd try Blake again. Maybe he was home by now. After several rings, he answered breathlessly.

"Did I catch you at an inconvenient time?"

"Kind of."

Karly pictured Blake and Madison snuggled together on his couch watching a movie. *Oh boy*! Karly pressed a hand to her stomach.

"Oh. Did I take you away from Madison?"

"You didn't take me away from anyone. I was just getting out of the shower. Why did you call? Are you still ticked about yesterday?"

"I'm trying to locate Madison. I assumed she was with you since you're the last person I saw her with."

"Well, you assumed wrong. I've had a long day and was getting ready for bed. I haven't seen your friend since last night." Blake sounded tired.

"Me neither."

"Are you serious?"

"She didn't come home."

"Is that unusual for her?"

"Yes."

"Try Raven. Maybe she knows where she might be. I saw them talking together earlier in the evening."

"So, you're being absolutely straight with me? Madison didn't spend the night with you?"

Silence followed for what seemed like a long time. When Blake spoke, his voice was heavy. "Don't you know me better than that? I'm not a 'one-night-stand' type of guy."

"People change." Karly shifted from one foot to the other. What would make her accuse him of such a thing.

"They certainly do, and I'd like to tell you all about that some time."

Karly frowned. "You're talking in riddles."

"I'll explain later. I need to get some sleep; I've had an exhausting day. I was caught in a vicious thunderhead, and I had to wait several hours for interior campers needing a ride. They weren't at their rallying point, due to the storm. All in all, it was a frustrating day. I'm going to have to let you go. I hope you have success locating Madison."

The line went dead before she had a chance to say another word. Now she was worried. She didn't have a phone number for Raven, but Harrison probably did. Karly threw on a light rain jacket and jogged over to Harrison's cabin, a soft drizzle coating her hair and cheeks. When he opened the door, she blew out a breath. "Thank God, you are home.

A grin lit up his face. "You missed me that badly?"

Not waiting for an invitation, she barged into his living room. In her haste, she hadn't noticed he was shirtless. Now, when she spun around to face him, warmth flooded her cheeks at the sight of his bare, muscular chest. She took a step backwards. "I'm sorry. You were obviously not expecting company. I should go."

Harrison chuckled. "Just give me a minute and I'll throw on a shirt. Don't go anywhere; I'll be right back."

Karly's gaze flitted to his television, then to the wooden units on both sides of it, DVDs lying haphazardly on the shelves—anything to keep from following his retreating physique. This was ridiculous. Why was she embarrassed? She'd seen grown men bare-chested at the beach many times.

"What's wrong? You look upset." Karly jumped. She hadn't heard him re-enter the room.

"I need Raven's phone number."

Harrison did up another button on his navy flannel shirt. "What for?"

"Madison didn't come home last night, and I can't reach her on her cell. I thought that maybe since someone saw them talking at the coffee bar last night, Raven might know where she is. In fact, Madison mentioned before we left last night that she may stay with Raven."

"Yes, I remember Madison mentioning that. It surprised me because I didn't realize they were friends." Harrison tightened his belt.

Karly's phone vibrated in her hand and she scanned the screen. It was her sister, texting about a fire in their home town, at a restaurant that had been their favourite while growing up. A twinge of sadness struck her, but Karly didn't have the time or mental energy to respond to the news. She tucked the phone in the pocket of her jeans, planning to talk to Katie later.

"Sorry to disappoint you, but I don't have a current number. Since we broke up, things haven't been good between us. We're barely on speaking terms. What about Blake? Does he know where she might be?" Harrison pulled a pair of sandals from the closet.

She shrugged. "He said he hasn't seen her since last night."

Harrison grabbed his keys. "Let's drive into town and find Raven. Maybe she'll be able to help."

Thirty minutes later, they pulled up to Moe's Diner just as the lights in the restaurant dimmed. Harrison rapped loudly on the front door until Raven made her way toward them, a perturbed look on her face.

"We're closed," Raven mouthed through the window, pointing at her watch.

Karly tugged a pen and paper from her bag and scribbled *We need to talk to you. It's very important* on it. She pressed the paper to the glass. Raven rolled her eyes, then unlocked the door and pulled it open. "What's up?"

Karly went into the diner. "Have you seen Madison?"

"No, why?" Raven wiped the table nearest the door.

"She didn't come home last night."

"So?" Raven picked up a menu that had fallen under a table. "Why are you worried? She's probably with Blake."

"Why would you say that?" Harrison cast a glance in Karly's direction.

"Maybe because of the way she threw herself at him? It was pretty embarrassing."

Harrison crossed his arms. "You sound jealous."

Raven glared at him. "Look, I'm busy. I don't have time for this." She grasped the knob and started to close the door.

Karly propped her running shoe against the door to hold it open. "I talked to Blake less than an hour ago, and he hasn't seen her since last night." She lifted a hand, palm up. "Please, if you can give me any information at all, I'd appreciate it. I'm really worried."

Raven snorted. "I don't know what Blake told you, but I'm pretty sure they left together."

"Really?" Karly's shoulders slumped. "He didn't mention that."

"Anyway, I've got cleaning to do. You need to go." Raven pushed harder on the door and Karly pulled her foot out of the way.

"What do we do now?" She looked up at Harrison as the door closed firmly in their faces, leaving them standing outside Moe's Diner in the dark.

"Let's head back to the park. I'll call an emergency meeting and see if anyone saw her today."

Karly scrambled to keep up with him as he jogged toward his truck. "Shouldn't we contact the police?"

"Let's wait and see what the meeting reveals. Maybe someone knows where she is, and we won't need to involve the authorities." A dark look flashed across his face, as though he'd had a painful experience with the police in the past. It came and went so fast, though, Karly wasn't sure she'd seen it. She opened the passenger side door and slid onto the seat.

Harrison fastened his seatbelt. "Maybe she's with Josh."

Karly managed a crooked smile. "I appreciate your attempt at humour, but that's not likely."

Harrison touched her knee. "Anything to see you smile again."

CHAPTER EIGHTEEN

An hour later they were no further ahead. The few employees they could locate on a Saturday night hadn't seen Madison since the end of the workday on Friday.

The tightness in Karly's chest grew more constricting, and now her stomach pitched and rolled. Her worry for Madison had not only squelched her appetite, but left a sick feeling inside.

After the door closed behind the last employee, Karly walked the perimeter of the small room, throwing worried glances at Harrison who sat calmly behind his large wooden desk. "What do we do now? I have a bad feeling about this."

Harrison leaned back in his black vinyl chair, clasped his hands behind his neck, and rested his feet on the desk. "Don't go jumping to conclusions. Maybe she came home late last night and decided to get up early and visit her family for the weekend."

Karly shook her head. "She would have told me, or left a note, not just taken off."

"Are you sure?"

"Madison may be impulsive, but she's not irresponsible. Or thoughtless. She would know I'd worry. Besides, although her family doesn't live too far away, Fort Francis I think, she doesn't have her own wheels. Someone usually comes to get her."

"A family member might have picked her up this morning while you slept. As for why she isn't answering her phone, maybe she misplaced it." Harrison rubbed his chin. "She's a grown woman, Karly. Give her some space."

"But ..."

"I think you're worrying too much."

"Maybe you're right, it's just that ..." Karly took a deep breath. "Madison had been experiencing this bad feeling lately. In fact, she warned me that something might happen, even last night."

"A bad feeling? She warned you that what might happen?"

Karly stopped her marathon trek around the room and faced him. "She wasn't specific. She didn't know herself." Should she mention that Harrison was the possible object of Madison's fears? No, that would accomplish nothing, except to upset him.

Harrison sat up and reached for a stack of registration forms and straightened them. "Like I said, I'm sure she's fine."

"Do you think we should phone her family and see if she's there?"

"That's not a bad idea." Harrison opened a drawer and tossed in the papers.

"What about the police?"

"I don't think they'd bat an eyelash. She hasn't even been gone a full twenty-four hours." Harrison closed the drawer and rolled his chair backwards. Then he stood, grabbed a folding chair, and stacked it neatly in the corner. "I'll get you the contact info for Madison's family. If they don't know where she is, and we haven't heard from her by morning, then we'll notify the police."

Karly lifted a folding chair and carried it toward the stack. "But if she's truly in trouble, then it could be too late. If Madison is just off gallivanting with some guy she met at The Cedar Canoe—although she's never done anything like that before—she could still be in danger. If he was a total stranger, who knows what he might be capable of?" The chair wouldn't fit into the stack, so she forced it. Bad idea. She trapped a finger and yelped at the blinding pain.

Harrison hurried to her side as she yanked her hand free.

"What happened?"

Karly grabbed her right wrist with her left hand and held it up, squeezing her wrist so tightly that her fingernails dug into her skin. "Somehow, I pinched it between the chairs," she gasped. The pain was so intense, her eyes blurred with tears.

Harrison reached for her hand. "Let me see. Which finger is it?"

"The baby." Karly dug her nails in deeper to mask the awful pain. One pain to cover up another.

"I don't think it's broken." Harrison tugged on her tightly clenched fingers. "Stop digging your nails into your flesh. You're going to make yourself bleed."

Was it the tender look in his eyes, or the accumulation of a stressful few days that finally hit her? Whatever the reason, she couldn't hold back any longer. Tears spilled down her cheeks.

"Oh, Karly. Does it hurt that badly?" Harrison let go of her hand and swiped at her tears with his thumbs.

"Um ..." Karly stumbled back, away from his intimate touch, her dangling finger throbbing at her side. "It's my own stupidity. I shouldn't have forced the chair. I'll be okay."

"Don't blame yourself. You were distracted with worry about Madison." His words were so kind, and she desperately needed compassion right now. She tried to squelch a hiccupping sob, but it didn't work. Now she was blubbering all over the place. This was so embarrassing. But she couldn't seem to stop.

She needed a distraction. Karly turned and tried to read the flyer hanging by one yellow stick pin on the bulletin board, advertising an upcoming canoe race. Unrelenting tears made it difficult to focus. What was wrong with her anyway? Karly never cried. Well ... hardly ever.

"Karly." Harrison placed a warm hand on her shoulder and squeezed.

Why couldn't she stop crying? Who knew a crushed finger could make her so hysterical?

Oh!

Her mind flashed back to the time she had slammed Blake's fingers in the car door and broke his middle one. How she had teased him about being a whiner. She really hadn't been very kind to Blake then, had she? Great! Now, she could add guilt to her growing list of reasons to bawl like a baby.

Karly took a swipe at her nose with the back of her hand. She really needed a tissue. Her mind backtracked to an earlier conversation. Had she really accused Blake of spending the night with Madison?

That ugly demon of jealously had clouded what she knew to be true about Blake, and about her roommate.

Harrison turned her to face him.

No. She didn't want to face anyone looking like a soggy, bedraggled mess.

"I think your tears are more for Madison, aren't they?" Harrison handed her a wad of tissues.

Where did those come from? No matter. She grabbed for the stack and dabbed her eyes and nose.

"Stop fretting, Karly. Madison will be fine. There's probably a good explanation for all of this and she'll come bounding into the park any minute, oblivious to the mayhem she's created."

Karly blew her nose. "Do you think so?"

"I think so." He stepped toward her and cupped her cheeks with his hands. "You have to stop worrying. We'll find her."

The tender look in his eyes had gone beyond concern. Blake was right. *He's in love with me.* She could see it clearly now. Had she unwittingly been encouraging him by spending so much time with him? Was he going to kiss her? Would she let him? Karly swallowed. Why shouldn't she? She enjoyed being with Harrison. And he was so incredibly good to her. If it was against company policy to date a co-worker, one of them could consider moving to another park. If Blake hadn't suddenly appeared on the scene, she wouldn't hesitate to get involved with Harrison. Would she?

"Excuse me?" A shaky female voice interrupted the moment.

Harrison dropped his hands as if he'd touched a hot stove and turned toward the middle-aged woman. "What is it, Heather?"

Karly squeezed the wad of tissue in her hand.

"I'm sorry to interrupt." Heather's face was beet red. "There's a police officer at the front desk, wanting to talk with the person in charge. Since the park superintendent is off, that would be you." She spun on her heel and fled into the hallway.

Karly's stomach twisted. "It's got to be news about Madison." She sprinted out of the room behind Harrison.

A tall, thin officer shifted from one foot to the other behind the main desk. His deeply-set, beady black eyes, long, narrow face, and cocky glare made the hairs on the back of her neck stiffen.

"I'm Harrison Somerville, how can I help you?" Her supervisor extended his hand across the counter.

"Officer William Neilson. Is there somewhere we can go to speak privately?"

"Here is fine. My employees are trustworthy, especially these two women."

The officer nodded. "Do you have an employee by the name of Josh Rutherford?"

"I do."

"We have a rather strange situation on our hands."

Crash! Heather's stapler clanged to the floor. All heads swung in her direction. "Sorry." Heather bent down and scooped up the stapler, her face an even deeper shade of crimson than it had been a minute ago.

"Strange? In what way?" Harrison propped an elbow on the counter and leaned into his hand.

"We found a man staggering along the shoulder of the highway a few kilometres east of here. When we stopped to question him, he appeared agitated and confused. At first, we thought he was inebriated, but a breathalyzer sample proved to be negative. Of course, there is the possibility that he's flying high on some illegal substance. He was visibly trembling, and he vomited twice after we found him. Other than his name and the fact that he worked here, he couldn't give us much information. He doesn't know why he was walking down the side of the road or how he acquired scratches and bruises on his arms and legs. Thankfully, he doesn't appear to be badly hurt."

Karly's thoughts whirled. Did Josh's bizarre behaviour have anything to do with Madison's disappearance? Harrison might have been joking last night, but maybe Madison really had gone off with Josh. *Or been forced to.* The thought made her sick.

But hadn't Raven said that Blake and Madison left together? Perhaps Raven was mistaken, and it was Josh. Karly shook her head at that thought. Blake and Josh didn't look the least bit alike. But, in a dark building perhaps Raven had been confused?

Harrison rubbed his chin. "He is a lone wolf, often wandering off, but that's odd behaviour even for Josh. Where is he now?"

"In the squad car with another officer. We're taking him to the hospital for a medical evaluation and drug screen. Since we had to pass by your main gate, I thought I'd verify if he was actually an employee of yours."

Harrison straightened up. "I'll follow you to the hospital."

"I'm coming too," Karly added.

"Are you sure?" Harrison looked at her, worry lines grooved across his forehead. "I can handle this. You've had a stressful day. Why don't you go back to your cabin? Maybe Madison will show up and put your mind at ease."

"Absolutely not. I have a strange feeling that Josh is the reason Madison is missing."

The officer held up one hand. "Who is Madison? I'm not aware of a missing person."

"That's because we haven't filed a report yet." Harrison squeezed his chin until his cheeks turned white. "We're not really sure she's missing." He sent her a warning look.

Karly bit her lip. Had she spoken out of turn? Harrison clearly wasn't ready to go to the police about Madison yet. Why was he hesitating?

Officer Neilson walked toward the exit. "I'll meet you both at the Aspen Ridge Hospital emergency."

Harrison held out a hand for her to go ahead, and Karly started for the door. *Just what is going on around here?* Her mind was as numb as her red and swollen pinky. Karly dabbed at a drop of blood on her wrist with her scrunched-up pile of tissue. If you combined all her physical injuries—the scraped knee, bruised arm, smashed finger and self-inflicted fingernail cuts—they still paled in comparison to the assault going on in her mind.

Josh found stumbling around on the side of a highway? Madison missing? Harrison's growing attraction toward her and now Blake's ...?

Blake's what? She frowned. It was hard to know what Blake felt. Had she ever been able to figure him out?

As she made her way to the park truck, Karly took a deep breath, desperate to inhale the tranquility of her natural surroundings. After all, the entire reason she chose this line of work was to escape her unfulfilling job and find solace in the peace and quiet of nature. Wasn't it?

Then why wasn't it working?

CHAPTER NINETEEN

Could this day get any worse? Karly stared at a pair of oncoming headlights, wishing she had super powers and could see inside the dark vehicle. Where was Madison?

As the sign for the Aspen Ridge Emergency came into view, Karly realized that Harrison hadn't spoken the entire thirty-minute drive. Was he just as worried as she was?

"Are you okay?" Karly glanced his direction.

Harrison lowered his window, took a ticket from the machine at the entrance to the emergency lot and waited until the arm went up. He drove through, searching for an available parking spot. "No, I'm not okay. But it's really not something I should discuss with you."

"Why? I thought we were good friends. You can tell me anything, Harrison. My day can't get much worse." Karly reached down and grabbed her purse from the floor between her feet.

Harrison sighed. "All right, you asked for it." He pulled into a spot, killed the engine, and slumped against his seat. "If Madison is missing, who do you think will be suspect number one on their list?"

Karly sat up straighter. She had been correct in her earlier suspicions that Harrison seemed uncomfortable going to the police. She had no idea what he had gone through before. Maybe she shouldn't have pressed him. To even consider that Madison could suffer the same fate as the other missing No Trace employee was so unfathomable, she really hadn't allowed her mind to go there. After what had happened with Jessica, though, Harrison had to have been dragged back into memories of the past.

His hands gripped the steering wheel tightly. "I knew I shouldn't have told you my concerns. You're worried enough without me putting such horrible thoughts in your mind."

"It's fine." Karly reached for the handle and pushed the door open. She started to climb out of the truck, then shifted to face him. "Besides, you have an alibi. You took me home last night. There were other people at the restaurant with Madison the police will want to question more than you." *Like Blake.* Raven did think she'd seen them leaving together. Blake couldn't have done anything to Madison, could he?

"I just don't think I have the strength to go through this all again ... not after Jessica." His voice broke as they walked toward the emergency entrance.

A chill came over Karly. Two female employees missing from No Trace Campground and Harrison knew them both. The odds were stacking against him. Did she really know Harrison as well as she thought she did? Had Madison been right about her suspicions? Karly swallowed the nervous lump in her throat as she followed Harrison through the automatic doors. *Pull yourself together, Karly. You don't even know if Madison is really missing.*

Officer Neilson met them in the waiting room with his note pad and, after learning everything he could about Josh, gathered information concerning Madison. He left after assuring them that he'd at least pass the word among the local detachment and they'd keep an eye out for her. If she still hadn't shown up by the afternoon tomorrow, then an official 'missing persons' report would be filed, and an investigation would ensue.

While they waited, Harrison phoned Heather at the campground and obtained Madison's contact information. Unfortunately, when Karly called them, Madison's parents informed her that they hadn't talked to their daughter since the Sunday before. Karly tried her best not to worry them, but it was unavoidable under the circumstances.

The next two hours with Harrison were awkward and uncomfortable. Neither of them spoke much, or even looked at each other. Karly finally picked up a two-year old entertainment magazine and flipped through it without taking in anything she was looking at. Harrison appeared laser-focused on a digital display on the wall across from him, announcing the wait time to be seen by a physician and didn't take his eyes from it. It was almost two o'clock in the morning before a nurse allowed them entrance into Josh's room.

Karly gasped at the dishevelled man. Josh's thinning hair stuck up at weird angles. The sickly white skin of his legs and arms were covered in fiery-red scratches and deep purple bruises. And his eyes were wide, his pupils dilated, as if he was in shock. Just what had happened to their summer student?

"What time is it, Karly?" Josh's eyes were large with ... fear?

"Two o'clock in the morning."

"What day is it?"

"It's Sunday, August the fifth." Harrison gripped the rails on the side of Josh's bed. "What happened to you, Josh? Did you meet up with a bear?"

"Huh?" Josh's forehead wrinkled.

"You're all banged up. Did you have a run-in with a wild animal?" Harrison leaned in closer.

Josh pulled the sheets up to his neck and turned a blank gaze toward him. "What day is it, Harrison?"

Karly exchanged a glance with Harrison, who shrugged his shoulders. For the next hour, Josh plied them over and over with the same two questions about the day of the week and time of day. He seemed unable to answer any other questions thrown at him, except those that involved long-term memories such as what was his hometown and who were the members of his family. Although he seemed to know that he was employed for the summer at No Trace, and he recognized the two of them, he had no recollection of any events that had occurred over the last few weeks.

Karly waved a hand to get Harrison's attention and pointed to the hallway. They had just gone out into the hall when a man in a long white coat approached them.

"I'm Dr. Peters. Are you family?" He held out a hand.

"Josh doesn't have any family in the area. I'm Harrison." Karly's boss shook the doctor's hand. "I'm his supervisor at No Trace Campground. I haven't been able to reach his family yet."

"I'm a co-worker of Josh's, Karly Foster." She cupped her aching pinky. No handshake for her.

"All indications lead me to believe your friend is suffering from *Global Transient Amnesia*," Dr. Peters explained. "This is a condition in which the patient has lost his or her short-term memory and often engages in repetitious behaviour."

"Josh asked us several times about the day and time." Karly nodded. "What would cause this condition?"

"Clinical possibilities include strenuous physical activity, acute emotional distress, or extreme cold temperatures."

Harrison frowned. "How long will he be like this?"

"This type of amnesia usually lasts anywhere from six to twenty-four hours. But I'll warn you, the patient normally has no recollection of the hours during or immediately preceding the episode when he comes out of it."

"So, even when he regains his memory, we may never know what happened to him?" Karly leaned a shoulder against the wall, her legs weak.

"That's correct. Because of the extremely agitated state in which he arrived here, we're keeping him sedated and admitting him overnight. He should fall asleep shortly, so I suggest that you go home and get some rest. You can check back in the morning." The doctor disappeared inside Josh's room.

Karly nearly had to break into a jog to keep up with her supervisor as he strode silently toward the emergency exit. Harrison was in one mighty hurry. It seemed he couldn't get out of here fast enough.

She glanced down at her throbbing pinky. Should she get it looked at while here in the emergency? She shook her head. Like Harrison said, it was probably not broken. Still, a strong painkiller would be welcome right about now. Once she got back to the cabin, she'd swallow a few Tylenol. That should dull the physical pain. If only she could fix the emotional pain as easily.

As Harrison pulled out of the parking lot and picked up speed, Karly leaned against the headrest and closed her eyes. She was terribly exhausted. She needed a break, mentally and physically. *Where are you, Madison?* She would pray, but that had never gotten her anywhere in the past. Why bother?

Thump! The truck jerked violently. Karly's eyes shot open. *What was that?* Her breath hitched in her throat as her heart pounded wildly.

She grabbed her door handle and screamed as the truck careened across the road, into the oncoming lane. Thankfully, it was empty at that time of night. When the vehicle skidded to a halt on the opposite gravel shoulder, Karly skittered her gaze to Harrison. His hands squeezed the steering wheel tightly.

"What happened?"

"We hit a deer." Harrison smacked the wheel before angling a worried gaze her direction. "Are you okay?"

Karly nodded, her hand on her chest. "Just scared out of my mind."

Harrison pressed both palms to his temples. "This is unbelievable. What else could possibly go wrong?"

She took a steadying breath. "I'm afraid to find out."

"Stay here. I'm going to check the damage." Harrison opened his door.

"You don't have to tell me twice." In the soft glow of the headlights, Karly watched as he bent down and examined the front driver side of the truck. Then he scratched his head and checked the ditch that ran along the shoulder of the highway.

A few minutes later, he climbed back inside.

"Well?" Karly asked.

"Good news for us. Only a slight crack in the headlight and a small dent in the fender. It sounded way worse than it was. I'm not sure how the deer fared, though. I couldn't find any carnage, so I assume it continued on into the woods." Harrison checked for traffic and pulled onto the highway.

"Hopefully, it'll be okay." Karly flopped her head against the back of her seat again, but this time her eyes scanned the highway surrounded by dense bush.

It was funny how, in daylight, the beauty of the area almost took her breath away. Now, an eeriness settled over her at the fear of what could be lurking in the darkness. Karly bit her lip. This was silly. It was not like her to be a worrier. But it just seemed to be one thing after another lately. When Karly thought about everything that had happened in the last few days, it almost seemed like a curse hovered over No Trace Campground. She felt like she was on the verge of cracking.

Just how much more could a person take?

CHAPTER TWENTY

As Blake sang the last verse of "How Great Thou Art", his peripheral vision caught a movement. Glancing sideways, he noticed a young woman scooting into a pew one row behind him and to his right. She caught his eyes and smiled. *Raven.* Blake struggled to tear his gaze from her as the words to his favourite hymn slurred in his mouth. A pink and white floral sundress flattered her petite frame in all the right places. With glistening ebony hair, her entire appearance was flawless.

Blake shifted from one foot to the other and forced himself to face the front of the church as he bowed his head for the closing prayer. Unable to concentrate on the pastor's words, his mind wandered. What did that mean, Raven coming to church? Was she a Christian?

Blake filed out of the church and somehow wasn't surprised to find Raven leaning against the side of his truck, twirling a lock of hair around her finger.

Oh boy!

"Do you always make it a habit of being late? You came in for the closing hymn." Blake stumbled over a cement barrier at the edge of the parking lot.

"I guess I overslept a little." She giggled and touched a finger to her full fuchsia lips. "I was surprised to see you here."

"Why was that?" Blake stuffed the paper church bulletin in his jean's pocket.

Raven bent down to adjust the strap on her shoe, and too much skin spilled forth from the bodice of her sundress.

For goodness sake.

Blake averted his eyes. Too much temptation. And in a church parking lot no less. An uneasiness settled over him. *Where is the pastor?* He could use some prayer right about now. And not only for his weak flesh, but because warning signs were popping up all over his brain.

"I didn't take you for a church-going man." Raven flipped her long dark hair off her shoulders.

"It's a recent change—one I should have made years ago. So, do you attend here regularly then?" Blake asked.

"As often as I can. Do you want to grab some lunch?" Raven placed a sizzling hand on his chest.

Bad idea, Blake. "I'd love to but ..." He fumbled for his keys just as his cell phone vibrated in his pocket. Saved by a text.

"Excuse me a moment, Raven." Blake read Karly's message and sobered. Josh spent the night in the hospital with a case of something called Global Transient Amnesia? And Madison was still missing? That didn't sound good. Of course, he'd like to help in the search.

Blake sent off a quick reply agreeing to help. Then he looked up at Raven, figuring it wouldn't hurt to ask. "Have you seen Madison?"

"No. She's still missing? That's terrible. Now I feel awful about my jealousy."

Jealousy? The early warning signs were now flashing bright neon colours.

"I admit that it killed me to see her dancing with you. In my anger, I said a few things I now regret."

This was ridiculous. Blake and Raven were not an item. And her bold flirting was a huge turnoff.

"Do I make you nervous?" She tickled his hand with a finely manicured, painted fingernail.

Not anymore. Blake bit his lip to squelch the unkind words, then reached in his pocket for his keys. "I need to go."

"Rushing off to your damsel in distress? I should have known. The old flame still burns, doesn't it?" Raven hissed—the sound as threatening as a Mississauga Rattler.

Okay, that did it. Blake met her cold gaze with a hot one of his own. "That's a little harsh, Raven. Since I'm off today, I thought I'd offer my support. There's a lot of serious stuff going on right now. Josh spent the night at the hospital with a case of ... I can't remember what it was called ... some sort of amnesia, and Karly and Harrison have a lot on their minds with Madison still missing. They need some help, so I'm heading over to the park. You're welcome to come along if you like."

"I would, but I promised Moe I'd help him with a ... shipment of vegetables." Her words tripped over each other.

"Suit yourself." Blake climbed in his vehicle, started it up and drove away—without so much as a look back.

The farther he got from Raven, the duller the neon flashes were. Blake sighed and relaxed into his seat. Had God put a check in his spirit? It was a very strong possibility. The more he learned about the seductive waitress, the less he wanted to know. In fact, the desire to run far and fast in the opposite direction possessed him. He couldn't get out of that parking lot fast enough.

And just what was going on in No Trace Campground? Was Madison truly missing? And what about Josh's mysterious illness? Were they connected? He prayed as he drove, for everyone involved and for answers to be found soon.

Then he added his daily prayer for Karly. As soon as she had re-appeared in his life, he had begun to make it a habit. He really needed an answer soon as to what to do with his conflicting emotions over his ex-girlfriend. And more importantly, he truly wanted her to find the love he had found in Jesus Christ.

Please God, hear my prayers.

CHAPTER TWENTY-ONE

Blake drove into No Trace behind a white campground truck and pulled into a parking space beside it. Harrison stepped out of the driver's side and a slightly built man almost collapsed as he tumbled out of the passenger door.

Blake hurried to the man's side and grabbed his arm. "How are you, Josh? I heard you spent the night in the hospital. How are you feeling?"

Josh flinched at his touch and yanked his arm away. "I really don't know what happened. Maybe I was hit by a truck."

Blake took a step back from the jittery man so as not to agitate him further. "That rough, eh? Well, I hope you feel better soon."

"Excuse me, I need to go lie down." Josh stumbled down the path toward his cabin.

"Do you think he'll be okay?" Blake asked Harrison, who was also staring after Josh. "Should someone go with him? He doesn't look well at all."

"I offered, but he refused. It's the oddest thing. He has no recollection of what happened." Harrison rubbed his temples as if he had a headache.

"I know. Karly filled me in on the strange occurrence." Blake shook his head. "Does anyone at the park know what his plans were for the weekend? Maybe that would give us a clue as to where he was and what might have happened to him."

"I'm going to hold another emergency meeting at three this afternoon to discuss Madison's whereabouts and Josh's mishap. Maybe we'll learn something helpful then."

Blake glanced at his watch. "Is it okay if I attend? I'd like to offer my assistance in finding Madison. I can scout out the area from the air and look for anything unusual."

"You're welcome to attend." A female voice from behind him sent Blake's heart racing. "We'll take all the help we can get. Can I go with you?"

He whirled to face her. Karly looked as if she hadn't slept in days. Her blue eyes were cloudy. Her long blonde hair hung sloppily in a sideways ponytail. Blake had never seen her so unkempt. But it did nothing to slow down his galloping heart. Perhaps he'd had too much caffeine today. How could her presence still rattle him so much?

The awkward and distressing scene with Karly from the Cedar Canoe flashed into his mind. Blake removed his cap and scratched his head. Why would he be excited to spend more time with her after that? He slapped the ball cap back on. He knew the answer. Because Karly needed help. Her good friend was missing. "Sure. We'll plan to go up once the meeting is over. Maybe we'll discover something that will be helpful."

Harrison's fists were clenched at his sides, but he didn't say a word. He didn't have to. His displeasure at the idea of Karly accompanying Blake instead of staying at the campground was written all over his face.

Blake pushed back his shoulders. It was Sunday and technically Karly was off work. She wasn't required to stay here with him. Harrison had no say over her decision.

Karly tilted her head skyward. "It looks like it might rain. I need to run back to my cabin and grab a light jacket."

"I'll come with you." Blake fell into step beside her, leaving Harrison standing by his truck. Although he couldn't see the man, Blake could feel the heat of Harrison's glare on his back.

"I'm really sorry about Madison. I've been praying she'll be okay." Blake picked up his pace. Karly could really move.

"If it makes you feel any better, go ahead. Personally, I don't think prayer will help much." Karly's fast walk turned to a jog.

Blake nearly choked on her dust as he struggled to keep up. "You sound rather cynical."

"I don't have much use for religion. It didn't help my mother when she was dying of cancer."

"I'm sorry to hear that, Karly, but sometimes God has other plans," Blake panted.

"Then I don't like his plans. Leaving young children without their mother seems cruel and unloving to me." Karly stopped in front of her door, tugged a key from her shirt pocket, and unlocked it. She stepped inside, grabbed her jacket, and re-locked the door.

Blake bent over and put his hands on his knees. Karly was in much better shape than he was. "That is very sad. I admit that I sometimes don't understand why God does what he does either. Of course, I'm new at this."

Karly threw her jacket over her arm. "Don't tell me you've become one of them. Kerrick finally got to you, didn't he?"

Blake started to laugh, but the action caused him to cough. His lungs hadn't fully recovered yet. "You make it sound like I was abducted by aliens or something. But yes, it was Kerrick who helped me to see the truth."

She stared him up and down.

"What?" Blake swiped at beads of sweat on his forehead, with the back of his sleeve. "I'm still the same guy I used to be." He lifted his cap. "I haven't sprouted antennae that I'm aware of." Blake ran a hand through his shoulder-length damp hair.

The corners of her lips twitched, which pleased him somewhere deep inside.

"Is this what you were referring to yesterday when you mentioned that you had changed?"

"Yes." Blake plunked the cap back on his head.

"Ah. Well, good for you." Karly spun on her heel and sprinted away from him.

She dropped that subject like a hot potato. Blake stared after her, trying to summon the endurance to jog back.

"Let's go. I don't want to be late for the meeting," she yelled over her shoulder.

Why does she have to run everywhere?

"For the record, you need to exercise more. You're really out of shape."

Blake struggled as he trailed after his ex-girlfriend. Yes, he was out of shape in the jogging department. But *she* wasn't. Out of shape. In any way. Nope. Not at all.

Blake stumbled over an exposed tree root. Arms flailing, he caught himself just in time to avoid a painful, embarrassing face plant. Phew! It was a good thing he was behind Karly.

Focus on the task, Blake, focus.

He smiled deviously. Karly might be in her element down here, jogging on solid ground.

But wait until he got her up in his Cessna.

CHAPTER TWENTY-TWO

As the Cessna lifted off the water and skimmed the treetops, Blake chuckled at the wild look in her eyes. "What's wrong, Karly? Does my flying make you nervous?"

"Are you kidding? This is exhilarating."

"How could I forget? You always were the thrill-seeker type."

"The scarier the better. Bring it on."

Blake laughed again. When she joined him, a jolt of pure pleasure raced through his being, bringing with it a profound revelation. But he pushed it away. He wasn't going there—not now and maybe not ever.

As he climbed higher, her squeals of delight bounced off the seaplane's interior. "This is more exciting than I ever imagined. It's so beautiful up here."

"I know."

"This reminds me of a poem I memorized in fifth grade. It was also one of my mom's favorites."

When she began reciting, he thought it was the most wonderful thing he'd ever heard come out of her mouth, even though he knew the poem well himself.

"Oh, I have slipped the surly bonds of earth,
And danced the skies on laughter silvered wings;
Sunward I've climbed and joined the tumbling mirth
Of sun-split clouds... and done a hundred things
You have not dreamed of... wheeled and soared and swung
High in the sunlit silence. Hov'ring there,
I've chased the shouting wind along, and flung

My eager craft through footless halls of air.
Up, up, the long delirious burning blue,
I've topped the windswept heights with easy grace
Where never lark, nor even eagle flew.
And while with silent, lifting mind I've trod
The high untrespassed sanctity of space...
...put out my hand and..."

When she stopped, Blake slanted a look in her direction. He waited for the ending. But it never came.

"*Touched the face of God,*" he finished.

"You know that poem too?"

"I've loved *High Flight* since the first time my grandpa read it to me when I was a little boy, and I've secretly wanted to be a pilot ever since. I'm really not into poetry, but that incredible piece by John Gillespie McGee Jr. is inspiring."

Other than the rumble of the engine, an awkward silence permeated the Cessna's small cabin. "Why didn't you say the last line, Karly?"

"I forgot it."

Blake wasn't buying it, but he kept that thought to himself. Karly had issues with God. Big issues. Were they insurmountable? Nothing was impossible with God, according to his brother-in-law, Kerrick. A flicker of hope ignited inside.

"Will an aerial search really help?" Karly stared out the window and he recognized the abrupt change of subject as strategy to avoid the topic.

"I hope so."

Neither spoke for a while until she tapped her head against the glass. "This is ridiculous," Karly complained, as she scanned below. "For the last half hour, all I've seen are trees, water, rocks, and more of the same." She straightened up abruptly. "Wait. There are people waving up at us. It looks like a little village or something ..."

"Those are my friends at Shadow Lake. I bring interior campers here all the time for guided tours of the wilderness."

"You do? That's so cool."

When Blake began his descent, her eyes grew large. "What are we doing?"

"Landing. Hang on." Blake guided the Cessna's pontoons down onto the tranquil, crystal-clear waters, and killed the engine at the dock. "I thought we'd check with my friends here and see if they know anything that might be helpful."

"Good idea." Karly released her belt.

Once ashore, the pair were greeted by several excited children. A small boy of about eight years of age, Henry's son, stared at Karly with enormous jet-black eyes and a full head of thick dark hair to match. Smudges of dirt marked his face, arms, and legs. It seemed he'd been playing hard. His little hands grabbed hold of Karly's fingers and he began to drag her away. "Come, I want to show you my collection."

"Okay ... but just for a moment." Karly glanced backwards over her shoulder, her eyes pleading with Blake for intervention.

Blake grinned. "See you later. Go easy on her, Dakota."

He approached Henry's modest home, which sat only a few hundred yards from the shoreline. What an incredible daily view this place offered. Blake would love to own a home in such a location one day. The more remote, the better.

Henry sat on a handmade rocker, constructed from vines and branches, outside his front door and waved at Blake as he approached.

"How's the backside feeling?" Blake taunted.

"Even fake moose can cause damage when they kick." Henry grimaced as he rose to his feet. "But enough about me. Mr. White Pelican Man is making very swift progress, I see."

Blake stopped at the bottom of the porch stairs and propped a hiking boot on the bottom step. "Huh?"

Henry pointed a few bungalows down to a pile of children gathered around Karly. "You brought future Mrs. White Pelican here to obtain my blessings."

Blake scratched the back of his neck. "Oh ... I ... no ... it's not what you think. Karly and I are searching for her missing friend, Madison. That's the reason for our visit. Maybe you've seen her? She's short with a thin build and purple, spiked hair."

"No, I haven't seen anything of the sort. I would remember such a spectacle." Henry folded his arms across his chest, but his eyes twinkled.

"Oh ... well ... will you keep your eyes open for her? Karly is her good friend and she's worried that something bad has happened to her."

"I'll be on the lookout and ask everyone I know. Now you better rescue your future bride from Dakota and his friends."

Blake turned to see Karly approaching. Panicked, he leaned towards his friend and whispered, "Will you stop with that future bride stuff?"

Henry threw back his head and laughed, which only made Blake even more uptight.

"That was interesting." Karly reached Henry's porch and cocked her head. "Hey, aren't you the man I sent flying into the wooden display?"

"One and the same." He extended his hand. "I'm Henry, and you met my boy, Dakota."

"Dakota is your son? He's adorable and has quite the snail collection."

The screen door banged open and a small, dark-haired woman stepped out. She delivered a playful slap across her husband's back. "I thought I told you to invite your friends in. My name is Shawna and I'm married to this big lug. I hope you can stay for tea and cookies."

Blake skittered a glance toward Karly, but before he could ask if it was okay with her, she accepted. "We would be delighted."

A few minutes later, after they'd all settled themselves around the big oak table in the kitchen, Karly swallowed the bite she'd just taken and held up what was left of her cookie. "These are the best oatmeal raisin cookies I've ever tasted, Shawna. Can I get your recipe?"

"Recipe?" Shawna refilled Dakota's glass from the milk pitcher. "I never make them the same way twice. I just throw in what I have in the house."

"Including snails," Henry said dryly.

Karly's hand froze with the last bite of her cookie inches from her mouth.

"Just kidding, White Pelican Lady. It was a joke. Blake says I should work at a comedy club."

Karly popped the last bite in her mouth. "Yes, you are quite funny. Can I ask you a question?" Without waiting for him to respond, she barrelled forward. "Why do you call me White Pelican Lady?"

"Why don't you ask him?" Henry winked at Blake.

Blake lifted his teacup to his mouth and drained the last few drops. Then he placed his palms on the table, pushed back his chair, and stood. "Thank you so much for your hospitality, but we should head out. We need to continue our search before we lose daylight."

Henry accompanied them to the Cessna and watched as they climbed in. "I hope you have success in finding your missing friend. Goodbye, White Pelican Man." He waved a hand, a devious smirk on his face.

Karly sat up soldier-straight and whirled to face him.

Blake felt her eyes boring holes in the side of his head, like a truth-seeking laser. He refused to make eye contact. He'd have to get back at Henry for that one. If Henry thought he was being funny, he was sorely mistaken. He should never have encouraged his friend with the comedy club suggestion. The engine roared to life and Blake concentrated on liftoff. Once they were airborne, her interrogation began.

"White Pelican Man?" she sang, all annoying and ditty-like. "Why does your friend call me White Pelican Lady?"

"Would you believe it's because you're tall and blonde like me?" Blake focused on his instrument panel, and checked his elevation. She wasn't the only one who could use avoidance strategies.

"What have you told him about us?"

"Absolutely nothing." Blake studied his fuel gage. Half a tank. Good.

"I'm not sure I believe you."

Blake sighed. He couldn't avoid her question forever. "Suit yourself. For some reason, he's bound and determined to find me a bride. Because he's so happy, he thinks I need to be married too."

"And he picked me as your future wife?"

Blake studied the landscape below. "Hey, I was as shocked as you when he started calling you White Pelican Lady that night outside The Cedar Canoe."

"He has no idea that we used to date?"

"I never shared that information with him." Blake chanced a look in her direction. "But that's not the worst of it."

"What do you mean?"

"He's bound and determined to have us married before the next full moon."

A snort flew from her mouth. "Like that's going to happen."

He frowned. "Hey, you could do way worse than me."

"I think we should concentrate our efforts on the search." Karly stared out her window.

"I agree. No more mention of white pelicans. I won't bring it up again, but can I ask you something?"

When she met his gaze, Blake touched a finger to his nose. "Do you think I have a big beak ... er, nose?"

A smirk twisted Karly's lips as she leaned close and studied him. Blake wished he could take his words back. Whatever had possessed him to humiliate himself like that? Sometimes he was his own worst enemy.

The familiar floral scent of Karly's shampoo sent old feelings charging through him, warming him from head to toe. When she ran a finger down his nose, he fought the urge to sneeze.

"What are you doing?" He snagged hold of her finger.

"I've never felt a beak before."

"That's not funny. Forget I asked. It's just that Henry's explanation for the nickname, 'White Pelican Man' was because I like to fish, fly in the clouds, have white-blonde hair, and a yellow beak."

Giggles erupted, first ripples, then large waves. Karly wrapped her arms around her stomach.

"It's not that funny."

"Yes, it is. And now you have a complex about your nose. Hilarious! After all that's happened lately, I really needed a good belly laugh."

"So glad the blow to my self-esteem can lift your spirits. But consider this." Blake held a finger in the air. "If Henry called you White Pelican Lady, then maybe it's because you look like me. Lean over here and let me check *your* beak."

CHAPTER TWENTY-THREE

By the time they landed and entered No Trace's main building, it was eight o'clock in the evening. At the sight of a police cruiser in the parking lot, Karly's insides twisted into a pretzel.

Without saying a word, Blake placed a warm hand on her upper back. It calmed her nerves a little. Once inside, the atmosphere of the lunchroom was gloomy, and her mood plummeted again. When her eyes connected with Harrison's, she could almost feel the weight he carried from the past. As hard as this was for her, she knew it was even more difficult for him.

Heather sat in a chair to his right, twisting an elastic band around her fingers. To Harrison's left, Officer Neilson wrote furiously in his note pad. Across the table sat a senior-looking policeman and a few other employees. The silence ate away at Karly until she couldn't take the stress. She walked over to the table. "So, have you contacted Madison's family, Officer Neilson?"

"Yes, and they're on their way."

"We carried out a search of the immediate campground and came up blank," Harrison offered solemnly.

"We took to the skies, but also nothing," Blake added.

The policeman cleared his throat. "And you are?"

"Blake Fenton. I'm the owner of Wilderness Bush Adventures."

"Can you explain to me how you are involved in all of this?"

"He's a good friend of mine," Karly jumped in. "When he found out Madison was missing he offered to do an aerial surveillance and look for anything unusual."

"Is that right?" The officer glared at Blake. "Did you know Madison?"

"Not well. I met her a few times through Karly."

"From a witness report, a Blake Fenton was the last person to have been with her on Friday night. In fact, you were seen leaving The Cedar Canoe with her."

Karly stiffened. Why had the officer acted like he didn't know who Blake Fenton was a minute ago? She didn't like the way this guy operated. Strange police methodology as far as she was concerned. Sneaky and rat-like.

"I don't know how I could have been the last person to see her. I did dance with her once, but left right after, about ten thirty. There were still plenty of people in the restaurant."

"What did you do then?"

"Went home."

"Where's home?"

"Fifteen hundred Gulliver Side Road."

"Can anyone verify your whereabouts after you left?"

Karly held her breath, waiting for his answer, as her earlier accusation that he had spent the night with Madison came back to torment her. She just had to know for sure.

"I live alone, if that's what you mean."

"Did you take Madison home that night?"

"Absolutely not. I told you I left her at The Cedar Canoe."

A loud ticking of a wall clock was the only sound in the room for what seemed like an eternity. Then the belligerent officer turned on Harrison. "Let me get this straight. You drove these young women, Karly Foster and Madison Springfield, to The Cedar Canoe Friday night."

"Yes."

"Did you take Madison home afterward?"

"No."

"Why was that?"

"I left with Karly and never thought about it."

Karly felt Blake's eyes on her, but refused to look over.

"Where did the pair of you go?"

"To a wolf howl."

"Can anyone vouch for you?"

"There were a few hundred people there. Let me think ..." Harrison rubbed his chin. "I remember running into Mike Wigglesworth. He could verify that Karly and I were in attendance."

Karly watched the officer record the man's name in his notepad. "Did it not occur to you that Madison would need a ride home?"

Karly opened her mouth to speak, but the officer held up his hand. "I'd like Harrison to answer please."

"If you knew Madison, you'd know she was an impulsive and independent sort. Recently, she's been staying with her friend Raven, from what I gather. If not, she would bum a ride from someone else. She had a cell phone with her, so I figured if she needed a ride she would call."

"What time did the pair of you get home from this wolf howl?"

"Around midnight."

"What did you do after that?"

"I saw Miss Foster home, then I retired for the night."

At that point, the senior officer who was sitting quietly stood, his chair scraping the floor. "I think this meeting is adjourned. Keep us informed if Madison should contact you or show up. In the meantime, we'll be carrying out our own investigation."

As the officers walked away, Karly overheard the senior policeman rebuking the younger. "Stick with the facts, William, and try not to be accusatory."

Karly bit her lip to stop from spitting out her snarky agreement.

As the group began to disperse, Harrison waved a hand to attract everyone's attention. "I mean no disrespect to Madison, and I know this will be difficult, but tomorrow is Monday morning and will be business as usual. We have a campground to run. See you all at nine o'clock sharp."

Harrison fled for the steps to the downstairs library and Heather followed him.

Blake spoke softly into her ear. "Come on, Blondie, I'll walk you home."

Her heartache lifted at the affectionate nickname as memories flooded back. Funny how that single reference could lessen the angst of the last few days, if ever so slightly.

Karly sighed. Why couldn't things have worked out with Blake? Was there any hope for them now? He said he had changed. Did that change mean there was more of a chance the two of them could work things out, or less?

Only time would tell.

CHAPTER TWENTY-FOUR

The weight of Madison's disappearance weighed heavily on Karly's heart—in fact, on her entire being—as she trudged wearily beside Blake. Perhaps he felt it too. He had been quiet, the whole way to her cabin—until they stood outside the door and he turned to her. "I wonder what really happened to Josh?"

Blake's question reminded her that Josh had also gone through something horrific. Karly searched a pocket for her keys.

"I have no idea. It's bizarre for sure. But if I were to hazard a guess, I'd say that he went off alone, like he often does, and had an accident."

"What kind of an accident?"

"Maybe a fall, or a run-in with a wild animal or a vehicle."

"I suppose that could explain it."

"Either way, I hope they can figure out what happened to him and he feels better soon. Josh can be annoying at times, but I hate to see him like this."

"I have hope that Madison will be found alive and well, and Josh will recover too." He placed a comforting hand on her shoulder and squeezed.

Karly bit her lower lip and sucked in a deep breath. "I wish I could share your optimism." As Karly inserted the key in the lock, she heard an odd gurgling, growling sound beside her. Blake pressed a hand to his stomach and looked at her sheepishly.

"Someone's hungry." Karly unlocked the door and stepped inside. The sound of his stomach reminded her that she was also hungry. "I can throw a frozen pizza in the oven. Would you like to stay?"

"I won't turn down that offer. I'm so hungry I could eat the box." Blake trailed behind her into the kitchen. "Do you think Josh had anything to do with Madison's disappearance?"

Karly turned on the oven to heat it up and pulled the pizza from the freezer. "That thought crossed my mind, but I don't think so. He wasn't even at The Cedar Canoe that night." Karly pulled the cardboard zip tag on the side of the box off and removed the pizza.

"Could he have arrived after you and I left?"

She reached for a knife and slit the plastic covering open. "I suppose. I guess we'll leave that for the police to determine."

Blake grabbed the piece of plastic when it came loose from the pizza, scrunched it up, and tossed it in the garbage pail. "The more I think about this whole situation, the more worried I get. I don't like the idea of you staying here alone. A dead body was discovered a few days ago and now Madison is missing. Josh encountered some sort of strange attack or something. What if you are the next target?"

Karly placed the pizza on the middle rack of the oven, closed the door, and set the timer. "I wasn't worried until now. Thanks."

Blake leaned against the kitchen sink and put his hands in his pockets. "What if I slept over? I'll stay outside on the front porch, so nothing looks improper."

Karly's eyes widened, and her stomach flipped at the thought. "You would do that for me?"

"Yes." The caring look in his eyes almost made her want to cry again—to let loose three years of pain and sadness—tears that had been threatening since the day in Moe's Diner when he declared he had never intended to break up with her. Karly's lower lip quivered, despite her best efforts to stop it. She whirled so that her back was to him.

"Karly?"

Warm hands touched her shoulders. Sobs built inside like molten lava. How did one keep a volcano from spewing forth? He turned her to face him. "Why are you crying?"

Get a grip, Karly. This emotional stuff had to stop. She drew in a ragged breath and tried to pull herself together. "I thought ..."

Her words came out in a garbled, blubbery mess. She buried her face in her hands as Blake pulled her against his chest. Wrapped in his arms, she cried softly.

"You thought what?" A hand tenderly caressed the back of her head. The steady thud of his heartbeat against her ear was painfully familiar as she recalled the times she'd fallen asleep leaning against him as they watched a movie together. She lifted her head. "I thought you hated me."

He brushed back the wet strands of hair stuck to her cheeks. "I have never hated you."

"No?"

"No."

"Even after I threw you in the cold lake and ruined your suit?"

"Not even after that."

"Are you sure?"

"Not even after you broke my heart." His eyes drooped, along with his shoulders. With the sight came the realization that her impulsiveness had caused him much pain.

A lump lodged in her throat, making it difficult to speak. "My heart was shattered that day too."

He pulled her against him again. Time froze as they stood wrapped in each other's arms.

"So, what do we do now?" He tipped her chin up to meet his probing gaze.

Karly wiped at her eyes. "I know it's been a long time coming, but I'm sorry for over-reacting that day at Maya and Kerrick's wedding. If I'd only listened and heard you out, everything would have been so different. Can you forgive me?"

The stove timer dinged and they both ignored it. Blake's eyes carried sadness, yet something else. Resignation perhaps? "I forgive you, Karly. I'm beginning to believe that everything happens for a reason. I guess it just wasn't meant to be."

Hope crashed—with jarring impact. What was he saying? That it was too late for them now? All because of her?

The timer dinged again, reminding her she'd better get supper out of the oven before it burned. For some reason, she'd lost her appetite. While she made a valiant effort of nibbling on her first piece, Blake managed to put away three quarters of the pizza.

"Are you sure you don't want that last piece?" Blake stared at the sliver on the plate.

"Help yourself. I guess I wasn't as hungry as I thought."

Blake finished the last slice, then took his plate to the sink and rinsed it. "Do you have a spare sleeping bag kicking around?"

"Why?"

"I'm staying the night and you can't stop me." He tipped his glass and downed the last of his water. Then he reached for the dishcloth.

"I don't have a sleeping bag." Karly snagged the dishcloth from his hands and scrubbed the table vigorously.

"You expect me to believe that?" Blake grabbed her hand, abruptly stopping her cleaning frenzy. "Look me in the eyes and tell me that. I know you have a sleeping bag. In fact, you probably own several top-quality brands."

Busted. Karly refused to make eye contact. She tugged her hand from his grasp, hurried to the sink, and rinsed the cloth free of crumbs.

"If you don't have one, I'll camp outside anyway, sleeping bag or not. But don't be surprised if I'm gone when you get up. I have an early-morning flight."

This was a very bad idea. Wasn't it? Karly shut off the tap, turned and finally faced him. "You're not sleeping outside. You'll be eaten alive by mosquitoes. You can sleep on the couch. I don't care what people think." Although she made a valiant effort at appearing nonchalant about his protective offer, inside she was pleased—ever so slightly. And just why had she invited him to sleep on the couch? Didn't she just tell herself that this whole thing was a bad idea? Talk about being conflicted. She reached for the pizza box.

"I care."

His serious tone caught her off guard. She jammed the cardboard box in the garbage pail and stared at him.

"You really have changed, haven't you? The old Blake wouldn't have cared what anyone thought. Isn't that the way it should be?"

"To a certain extent, you're right. But I'm learning that you need to go with your conscience. I don't want to mislead anyone. Not to mention that your reputation is very important to me."

"It is?"

"It is.

Karly didn't know what to do with that. Hope of the smallest degree simmered, despite her desperate attempt to squelch it. Exhaling loudly, she strode to the closet and dug around in the bottom of it until she located her sleeping bag.

When she handed it to him, Blake started for the door. Karly followed him. "Do you think you'll be safe out here?" She searched the darkness.

"I'll be fine. Lock the door behind me."

"Okay."

Karly had just crawled into bed when rain slammed against her window. She tossed her blankets off and jumped out of bed. After hurrying to the front door, she whipped it open.

Karly screamed as a large dark figure loomed in the doorway, the whites of a pair of eyes staring at her. It took her a second to realize she was looking at a cocooned Blake, wrapped from head to toe in the black sleeping bag.

"It's only me, Karly." He brushed past her and tore off the soggy sleeping bag.

"You scared me half to death."

"I'm sorry. I didn't mean to. I was just protecting myself from the rain and the mosquitoes. Where can I put this?" He held up the dripping sleeping bag.

Karly pointed to the washroom. "Just drop it in the bathtub for now. I'll hang it out to dry tomorrow."

While he headed toward the tub, she dug out a pillow and some extra blankets from the closet and tossed them on the couch. When he emerged from the washroom, rubbing his head vigorously with a towel, her stomach fluttered like a swarm of migrating monarchs. *Stop it, Karly. It wasn't meant to be, remember?*

"I guess you got your wish after all." His mouth hitched at one corner.

"My wish?" Karly rubbed her stomach. Those monarchs were agitated.

"To have me sleep indoors." A large grin lit up his face—which didn't help matters at all. Three years had increased Blake's looks exponentially, large beak or not. Karly bit her lip as she studied him. Or did it have more to do with the change inside him?

Karly held a finger in the air. "Wait a minute. You're twisting this all around. I didn't feel it was necessary for you to guard me in the first place. You were the one that offered."

"If I didn't know any better, I'd think you had some sort of deal going with God to whip up this drenching." Blake stopped in the bathroom doorway, leaned back into the room to toss the towel in the tub, then walked over to the couch.

At the mention of God, Karly's stomach knotted as if the large swarm of butterflies had congealed in the middle in one large mass. "If that was the case, I'd be making bigger deals than weather-related ones. Something about Madison being found safe and sound, for example. And speaking of which, don't flatter yourself. I only wanted you inside for safety reasons—your safety. There was no ulterior motive involved."

"You keep telling yourself that, Blondie. Deep down you were hoping I'd stay." Blake crossed his arms and watched her as she spread out his blankets. She could feel his gaze on her and warmth spread up her neck.

Karly stopped what she was doing and looked up at him. His flirting was driving her crazy. Of course, she'd never let him know that. Before she could stop herself, old, impulsive Karly reached for the pillow, whammed him across the chest, and took off like a bullet to her bedroom. His footsteps sounded close behind her. Adrenaline pumping and heart thumping, she slammed the door just before he caught up to her, and leaned her weight against it … just in case.

"You may be safe for now," he yelled, "but you'd better keep watch. I'll get you when you least expect it."

Her back still to the door, Karly slid down to the floor, smiling.

✤

Loud banging on her bedroom door startled her from a deep sleep. Karly bolted upright.

"Are you awake?" Blake's voice was muffled.

"I am now. What is it?"

"I'm leaving for work. I'd like you to get up and lock the door behind me."

Karly yawned and shoved back her covers. "I'm coming."

Rubbing her eyes, she opened her door and staggered sleepily into the living room. When Blake stared at her oddly, she froze and looked down. She was dressed only in her pajama shorts and a tank top. She snatched a blanket off the couch and wrapped it around herself.

A devious look crossed his face, but her groggy mind couldn't quite process what was going on. Until it was too late.

The blow hit her across her left shoulder. She stumbled backwards at the force of the pillow. "Hey!"

"Revenge is sweet." Blake grinned.

"Yes, so sweet when your victim is half asleep and her arms are trapped under a blanket."

Blake laughed and headed for the door. "By the way, I signed us up. We'll be great together. No one will catch us." He clasped the knob.

"What are you talking about?"

"The No Trace canoe race. You're my partner." The door slammed behind him and he disappeared into the dim light of early dawn.

Karly stared at the closed door. Suddenly it flew open again, making her jump. "What now?" she croaked, her heart skipping a beat.

"You didn't lock the door."

Karly pointed. "Get going, you'll miss your flight."

"Hardly, since I'm the pilot."

She shook her head at his teasing grin. When she took a step forward, she stumbled over the pillow Blake had whacked her with. Karly kicked at it, sending it airborne.

"Hey, that was a one-yard kick. You must have played football in preschool."

"Go." Karly couldn't help but smile at his attempt at humour as he disappeared again. She closed the door after him and slipped the deadbolt in place. She didn't have a clue what any of it meant, but for the first time in forever, despite her reservations, hope flickered—ever so faintly.

Then the comment she'd made to Blake, that she should be making a deal with God about bringing Madison home safely, flitted through her mind, and her smile disappeared as quickly as it had come.

CHAPTER TWENTY-FIVE

"I'll have the halibut and home fries. And don't forget the tartar sauce, please." Blake held out the menu.

The middle-aged waitress finishing scribbling down Blake's request, then smiled politely as she took his menu and headed toward the kitchen.

Thankfully, Raven didn't appear to be working tonight. Steering clear of her would be wise. She was good at offering herself up as bait. Like a hungry fish, though, he knew that if he bit, he'd be hooked, never to be free again.

But *Moe's Diner* offered the best food at the best prices. Since opening a can of soup or throwing a frozen dinner in the microwave summed up his cooking abilities, eating here was his best option. Besides, it was a small town and he couldn't avoid her forever. Might as well face her now so he wouldn't have to worry about running into her later.

While waiting for his meal, he reached across the aisle to the empty booth and snatched the Aspen Ridge Daily Newspaper. The headlines jolted him: *Forensic Testing on Body Found by Local Pilot Could Take Weeks.*

The article stated that local pilot, Blake Fenton, had come across a body while fishing at Potter's Lake and that it could take weeks for forensic testing to reveal the identity of the victim. It also mentioned that there were unconfirmed speculations that the body could belong to a young female No Trace Campground employee who had gone missing two years earlier. Blake put down the newspaper just as his meal arrived. So much for anonymity. When the story first broke, late Friday, they hadn't revealed his identity. Not so any longer.

Having eaten last around ten that morning, and then only a banana, two granola bars, and a thermos of coffee, he was famished. As he dug into his food, he couldn't help but notice an older couple whispering and looking his direction. Several teenage boys at a nearby table were also staring at him. What in the world was going on? Then it hit him. It was a small town and news traveled fast. If they didn't know who the new pilot was before, they did now. His *Wilderness Bush Adventures* T-shirt and cap identified him clearly. And after everyone had seen his picture staring back at them from the front page, there would be no doubt as to his identity.

"Hey, are you Blake Fenton?" A boy of about fifteen years of age with a head of wavy blonde curls yelled at him from two booths down and across the aisle. "What was it like to find a dead body?"

"It was pretty awful." Blake muttered the words before dropping his gaze to his plate, hoping to discourage any further interaction. The few remaining home fries held no appeal. He tossed his napkin on to his plate and slid to the end of the bench. He didn't want to wait for the server to bring him his bill, so he tugged a twenty from his wallet and dropped it onto the table. Pretty big tip, but a small price to pay to get out of there fast.

Seconds later, he was out the door and breathing a sigh of relief. He didn't care for that type of attention. Not at all.

Hurrying to his truck, he opened the door, slipped inside, pushed the locks and sighed. Ah, safe in his aging pickup. He turned the key and adjusted the air-conditioning. While he waited for cool air to come, he tipped his head back against the headrest and closed his eyes. So much had happened in the last week. The reappearance of Karly, the discovery of a body, Madison missing and Frank's ... mishap. And then Raven.

Blake leaned forward, grabbed the steering wheel and banged his head against it. How had he allowed his good judgement to be so clouded by Raven's feminine wiles? He was not only angry with himself but embarrassed. He really needed to deal with her. But how? He banged it one more time in frustration.

A knock on the glass brought his head up sharply. Karly cocked her head at him as Blake rolled down his window.

"What's wrong? Do you have a headache? If you didn't before, you will after all that head-banging." Karly's eyes twinkled with amusement.

Yes, and her name is Raven. "I'm fine." He really couldn't tell her what was troubling him. She'd never understand. When Harrison appeared behind her, Blake's shoulders sagged. Now he really *did* have a headache. Why were those two always together?

"We're here for supper. Why don't you join us?" Karly gestured toward the diner.

"No, thanks." *Three's a crowd.* Besides, he didn't want to expose himself to more questions about his upsetting discovery.

"I saw the newspaper article," Harrison commented. "Sorry you had to experience that." Harrison turned to Karly. "Moe's is filling up. I'll head in and get us a table."

"I'll be in shortly."

Harrison nodded and walked away.

"So, what's really wrong?" Wrinkle lines had appeared on Karly's forehead when she turned back to him.

"I look that bad, eh?" Blake ran a hand through his hair." It's nothing you'd want to hear about. How are you holding up? Any news about Madison?"

"No."

"What about Josh?"

"He showed up for work, but was extremely quiet most of the day. Very odd for him."

"I'd better join Harrison for supper." Karly took a step back, then hesitated. "When are we going to practice?"

"For what?"

"The canoe race you signed us up for."

Blake's spirits lifted suddenly. "Oh that. When are you free?"

"Does Saturday morning sound good to you?"

"Yep. And be prepared." Blake straightened in his seat, feeling his old self returning.

"For what?"

"This will be the hardest workout you've ever experienced in your entire life, Blondie. You may be able to out-jog me, but when it comes to canoeing, I can out-paddle you any day of the week." Blake flashed her a teasing grin.

Karly flapped a hand. "Ha! Did you forget I used to teach canoe courses at the YMCA?"

The tension eased from Blake's body. He rested his arm on the window ledge. Bantering with Karly was always enjoyable. He hadn't even realized how much he'd missed it. "Knowledge is one thing, but physical strength and endurance are something else altogether."

'Bring it on. I can handle anything you throw my way." Karly raised both arms and flexed her muscles.

Blake threw his head back and laughed. "When I get through with you, those arms will ache so badly, you won't be able to lift a fork to your mouth."

"Is that right? Well, when I get through with you, you'll be so exhausted you won't be able to portage a pretzel." She reached through the window frame and poked him in the shoulder. "So there." She whirled and hurried off, her long blonde hair flying behind her.

Portage a pretzel?

He chuckled again and watched her until she disappeared inside the restaurant. His mood had lightened considerably since Karly tapped on his window. He really needed that laugh. Actually—a sudden revelation jolted through him—maybe what he really needed was her.

CHAPTER TWENTY-SIX

Karly reached for the sleeping bag that she'd sprawled across the rickety back-porch railing earlier that day. She patted it in several places. Good. It was dry. If it wasn't, it wouldn't matter anyway, as it was late in the evening and the dampness would seep back into it if she didn't bring it inside soon.

A movement caught her eye and she flicked off a daddy-longlegs that had been running across the top. Her best friend Maya had been terrified of spiders. Karly sighed. She really missed Maya. As soon as they could find Madison, she'd contact her. Maybe even arrange to see her.

The woods behind the cabin were thick and dark as dusk began to fall. It was eerily quiet in the campground. Karly and Madison's cabin had been the last one in a row of cabins and quite a distance away from the rest. Although the seclusion had always bothered Madison, Karly loved it. Usually.

As Karly gathered the sleeping bag into her arms, a twig snapped behind her. Probably just a squirrel or raccoon.

But when she turned, and a large figure loomed in front of her, Karly jumped. "Harrison. You scared me half to death. What are you doing here?"

He pulled a hand from behind his back. A bunch of wild flowers appeared in front of her face. "These are for you. Sorry if I startled you."

"But you just dropped me off. How did you have time to pick flowers?"

Harrison shrugged. "They're wildflowers, Karly. They grow in abundance. It only takes a few minutes."

"That was very thoughtful of you." Karly crossed the back porch, her arms full of the sleeping bag. "It's been a rough week. I'm accustomed to Madison's lively personality. Things just aren't the same without her."

Karly stopped at the door. The old screen door creaked as Harrison opened it and held it for her. "I get that. I wanted you to know that I'm thinking of you."

Karly stepped inside and tossed the bag on the couch to be rolled and stuffed into its case later, then joined Harrison in the kitchen. "Your bouquet is perfect timing." Karly pulled the drooping, wilted flowers from the juice jug—the arrangement that Harrison had left her the week before. "It's time to replace these."

"I called the police to see if they've made any progress yet." Harrison leaned against the sink, crossed his arms, and watched her dump the old water and rinse the container.

"And?" Karly filled the jug with fresh water from the tap.

"They're not really saying much other than that Madison's parents are staying in Aspen Ridge. Have you met them?"

"Yes, a few times, but only briefly when they came to pick Madison up to take her home for a weekend. They seemed nice. And Madison got along well with them. I can't imagine what they must be going through."

Harrison stepped behind her as she arranged the handful of Queen Anne's lace, rosy coneflowers, purple asters, and yellow rudbeckia.

"They're very pretty."

"Like you." He leaned over her right shoulder, his breath tickling her cheek.

Karly shifted uncomfortably, pulled out a pink coneflower, and moved it to another spot in the arrangement. Anything to busy herself and avoid Harrison's words of affection.

"I'm a little worried about you, Karly. We have no way of knowing if there is a killer at large. It could even be Josh."

So, he was worried about her too? Maybe she should take Blake and his concerns a little more seriously. "That thought has crossed my mind, but I doubt it's Josh." Karly tried to move, but his arms had her trapped against the sink.

She turned to find him standing very close. Too close. "Josh doesn't seem the type. Besides, he's pretty small; I could probably take him."

"You probably could at that." Harrison's eyes darkened. "I lost Jessica once. I couldn't bear it if anything happened to you." He slid a finger under her chin and tipped it up. "I think you know how I feel about you, Karly."

"I ... um."

A finger touched her lips. "It's okay, I know you're not there yet. I hope in time that you'll feel the same, but in the meantime, I'll wait for you. Forever. If it takes that long. Or until you tell me to take a flying leap. Will you promise me that you'll at least think about giving me a chance?"

She pulled his finger away. "I guess I can do that. It's getting late, though, and I'm really tired." She slipped away from him and hurried through the living room, hoping he'd take the hint.

"Karly?" He trailed her to the front door. "Can I ask you a rather personal question?"

Karly swallowed the lump that had formed in her throat, since Harrison told her she was pretty ... again. Normally, she'd be flattered but ...

"I happened to notice Blake's truck leave the campground early this morning. You can tell me this is none of my business, but did Blake spend the night with you?"

Karly stiffened. Blake's advice about protecting her reputation was coming back to haunt her. Maybe there was some truth to what he had said after all. Should she tell Harrison or leave him wondering? Frankly, she was annoyed. But she couldn't really pinpoint why. Was it because Blake had been right? Or because Harrison had dared to ask?

Karly sighed and pointed to the couch. "Blake slept there. He insisted because he was worried about me." She folded her arms across her chest. She knew her words were clipped, but since he was being nosy, she couldn't bring herself to feel badly about it.

"Thanks for telling me. I feel better now. Good night, and lock this door behind me." Harrison slipped outside and shut the door.

She secured the lock, leaned her back against the door, and sank to the floor. She drew her knees up to her chest and rested her head on them. She couldn't deal with any of this right now. Especially Harrison's feelings for her.

Not that he wasn't saying and doing the right things. Twice in the span of a week he'd brought her flowers. And twice in that same time, he'd told her she was pretty—the first time down by the lake in the moonlight.

Still, his persistent affections were starting to grate on her nerves, like fingernails on a chalkboard. Why was that? Was it because she was worried sick about her missing friend and really couldn't think about a relationship right now? Or the fact that strange things continued to happen in the campground? Or did it have to do with Blake's reappearance in her life?

One thing she knew for sure.

She was not going to make a hasty decision concerning Harrison. He may have to wait forever. No. That wouldn't be fair. She'd tell him as soon as she could figure things out herself. And who knew how long that could take?

Blake's teasing grin flashed into her mind, along with his threat about pushing her so hard she wouldn't be able to lift a fork to her mouth. Despite all her worries, she smiled. She was really looking forward to canoeing. Or was she really looking forward to spending time with Blake? She desperately needed something or someone right now.

Was it Blake?

CHAPTER TWENTY-SEVEN

Karly sat in the conference room, rubbing her temples. The headache she had acquired last night, after Harrison left, just wouldn't leave. She really should pay more attention, but it hurt to think. Thankfully, Blake sat beside her listening keenly to details about the canoe race.

"In just two weeks, the No Trace Marathon Canoe Race will take place. We already have a dozen teams signed up and are hoping for at least another dozen. So far, our entries range from novices to world pros. It's important that you read about, and are prepared for, the potential hazards of wilderness travel. Don't forget to study your information packages. Are there any questions?" Harrison scanned the room.

Josh raised his hand. "I don't have a partner."

"Do we have anyone in attendance who needs a partner?" Harrison asked.

When no one volunteered, he continued. "I wouldn't worry about it, Josh. I'm sure there will be some future entries that need pairing up. I'll keep my eyes open for you."

As the group dispersed, Josh made his way towards them.

"How are you feeling?" Karly asked.

"I'm okay, but I was wondering where Madison is. I haven't seen her around."

Unexpectedly, her eyes filled with tears and her lower lip trembled. His question had caught her off-guard. When she didn't immediately answer, Blake glanced in her direction. "Haven't you heard the news? Madison has been missing since Friday night," he offered solemnly.

"What?" Josh collapsed into a nearby chair. "How did that happen?"

"No one knows for sure. She was at The Cedar Canoe that night and hasn't been seen since."

Josh blanched. He looked as pale as he had that night in the emergency room. "I think I need to go and rest for a while." He stood and tipped to one side.

Blake jumped out of his seat and caught his arm to steady him. "You okay, man?"

Josh jerked back, almost skittishly, from Blake, and pressed a hand to his forehead. "I was a little dizzy for a moment. It happens if I get up too quickly. It's passed now."

"Do you want me to help you back to your cabin?" Blake offered.

Josh shook his head. Then he turned and staggered toward the exit, mumbling something as he fled. Blake stared after him for a moment, then he looked down at her, his eyes warm with concern. "Are you okay?"

Karly sniffled. "I'm fine. I wasn't prepared for his question about Madison. But, if Josh doesn't feel better soon, he won't need to worry about finding a partner. That race is physically grueling. He certainly won't be up to it." Karly wiped at a renegade tear that trailed down her cheek. "And I didn't realize he had no idea that Madison was missing. Did you see his face when he found out?"

"Yes, I did. I could be wrong, but I think Josh has feelings for Madison. Hearing that kind of horrific news would do that to a guy. Trust me, I know. I remember the day I discovered it was *your* injured body lying at the foot of the fire tower, shot, broken, and barely alive. My legs gave out from underneath me, although I didn't remember that until Kerrick told me." He shook his head. "That's when I first realized ..."

Karly waited for him to continue, but he didn't. His lips pressed tightly together like a jail door slamming shut. He reached for his information packet and began flipping through it. Her heart pounded erratically in her chest. Was he inferring what she thought he was? That he had been in love with her then? He couldn't leave her hanging like that. Sure, they began dating shortly after her accident, but in the time that they were together, he had never, ever, told her he loved her—never said those three monumental words.

Ding! A bell clanged loudly in her brain.

Perhaps that was the main reason she had jumped to the conclusion that he wanted out of the relationship that day on the dock at Maya and Kerrick's wedding.

She had to ask him. She just did. Had he been about to tell her that he loved her?

"What did you realize?"

"It's insignificant now." Blake appeared to be studying one page diligently.

Insignificant now? It wasn't meant to be?

Karly felt sick. She pressed a hand to her stomach. Now, she not only had a headache, but an upset stomach. The topic of 'them' was clearly closed.

For now.

Her mind wandered back to Blake's statement about Josh possibly being in love with Madison. Safer territory. "I think you're wrong about Josh liking Madison. They were always fighting."

One corner of Blake's mouth hitched. "Kind of reminds me of another couple I once knew. In fact, one of them still has the scars to prove it." He held up a slightly crooked middle finger.

Impulsively, she grabbed the digit and gave it a little twist. Then she felt horrible as she remembered the pulsating pain her own pinky had experienced lately and the remorse she'd felt over her taunting of his injury. What was wrong with her?

"Ouch, Cruella. What do you think you're doing?"

"Reconstructive surgery?" She threw her hands in the air. "I'm really sorry. I shouldn't have done that. But I don't deserve that nickname."

"Really? Your actions just proved otherwise."

"I see you guys are partners." Harrison walked over to them and stopped beside Blake, his arms crossed, feet spread wide apart, a serious look on his face. "What do you know about portaging and canoeing?"

Blake squared his shoulders. "Not that I need to defend myself to you, but actually I'm very experienced. Over the last fifteen years, I've spent a lot of my spare time canoeing, kayaking, and white-water rafting. I've taken courses and I even did some instruction at a provincial park for a few years."

"Just making sure, since you'll have precious cargo aboard."

The air was so thick with testosterone Karly could almost cut it with a knife.

"I can take care of myself, Harrison." Karly straightened in her chair. "Don't worry about me."

"Do you both realize that this canoe race will involve one night in the bush together—two if you get yourselves lost?"

Karly's gaze flew from Harrison to Blake. How would he respond, since he was so keen on keeping her reputation untainted?

"My actions toward Karly have always been honourable. I can assure you they will remain that way." His bold, firm reply warmed her through and through.

Harrison guffawed. "Do you expect me to believe that?" He nudged Blake in the shoulder. "Maybe you're not interested in women."

Blake rubbed one hand around a fist. Was Harrison going to be on the receiving end of some intense facial pain? Before she knew what was happening, Blake leaned forward and kissed her. Long and passionately. When he pulled back, he looked up at Harrison, a smug look on his face. "Women suit me just fine ... especially this one."

CHAPTER TWENTY-EIGHT

Had his lips cast some type of hypnotic spell over her? Even after Blake flew from the building as if it was on fire, and Harrison stomped away in an angry huff, she sat as though her bottom was glued to the chair. Her fingers reached up and touched her lips.

She was numb. From head to toe. That kiss had left her reeling and had ignited a fire in her belly, which spread to her entire body. One that she just couldn't seem to extinguish.

Why did he kiss her? Hadn't he just said that the past was insignificant now? And that it wasn't meant to be? Terribly confused, she rose to her feet. Like a zombie, she wandered toward the exit, opened the door, and took off running through the parking lot.

As if following an invisible beacon, she sprinted toward the main gate, across the highway, and began her climb up the steep Lookout Trail. Due to the sharp slant, her sprint slowed to a jog, then a slow, arduous walk.

Ten minutes later, her breaths fast and hard, she reached the summit. This was the highest elevation for miles around and worth every calorie burned for its spectacular scenery. Karly plunked herself down and leaned against a large rock outcropping.

She relaxed until her breathing returned to normal. Why hadn't she taken the time to grab some water? She could use a cool drink of water right about now. Since it was noon, the sun was high overhead and hot.

Karly glanced around her and sighed. Northwestern Ontario was more beautiful than she would have ever imagined. With its untamed wilderness, hidden lakes, abundant wildlife, and soothing solitude her heart would normally be at peace. But not since Madison had gone missing. And not since Blake had shown up, disrupting her life. Especially not after that kiss. Why did he kiss her if things were not meant to be and the past was now insignificant?

Karly pressed both palms to the sides of her head and held tightly, as though that would help to contain her racing thoughts. To be honest, she was a mess. Her life was in shambles. So many things were wrong. No amount of amazing or spectacular scenery could change the turmoil inside.

Her fingers trembled as they touched her lips again. She closed her eyes and remembered his kiss. Was she in love with Blake? Had she been all this time? To say that his impulsive and unexpected display of affection had impacted her was an understatement.

What about Harrison? He was kind, thoughtful, and handsome too. But lately, she had felt pressured by his continual affections. He freely declared how he felt about her, although he also had never uttered those three special words of endearment. He loved her, didn't he?

No one had said those words to her in a very long time. She loved her father. He was a kind, strong man. But not outwardly affectionate. Oh, how she missed her mother. All the time that had passed hadn't replaced the deep loss.

Karly would cry, but she had no tears left in her. It seemed all she had done was cry the last few days. Instead, she leaned her head against the rock and groaned aloud. A picture of Blake banging his head against his steering wheel the night before popped into her mind. Maybe he was just as frustrated as she was. But over what?

She was tempted to bang her head too. But that wouldn't be wise with her already pounding headache. She drew her knees to her chest and dropped her head against them. A habit she seemed to be doing a lot of lately. She'd never felt this despondent her whole life, except for the time her relationship with Blake had ended. But this was even worse. How could one feel so alone and unloved in a world with over seven billion people?

I love you, Karly.

Karly's head shot up, her eyes wide with surprise. She looked around. "Hello?"

Silence. In front of her was only a deep gorge. Bushes and rocks covered the ground to either side of her. The voice must have come from behind, where the trail was.

"Hello? Is someone there?"

Curious, Karly stood to her feet. The words had been so clear. She couldn't have imagined them. A cool, brisk wind whipped up suddenly, whistled through the fir trees, and blew her hair around her face.

Karly took a few steps down the trail, searching for a hiker or anyone nearby. "Hello?"

Silence. Again.

Was she losing her mind? That must be it. The stress of the last week had finally gotten to her. Or that headache was making her delusional.

But no. She was certain she had heard those words. And this was crazy, but ... they were so soft, kind, and gentle, they stirred something inside her—hope maybe?

A crazy thought popped into her brain. Was God speaking to her? Ridiculous. God didn't speak audibly to people. Did he? Besides, what would God want with her? It was only her mind desperately conjuring up those three words her heart longed to hear. Besides, she didn't need God. She had made it this far without him.

Have you looked at yourself lately, Karly? You're a mess.

Oh great, now she was arguing with herself. Yep, she was losing it.

As she paced the summit, her mind wandered to Blake. Apparently, he thought God was someone worth knowing. Now that she thought about it, Blake really had changed. She'd always been attracted to him, but now she found him even more appealing.

The wind continued to refresh her. Funny, something felt different with her too. All her problems still existed, yet ...

Everyone would be wondering what had happened to her. Karly turned to head back, but something large and dark appeared in her peripheral vision. Several turkey vultures hovered not far from the cliff face. Were they targeting fresh carrion?

Carefully, she stepped to the edge and peered down, expecting to see the dead carcass of an animal. Or possibly nothing at all, since she was quite a distance up. A shiny bright object glimmered far below.

What is that? She inched along the rock edge to try and get a better view. The sun went behind a cloud briefly, temporarily removing the brilliant glare. A splotch of glittering purple caught her eye.

And it was attached to a body.

"No." Her shaking hands flew to her mouth. A tremor ran through her. She stepped back from the edge as her knees gave out from underneath her. She collapsed onto the dirt. It couldn't be.

But Madison had worn a large gold belt buckle and a wildly-coloured purple top to match her hair that night at The Cedar Canoe. Even at this elevation, Karly knew the horrifying truth deep inside. Below was the twisted, broken form of her friend.

Karly had no idea how much time had passed as she sat in a stunned stupor. Poor Madison. How did she end up down there in that deep valley? Did she fall? Was she pushed? Whatever had happened, one thing was clear: Karly would never again have the privilege of seeing her friend alive. She tried not to imagine the suffering her friend must have endured. She had to tell someone.

Pull yourself together, Karly.

An eerie feeling hovered over her, causing the hairs on the back of her neck to prickle. It was probably just the circumstance she found herself in. Anytime she watched Dateline or The Fifth Estate about true life murders, she had the same feeling. Why she continually watched those shows and freaked herself out was beyond her.

She needed to get out of there and tell the authorities about Madison. Karly stood and brushed dirt from her shorts. Slipping her hand into the pocket of her shorts, she felt for her cell phone.

It all happened so fast, her mind spun. The bushes rustled, then a figure charged toward her, holding a thick branch above his head with both hands. The maniacal expression on his face was terrifying.

Karly screamed and threw her hands up to protect herself. "Josh! What are you doing?"

"You'll pay for what you've done." His twisted, angry face sent horror racing through her body.

Fear froze her to the spot. Then her adrenalin kicked in. Diving for cover behind a large boulder, she ducked just in time to miss his violent swing. The blow connected with the gigantic rock with a terrible thud and the stick fell from his hand. Before she had a chance to think about getting away, he retrieved it, swinging it in her direction again.

"Don't do this, Josh. Why do I need to pay? I don't know what you're talking about."

Another hard smack slammed brutally against the rock, this time cracking off a piece of his weapon. The force threw him off balance briefly and he landed on his butt. Seizing her opportunity, Karly bolted for the trail.

She didn't make it. Josh was small, but he was super-fast. Her assailant leapt on her back, his unexpected weight causing her to hit the dirt.

A wrestle ensued. She kicked her legs, swung her arms, and fought with everything she had, but his agility made up for his size. Somehow, in the scuffle, she had flipped onto her back. Now, as he sat on her stomach, his hands found her throat and applied horrific pressure.

Gasping for oxygen, her vision blurred. Her arms dropped to her sides and her right hand closed over a palm-sized rock. Digging deep for strength, she lifted the rock and slammed it against his temple.

His eyes bulged, his hands loosened their death grip on her throat, and he tipped sideways, landing on the ground. Coughing and gagging, Karly fought for oxygen. She sat up and studied her attacker. A trickle of blood ran down his head as he lay in the dirt, not moving. Had she killed him?

He groaned and opened his eyes. She had to get out of there. Now.

On all fours, Karly crawled toward the trailhead, scrambling to get to her feet. A rustling filled the air behind her and terror flooded through her again. Hands grabbed her ankles and yanked her backwards, knocking her flat on her belly. She dug her elbows into the dirt and tried inching forward, to no avail. She reached for a sapling and held on, but it tore loose as he dragged her. At this rate, she'd be hurled over the cliff to her death very soon. Would she end up like Madison? She didn't want to die. She had so much more to live for. Didn't she?

The incredible hope-filled words she'd heard a few minutes ago, whether imagined or not, gave her the determination to fight. In desperation, she yelled, "Save me, God."

In the struggle, her running shoes and socks had come loose and her bare toes now dangled over the edge or the cliff.

"If you're praying, don't waste your breath. It won't help. There is no God."

The words had no sooner left his mouth than the unimaginable happened. Backing toward the gorge, Josh stumbled over something in his path. He staggered for a few seconds, teetering at the edge of the deep chasm. His arms wind-milled wildly as he attempted to regain his balance.

Then he was gone.

Karly stared at the splintered piece of weapon that Josh had intended for her demise. Ironically, he had tripped over the broken branch and fallen to his own death.

It was over. Exhausted and relieved, her head flopped back against the warm dirt. She lay completely still, her bare feet still dangling over the edge, utterly amazed that somehow, she had survived. Was there really a God who loved her and had saved her from impending death?

Finding a new source of strength, she inched herself forward, digging her tender, scraped and bleeding elbows into the earth, until she was a safe distance from the edge. She crawled to her original leaning spot against the boulder and stared, trance-like, into the sky. It was nothing short of a miracle that she had survived.

"Thank you, God," she whispered. "I owe you my life."

CHAPTER TWENTY-NINE

Nearly sick with worry, Blake drove faster than he knew was either legal or wise. He'd just arrived home when he got Karly's text message for help. It said, 'Bring police, top of Lookout Trail. Please hurry.' What could possibly have gone wrong? He'd just left her thirty minutes ago.

After making the emergency call to police, he raced back to his truck and sped down the highway. He parked at the entrance to the campground and heard sirens approaching as he exited his vehicle. One cruiser pulled into the lot, followed by another close behind.

Officer Neilson stepped out of his vehicle and hurried toward him. Another policeman sat in the squad car talking on the radio. "Do you have any idea why we're needed at the top of a trail? And where's Harrison?"

A couple in their fifties with binoculars around their necks walked past, heading toward the trail.

"Excuse me," Officer Neilson said. When the couple looked at him he continued. "It would be wise if you picked another trail for today."

The couple seemed surprised, but nodded and headed back into the campground.

Another officer emerged from the squad car and joined Blake and Officer Neilson.

"I have no idea where Harrison is, but we're wasting valuable time standing here. It's been thirty minutes since Karly's text. I'm not waiting any longer." Blake checked the highway for vehicles and ran across, heading for the trail.

Officer Neilson yelled as he ran behind him. "Don't be going up there ahead of us. You have no idea what you might face."

Blake ignored him. If Karly's life was at stake, he was going up the trail, no matter what anyone said. Holding his sides from exhaustion, he finally reached the top. He stepped through the heavily treed path and broke into a clearing. The first thing he saw was Harrison and Karly locked together in an embrace. Anger surged through him. What kind of a cruel joke was this? "Karly?"

She turned, and he immediately felt horrible for his assumptions. Something terrible had happened up here. Karly's knees and elbows were scraped and bleeding, and her throat was covered in nasty purple bruises. She was dirty, and her clothing was torn.

White-hot rage poured through him. "What happened?"

She pulled herself away from Harrison and flew into his arms. Burying her head on his chest, she trembled against him.

"I'm here now. It'll be okay." As he stroked her hair, he couldn't help but notice the look of frustration on Harrison's face. He would have gloated had the circumstances not been so grim.

The two police officers burst onto the scene, hands on their holsters. "What's going on? Did you place an emergency call? Do we need to call an ambulance?"

Karly looked toward them, but stayed pressed against his chest, as if it would take too much energy to lift her head. "I did place the call and no to the ambulance."

Officer Neilson frowned. "What's the emergency?"

"Madison's body ... is down there." As she gestured toward the valley, her arm shook. "Josh too."

Blake's eyes widened. Madison and Josh were both lying dead in the valley below? What horrors had transpired at the top of Lookout Trail? He tightened his hold on Karly.

Harrison stepped toward them and placed a hand on her arm. "Come, Karly. Sit down on this boulder and tell the officers what you told me."

Reluctantly, Blake let her go and watched her stumble away barefoot in the dirt. It disturbed him to see her socks and shoes scattered across the ground. Had Josh assaulted her? A knot formed in Blake's gut.

He listened in disbelief, as Karly told of her accidental discovery of Madison's body and her fight to the death with Josh. The fact that he had fallen over the edge by tripping on the weapon he had intended for Karly's harm was almost beyond belief. *Thank you, God, for protecting Karly.*

"That does it." The officer flipped his notepad shut. "Josh was obviously Madison's killer. It's nothing short of a miracle that you survived, Karly. And thanks to you, we've solved the missing person case and caught the killer all in one day."

Blake chewed on the officer's words, mulling them over in his brain. Officer Neilson's assumptions certainly made sense, given the way events had unfolded. But something wasn't sitting right, and he couldn't figure out what it was. Maybe when he had more time to think, things would become clearer. Right now, his major concern was Karly. She'd been through a horrendous trauma.

Just as he stepped toward her, Harrison grabbed Karly's hand and pulled her to a standing position. "I think this woman has had about all she can take." He looked at Officer Neilson. "If you're finished with her, I'd like to escort her home and see that she gets some rest."

"We've gotten enough information for today. She's free to go. We'll contact her if we have any further questions." Officer Neilson turned away and began waving his arm through the air, barking orders to his partner about securing the area and calling in a recovery team.

Blake stepped aside to let Harrison and Karly pass. He couldn't help but notice the way Harrison's arm was wrapped possessively around her waist. He really wanted to be the one to offer consolation after the horrific events she had just experienced.

Harrison leaned closer to Karly. "Let's get you home, honey. You've had a traumatic day."

Blake's fists tightened. Under another circumstance, Blake might have spoken his piece. But Karly didn't need a couple of idiots fighting over her right now. Instead, he opted to gather her socks and shoes.

When he had them in hand, he paused and surveyed the area, trying to imagine the whole nightmarish scenario and the sequence of events. How did Josh and Karly both end up at the top of this rock today? Had he followed her here to murder her, just as he'd murdered Madison? It was possible, although he never would have pegged Josh for a murderer. Of course, there was no exact mold. Was there? Not according to any crime shows he had ever watched, except that it was often the one you'd trust with your grandmother.

Harrison.

The guy seemed nice enough on the surface. But what about the case of the missing female campground employee? Rumours still circulated that he was her killer.

Blake shook his head to clear out the cobwebs and stop his imagination from running wild. Autopsy results would be in soon on the body he had discovered. DNA testing could reveal a lot nowadays. He hoped and prayed that the evidence didn't point to Harrison Somerville being the killer.

Karly's life could depend on it.

CHAPTER THIRTY

Karly spent the next few days in a blurry, trance-like state. Madison's parents came by the cabin and talked to her. They were holding up amazingly well, considering the circumstances. Way better than she was. They expressed a deep faith in God, which they said was carrying them through—that and the prayers of friends, family, and their local church.

Blake and Harrison paid Karly a few visits, along with many other park employees, but she couldn't shake her depression. She slept most of the time, rising only for brief periods to accept visitors with flowers, food, and heartfelt condolences.

On Friday morning, the day of the funeral, Karly dragged herself from bed and crawled into the shower. After toweling off, she searched the closet for her black dress. She could barely summon up the energy to pull herself together.

A knock on the door reminded her it was time to go. Harrison looked handsome in his dark suit and tie. Come to think of it, she'd never seen him dressed up before today.

He tugged at his tie, as though he wasn't used to wearing one and wasn't entirely comfortable in it. "Are you ready to go?"

Karly shrugged. "As ready as I'll ever be."

It was a two-hour drive to Fort Francis where the funeral was being held. Once inside, Karly was surprised at the large gathering of people that had come to pay their respects from family, neighbors, church-goers, friends, and co-workers.

The service began when a pretty young woman sang a beautiful hymn. Then a middle-aged man led the singing. The words were displayed on an overhead screen, so Karly studied them as they sang. The choruses were inspiring. Wasn't most church music slow and boring? There was just something unique and appealing about the melodies. It warmed her heart in ways she never imagined.

The pastor shared comfort and encouragement from the Bible, reading some of Madison's favourite verses. A huge smile came over his face as he talked about the lively little girl, Madison Springfield, who had grown up in the church and youth group of Grace Community Church.

"I recall the day Madison approached me after the service and asked to be baptized. She told me that she believed Jesus had died on the cross for her sins, after the message was shared at pre-teen camping event." The pastor's face lit up. "Madison was so eager to be baptized and tell the world about her decision. I remember her hurrying towards the front, practically skipping past the congregation filing out."

"Because of her decision, we are confident that Madison is now with Jesus, basking in his love and rejoicing with the angels. Although her life was short, it was meaningful, and her joyful personality and faith in God impacted many lives."

A tear trailed down Karly's cheek. She quickly swiped it away with the back of her hand. Oh, how she would miss her friend. But if she believed the pastor's words to be truth, then Madison was happy right now. That thought brought solace and comfort. Whether it was truth or fiction, for now she would choose to believe it.

With remorse, she remembered the day that Madison had tried to talk to her about her faith in God, but Karly had grown uncomfortable and quickly silenced her. Come to think of it, Madison had lived a life of honesty and integrity, and her beautiful, happy personality drew Karly to her instantly. No, she wasn't perfect, often putting her foot in her mouth and speaking hastily without thinking, but everyone had faults. Didn't they? Karly reached into her purse for a tissue as tears threatened again. Harrison's hand closed over hers.

Before she knew it, the service was over, and a lunch reception put on by the ladies of the church was being held.

Many people flowed into the gym and a lengthy line formed at the food table. Hunger pains gnawed at her insides. Food still didn't hold any appeal, but Karly knew she needed to eat something.

Harrison excused himself for a moment and hurried away to talk with someone. Her eyes scanned the room and connected with Blake's. Even across the crowded gym, she could feel genuine compassion in his eyes. Blake stepped toward her, but was intercepted by a small, dark-haired woman. Raven. Disappointment shot through Karly.

She moseyed along with the line, and in a few minutes, was filling her plate with small triangular sandwiches, salads, veggies, and dip.

Soon Harrison joined her, his plate overflowing. His appetite didn't appear to have been affected. "It was great seeing my old teacher, Al Green." Harrison spoke in between bites of his sandwich. "He hasn't aged at all."

Karly listened as she nibbled on a celery stick. Although she was hungry, food just didn't want to go in. The few bites that she had managed weren't sitting well. "I'll be right back." She excused herself and left in search of a washroom.

Once inside, she leaned against the starkly cold wall, feeling weak and unwell. Dragging herself to a sink, she cupped cool water with her hands and dipped her face into it. It was then that she heard the words again.

I love you, Karly, as a mother loves her child, and I'll comfort you.

She must be losing her mind. She straightened up and stared at her pale, sad reflection in the mirror. Had grief from her good friend's murder caused her to snap? She had to stop imagining voices or she'd need to see a psychiatrist.

When she left the washroom, she ran directly into Mrs. Springfield. Madison's mother rested a hand on her arm. "How are you holding up, honey? You didn't look so well when you came in earlier."

"I'm okay. The service was good." Karly managed a small smile. "It really helps to know that Madison is in heaven and is happy."

When Mrs. Springfield impulsively pulled her into her arms for a long hug, Karly was surprised at the depth of emotion welling up inside. For a brief instant, she could have sworn she was a little girl in her own mother's arms. Then it hit her. God had just provided the motherly comfort she so longed for, that he had just promised. An incredibly warm peace settled over her.

Madison's mother stepped back, but left her hands firmly planted on Karly's shoulders. "Are you a believer too?"

She swallowed. "Actually, no. I don't think so. At least, I'm not sure what I believe anymore."

Mrs. Springfield's smile was warm. "We take great comfort in the fact that Madison was a Christian. We know without a doubt that we will see her again one day. I hope you find God's love. There's no earthly love that compares."

Karly nodded as a surreal feeling flowed through her.

"Come by and see us sometime. We would really like that, Karly."

She nodded again, unable to find the words to express the sudden joy that filled her until she felt as though she might burst. Odd, considering the circumstances.

Karly practically floated through the gym and found her seat beside Harrison. She didn't have a clue what was happening to her, but it felt so wonderful, she didn't want it to end.

"Are you okay?"

"I'm fine." She smiled up at Harrison. "Thanks for asking." There was no sense trying to explain. He might not understand and insist she see a doctor. Even she couldn't explain what had just transpired.

Suddenly ravenous, she reached for her egg-salad sandwich. Food had never tasted so good. In need of a caffeine fix, she excused herself and made her way to the large metal coffee pot. Watching the steaming brown liquid dribble into the Styrofoam cup, she was totally taken aback when someone bumped her from behind, sloshing the hot brew over her fingers and into a puddle on the floor.

She turned. It was Raven. "Oh, excuse me, Karly. I didn't see you there." Her apology was nullified by a sassy smirk.

"It's okay, accidents happen." Karly refused to engage in any type of confrontation. She'd just let it go. Nothing was going to steal her joy right now.

"Blake is taking me up in his floatplane this evening."

"That's nice." Was Raven trying to bait her? "You'll really enjoy it. I did."

Raven crossed her arms. "Blake took you up?"

Karly nodded as she added cream to her coffee. It wasn't nice to gloat.

"Well ... Blake brought me here today."

"That was nice of him."

"He treats me extremely well, if you know what I mean. And vice versa."

"Yes, I remember your offer of free scrumptious desserts."

The verbal sparring, although humorous to Karly, seemed to irritate Raven.

Raven's eyes grew into narrow indigo slits and her bright fuchsia lips scrunched together tightly.

Clearly unaware of the friction hanging in the air, Blake arrived and reached for a cup.

"There you are, silly bear. Your tie is crooked." Raven reached up to adjust it.

Blake squirmed and pushed her hand away. "Stop, Raven. My tie is fine." When his eyes caught Karly's, he looked like a trapped animal, desperately searching for a way of escape.

She bit down hard on her lip to squelch her amusement. Then she remembered their date to practice for the canoe race. And couldn't help herself. "I'll see you tomorrow morning, bright and early, silly bear. Get a good night's rest. You'll need it." Karly turned and walked away, but not before catching the fact that Raven's jaw dropped open.

Which was worth every bit of the residual lingering discomfort that the hot scalding coffee had inflicted.

Karly didn't know what was happening inside her, but she liked it. Could it be God reaching out to her? And at her friend's funeral? No, that would be bizarre.

Wouldn't it?

CHAPTER THIRTY-ONE

Wide awake and raring to go, Karly paced the dock. Where was Blake? She was about to grab her cell to send him a text when she heard the noisy rumbling of his aging pickup's engine.

"You're late. Did you sleep in?" Karly fired the question at him as he clambered toward her, carrying his gear.

"Hardly. I've already flown some interior campers into Shadow Lake for a five o'clock start with Henry. Things just ran a little later than expected."

"Under the circumstances, I guess you're excused." Karly pointed to her red Kevlar canoe bobbing beside the dock. "That one is mine."

"Thanks for your understanding, Cruella. And yes, I recognize your canoe."

"You're quite welcome, silly bear."

Blake tossed a life jacket at her. "Please don't call me that."

"If you promise to stop calling me, Cruella, I'll consider it." Karly crossed her arms and tapped a foot on the dock.

"That's a tough request." Blake's eyes twinkled briefly, before he held out a hand. "Deal!"

When he clasped her hand, holding it a little longer than necessary, electrical charges zipped and zapped the length of her arm.

"Besides, I have several other affectionate names for you." Blake let go of her, grabbed his backpack, and dropped it into the canoe.

Karly shook her arm free of tingles and handed him the paddles. "If you consider 'Cruella' affectionate, I'd hate to hear what names you'd come up with if you were truly angry with me." She pulled a map from her pocket.

Blake waved a hand through the air. "Put it away, I've got one." He held the canoe while she climbed in. "In fact, I have our itinerary planned for the day."

Her eyebrows drew together. "I do too." Why was he suddenly taking control?

"Let's hope they jive." Blake's playful taunt echoed across the water. "Otherwise, we're doomed. It'll be pretty hard if you're heading in one direction and I'm heading in the other."

"Need I remind you who owns this canoe?" Karly tossed the remark over her shoulder. She made her way to the bow before he could stop her. He could steer at the stern for now. No way was he going to prove he was stronger than her today.

"Need I remind you who signed us up as a team?" Blake responded sassily behind her.

For the next three hours, they followed the proposed route laid out in the pamphlet that the race would follow. They agreed that sticking to this plan would give them an advantage over teams that wouldn't have the opportunity to navigate and portage the area. Although unfair, it was a reality. Home teams did have an advantage.

The muscles in her arms were growing tired and putting up a protest, but she'd never admit it to Blake. When they approached land and Blake suggested they stop for a snack around nine o'clock, she was relieved.

Karly had barely finished the last bite of her apple when Blake jumped to his feet. "Let's go," he barked.

After portaging the narrow peninsula, they reached the water again and dropped the canoe into the lake. Blake faced her. "Why don't we switch positions for a little while? You can take the stern."

"Aye, aye, Captain." She saluted. "If you insist." Inside Karly was relieved. Steering the craft would give her arms a little break. Had Blake sensed she was growing weary?

"Your canoe runs on water." Blake looked back over his shoulder.

Karly stared at his bulging arm muscles. She liked the view from behind him. In fact, it had been hard to take her eyes off them since they'd switched positions. She blinked and tore her gaze away. "Huh? It runs on muscle power too."

Blake chuckled. "That isn't what I meant. I was reminding you of what's written all over your shirt, Blondie. It says, 'My canoe runs on water.'"

Karly looked down, but couldn't see her T-shirt because of her life jacket. Then she remembered what she'd slipped over her head earlier this morning. "Oh right, the campground is selling these. Did you know they're eco-friendly and made from recycled water bottles?" Interesting that he'd noticed what she was wearing.

"Really. A T-shirt made from water bottles. What will they think of next? I suppose it's much better than filling up a landfill with them."

So far, the morning had been pleasant with great weather, a light breeze and even a moose sighting. But as the noon hour approached, the sun grew more intense. Karly's stomach felt slightly nauseous and perspiration had begun to drip from her forehead and sting her eyes. It was time for a break.

They had portaged seven times and only reached Bass Lake. "Are we stopping for lunch soon? I'm famished." Admitting her exhaustion was out of the question. She'd rather collapse from heat stroke first. Wait. No. That was foolish thinking. She didn't want to go there again.

Of course, she'd been her own worst enemy. While portaging, she had suggested that they sprint. Was she out of her mind? But she knew the competition would be fierce. Getting in shape was very important.

"Wise decision. After lunch we'll turn back. We've been out six hours already, and another six will take us to the dinner hour. I think it's best that we head home."

"I agree. Twelve hours for one day is plenty. Overdoing it can lead to mistakes, accidents, and injuries."

After disembarking, Karly trudged wearily toward a large piece of driftwood on the shoreline, near a silver birch. After settling on it, she reached for her insulated lunch bag and immediately downed her entire bottle of water. Wisely, she had packed several extra ... and a large ice pack as well.

Blake plunked down beside her and pulled out three peanut butter sandwiches and a large thermos of water.

"A little hungry, are we?"

"Yep."

"Bears do eat a lot."

"Hey," he mumbled between bites, "you promised."

Karly pulled out her cheese and crackers and veggie sticks. "I couldn't resist. What's with that ridiculous name anyway?" She wiped at a dribble of water on her chin.

"Who knows? I hate it."

"It sounds rather intimate." Karly crunched into a celery stick. "And her actions at the funeral were very possessive of you. Didn't you bring her? It kind of looks like you guys are together." She knew her words sounded a bit jealous, but she couldn't resist confronting the issue.

Blake tipped his head back and downed a large gulp from his thermos. When he'd finished, he set the thermos down on a flat rock and wiped his mouth with the side of his hand. "Raven begged and pleaded for a ride. Apparently, she didn't have any way of getting to the funeral. I felt it was the kind thing to do since she and Madison were friends." He finished the last bite of his sandwich and reached for a second. "And just for the record, I'm not taking her up in my Cessna. Let's change the topic. How are you holding up?"

"Okay, I guess." Karly pulled out a chunk of marble cheese and bit into it. "By the way, did you know Madison was one of your kind?"

"What kind? Of the White Pelican family?"

"Very funny." Karly reached for a carrot stick. "I think *believer* was the term Mrs. Springfield used."

"Yeah, I gathered that from the funeral. Evil hasn't triumphed after all."

Karly tossed her empty plastic container back into the lunch bag. "What do you mean?"

"Josh may have thought he won by killing Madison, but she's happier than she ever was here on earth. She's celebrating in heaven with Jesus, never again to face any sorrow, pain, or heartache."

Blake's words swam around in her brain as she tried to make sense of them. She grew reflective as she remembered her divine encounter. "Blake?"

"Yes?" By now, he had finished his lunch, dropped from the log, and stretched out on his back under the shade of the overhanging birch branches.

"I have something interesting to tell you." Karly moved so she sat cross-legged beside him. "I hope you won't think me crazy, but I had an unusual experience. I think God might have spoken to me."

"Really? What did he say?" Blake propped himself up on his elbows, his eyes large.

"I love you."

"That's incredible. When did that happen?"

"At the top of the Lookout Trail just before Josh appeared. I was having a very emotional time, feeling confused and ..."

"Is that why you were up there? Was that just after I kissed you?"

"Yes." A flush of heat flooded her neck and face.

Blake sat up, reached for a nearby twig, and snapped it in his hands. He wouldn't make eye contact with her and seemed fidgety. "I'm sorry about that. I was out of line. I was trying to best Harrison because he was making me so mad." He picked up a larger branch and tossed it toward the lake.

He was sorry that he kissed her? Her lunch rolled into a cheese ball in her stomach. "You don't have to apologize."

"Yes, I do." Blake's eyes, tender now, met hers. "I took advantage of you." He reached for her hand. "If I hadn't behaved so impulsively, you wouldn't have ended up in a predicament where you almost died."

Karly revelled in his touch. He could hold her hand all day. "Maybe that's true. But you couldn't have known that kissing me might endanger my life. Besides, it resulted in discovering what happened to Madison."

"I suppose." A gigantic grin lit up his face. "From what I remember, kissing Karly Foster always bordered on the life-altering."

Her mind flashed back to the memory of their first magical kiss. She had been lying in a hospital bed with a gunshot wound and a leg fractured in two places. The Monarch butterflies inside her were on the move again. Now they flitted around in her cardiac chambers.

"I'm sorry I interrupted the story of your encounter with God, please continue."

Her heart was acting so strangely; Karly took a deep, steadying breath. It wasn't just Blake that had her heart palpitating. The memory of her ethereal encounter was also impacting her. "I was shocked when I heard those three words. I jumped up, thinking someone was behind me."

"You heard them audibly?"

"Yes. Does that mean I'm going crazy?"

"No. It may be unusual, but God works in mysterious ways." Blake shrugged. "If he can create the universe, I don't think speaking aloud would be too much trouble. Do you?"

"I guess not. But that's not the best part. When Josh attacked me, and dragged me toward the edge of the cliff, I thought my life was over. He was stronger than I expected, and I knew I was losing the fight. It was then I remembered those words, and pleaded with God to save me."

"And he did." Blake massaged her hand with his thumb. The tender action was calming. "And I can't tell you how glad I am."

Karly stared down at their hands. "That's not all. At the funeral lunch, I was overcome with grief. I ran into the washroom to hide. It was then that I heard those words again, loud and clear. It seemed that God was promising to comfort me as a mother comforts her child. I stood there, staring into the mirror in shock. How did God know I was missing my mother?"

Karly's words were slurring with emotion as her lower lip began to tremble. Could she even finish?

Suck it up, Karly. No more tears.

Blake squeezed her hand tightly. That action gave her the courage to continue and find her voice. "I left the washroom and ran directly into Madison's mother. The first thing she did was ask me how I was. Then she embraced me. I felt like I was in my mother's arms again after all these years. There's just something so special about a mother's love."

Blake edged closer, so he could wrap an arm around her shoulder and pulled her against his chest. Karly pressed her eyes closed with her fingers to ebb the flow of tears. There was no way she was going to cry again. She'd cried a lifetime of tears lately, especially the days following the discovery of her friend's body.

"Thank you, God, for answering my prayers," Blake whispered against her hair.

Karly sat up so suddenly, Blake's arm fell from her shoulder. "You've been praying for me? Why?"

"I knew you and Madison were close and I couldn't imagine how difficult it would be to lose your good friend the way you did."

"I don't know what to say, I'm blown away by all of this. Thank you."

"You're welcome. God also got my attention. Not audibly, but in a vision. At least, I think that's what it was."

That floored her. "He did? When?"

"The day Maya and Kerrick's baby was born."

Karly's eyes widened. "Maya and Kerrick have a baby?"

"Yes, a son named Noah. You mean you didn't know? He's about two months old."

Karly's shoulders drooped, and she stared at an ant that was crawling on the edge of her sandal. "I haven't talked to Maya in a long time. When you and I broke up, I didn't talk to anyone for weeks. I took a leave of absence from work and got some counselling. That's when I realized I needed to make some changes in my life. I've always had a passion for the outdoors. So, here I am."

"Let me get this straight. Because you were mad at me, you cut off all ties with your best friend, Maya?"

"I know. It doesn't make sense now, but at the time I needed—"

"To run away from life. Been there, done that."

His profound words were startling. Is that really what she had done? She flicked the ant off her shoe. How could he know her so well? Somehow, he exposed even her inward motives—motives she hadn't been aware of herself.

Karly drew her knees up to her chest, and watched another large black ant staggering under the weight of an enormous load. His oversized burden, a fallen crumb from one of her crackers, caused him to travel repeatedly in circles, making very little progress in his journey. Was that an analogy of her life? Had she really thought that leaving the past behind and changing occupations would bring her the happiness she longed for? "I feel so guilty. I should have kept in touch with Maya."

"It's never too late to reconnect with her."

"I hope not." Karly clasped her arms around her knees. "How did you see God in a vision?"

"The day Noah was born I went to the hospital to visit them. When I held that newborn baby in my arms and saw the love that Maya and Kerrick had for their little one, I fell apart. My whole horrible life flashed in front of my eyes, from the neglect my sister and I suffered by two physically and emotionally abusive parents, to my juvenile delinquency, to losing you. I handed the baby back to Maya, left the room, and practically sprinted down the hallway. Kerrick found me in the waiting room."

He paused a moment before he continued. "Kerrick knelt beside me and put a hand on my shoulder. I didn't look up. I knew it was him, but I was so distraught, I kept my face buried in my hands. Thankfully, I didn't have to say anything. Kerrick began to pray. Words that I will never forget."

His voice broke and Karly placed a hand on his arm. "He asked God to reveal himself to me. In my mind, I instantly saw a picture of Jesus with scars on his hands and feet, tender love in his eyes, and his arms stretched wide, as if He wanted to hold me."

Blake grew quiet as he stared out over the water. "The day of Noah's birth, I accepted Jesus and his love. That moment was so remarkably life-changing, I will never, ever go back to the old Blake." His words were whispered, reverent, and full of emotion.

Karly touched his cheek. "From the first day in Moe's Diner when you re-appeared in my life, I sensed something was different. Now I know. So, you're saying you think there really is something to all of this God stuff?"

"If you never trust me on anything else in this life, trust me on this. It's the most spectacular thing in the entire world. God is for real—so real that there's nothing, or no one, that compares." Blake leaned his forehead against hers.

The intimate act nearly undid her. Wow. Blake sounded so convincing. With everything in her, she wanted to believe him. Their foreheads still together, something passed between them. She knew he felt it too.

Blake pulled back and looked directly into her eyes. His intense gaze carried something so deep. So precious. So loving.

Entranced, enthralled, mesmerized ... there were no words to explain the occurrence. It passed all understanding, but it was tangible and swallowing her whole. Was this love? Two people sharing and caring so deeply?

The enchanting moment intensified at the landing of a stocky white bird about a dozen feet away on the shoreline. Blake's mouth opened to speak, but she pressed her finger to his lips and whispered in his ear. "White Pelicans startle easily. Remain as still as possible."

Blake's eyes narrowed. "What are you talking about?"

"Just behind you." She took her finger from his lips and pressed it to hers to reinforce the need to be silent.

Blake shifted around slowly so he could see. Together, they watched as several birds joined the first. Excitement raced through her as she pressed against Blake's shoulder. He leaned close and spoke quietly. "Did you know that groups of foraging pelicans can herd fish into schools, and that in a single scoop a pelican can hold up to twelve litres of water and fish? The fish are held in the bird's bill while the water drains out."

Karly desperately wanted to kiss his cheek, but she restrained herself. Whatever had happened between them in the past seemed a distant memory. "Of course, I knew that silly. But I didn't know that you did."

"A wonderful bird is a pelican; his bill will hold more than his belly can." Blake laughed aloud.

Karly covered his mouth with her hand, but giggled despite herself. "Shush! You're going to startle the colony." Her eyes met his and her breath caught when she saw the emotion there. Really, who cared about birds?

Karly felt herself free-falling. Her head swam dizzily as everything around her blurred. The hunger for his kiss consumed her. Her eyes drifted shut as he leaned in close.

When it landed, it came as a large, warm, sloppy smack on her forehead, not at all what she expected. Aghast, she opened her eyes as something began dripping down her face. A loud chorus of flapping wings, accompanied by Blake's hilarious laughter, drew her gaze to the sky, just as a white pelican flew directly overhead.

Reality hit. She'd just been kissed by a *Pelecanus erythrorhychos*.

CHAPTER THIRTY-TWO

Blake placed a hand on Karly's back and steered her to the only empty booth in the far back corner of The Cedar Canoe. He worried that this venue wasn't a wise choice, but they couldn't avoid it forever.

"This establishment doesn't carry fond memories for me." Karly closed her menu and stuck it in the holder on the table after they placed their orders. "I broke an outdoor display, was threatened by the owner, and worst of all, it's the last place I saw Madison alive."

"I understand, but neither of us has the energy to cook tonight after that grueling canoe practice."

"We probably could have gotten a seat at Moe's." Karly took a sip of her ice water and looked at him over the top of her glass. "We didn't even try. Why was that?"

"It's a Saturday night. Most of the town is out for supper." He tore his gaze from her and shifted uncomfortably in his seat. Did she suspect he was avoiding the petite waitress? He really needed to deal with Raven. And soon.

The server placed their meals in front of them and left. Blake heard an audible groan as Karly reached to the end of the table for the salt shaker. She liberally scattered salt across her French fries.

"I'm waiting," he teased.

"For what?"

"To see if you can lift that fork to your mouth."

"Very funny." She reached for the fork, stabbed a fry and ate it. "Although I managed to complete my challenge, I hate to admit it, but you win. I wasn't in as good a shape as I thought I was. I can't believe how sore I am."

Although he knew he shouldn't, he did it anyway. Blake reached in his pocket, tugged out the item he'd stuck in there earlier, and lifted it high above his head.

"What are you doing?"

"Portaging a pretzel."

"You're a barrel of laughs today. You thought that one out ahead of time, didn't you? Unless you normally carry pretzels in your pocket."

"I think the laughs are on you today, oh Poop Queen." Blake flashed a teasing grin.

"It's wasn't that funny." Karly dipped the tips of her fingers in her water and flung the cold drops at him.

"Did you forget I was there? Believe me it was hilarious." He shook a drop of water from his french fry before swiping it through a blob of ketchup and popping it in his mouth.

Karly swirled her chicken finger in plum sauce. "If I were you, I'd be a little nervous. That massive pooping pelican could have been bombing the competition, Mr. White Pelican Man."

His forehead wrinkled. "So, let me get this straight. Are you saying that the pelican was female and got jealous when you and I were ... um ...getting close? That she dropped a load on you to scare you off, so she could have me all to herself?"

Karly slid him a sly smile. "Maybe she was attracted to your large yellow beak."

Blake paused with his burger in his hands. "Maybe it's you that's jealous. Do you see yourself in contention for the honorary position of Mrs. White Pelican?"

It was fantastic watching the flush creep up her neck and into her cheeks. He loved every moment of it. Gloating from his witty reply, he waited for her stinging rebuttal, but it never came. Instead, he watched her eyes grow large as footsteps approached.

"Thanks for the payment. And even early to boot." Moe barked roughly, as he stopped at the end of their booth and crossed his arms over his massive chest. "I didn't think you'd do it after the way you were acting last week. I guess my persuasive techniques worked."

Blake's eyes narrowed. "If you're referring to your physical and verbal abuse, then you're not much of a man. Didn't your mama ever teach you how to behave around a woman?"

Moe kept his glare fixed squarely on Karly. "My business is with the lady, not you. So, if you know what's good for you, stay out of this."

Blake stood to his feet. He towered over the portly middle-aged chef. "Karly is a friend of mine and she *is* my business. So, if you know what's good for you, never, ever, threaten her again, verbally or physically. You've got your money, now leave."

The chef didn't budge from his spot, although he did finally look over at him. "I have a mind to throw you out of my establishment right now."

"But you won't because you want our business and everyone else's in Aspen Ridge for that matter." Blake waved a hand over the crowd.

The owner glanced around the coffee house. Many patrons had stopped eating and were looking in their direction. Moe stared at him belligerently a moment longer before turning on his heels and storming off.

Blake plunked himself down, his heart hammering in his chest.

Karly reached over and covered his hand with hers. "Thanks for sticking up for me." Her heartfelt appreciation—and soft, warm hand on his—calmed his frenzied, fiery emotions. Taking a deep breath, he sank against the back of the booth, trying to slow his pulse. Blake had never liked confrontations. But sometimes they were necessary. Especially when it came to protecting Karly from that man.

"I'm confused." Creases appeared on her forehead. "I didn't pay him any money. In fact, with everything that has happened with Madison over the last week, I totally forgot. Did you pay him?"

"Me? I don't have that kind of money." A stab of jealousy knifed him in the gut. If she hadn't paid the money, then who did? In his heart, he knew the answer. How could he compete? Should he even try? He stared at the half-eaten burger on his plate, then began a drum roll on the edge of the table.

"What's wrong? You always do that finger-banging thing when you're uptight."

He couldn't tell her. Impulsively, Blake reached for his burger and jammed an over-sized bite into his mouth. Couldn't let his meal go to waste.

"I wonder if it was Harrison." Karly took a nibble of her chicken finger and her eyes took on a far-away look.

Blake gagged. No matter how much he chewed the beef patty it stuck like glue to the roof of his mouth. He reached for his root beer and swallowed a large gulp.

Karly thought it was Harrison too. Blake punched his chest with a closed fist.

"What's wrong?"

"That last bite went down the wrong way."

The rest of the meal passed by awkwardly, at least for him. Finally, he tossed the cold fry he'd been about to choke down onto his plate. "Come on, Blondie, let's call it a day."

Just as Blake slid to the end of his bench, his cell vibrated. He reached in his pocket and checked the screen. Raven. And she was pestering him again about a ride in his plane. Did she ever quit?

Blake sighed and pushed to his feet as he shoved the phone back in his pocket. He was tired from his day canoeing and portaging. He couldn't deal with her tonight.

"Was that a message from Raven? "Why don't you just give her a ride in your plane and be done with it?" Karly followed him to the front of the restaurant.

"No, it was a telemarketer." How in the world did she know that message was from Raven? Blake's shoulders drooped as he paid the cashier. What was wrong with him? Why did he feel the need to lie to Karly?

After Karly inserted her debit card and paid for her meal, Blake pushed open the heavy wooden door. "Yes, it was Raven. Sorry for the lie. It's just that she's been driving me crazy."

Once they were seated inside his truck, her taunting began.

"Please, pretty-please, will you take me up in your floatplane?" She batted her eyelashes and flipped her long hair off her shoulders, mimicking Raven's mannerisms.

Blake scowled.

"What's the matter? Have I upset you, silly bear?"

Then suddenly it came to him. "You're jealous." He banged the steering wheel with his palm.

Karly jumped. "I'm what?"

"My friendship with Raven makes you insecure."

Karly snorted. "In your dreams. Why should I be jealous of Raven?" She wiggled in her seat. "Something's poking me." She reached behind her and pulled out a colourful peacock feather earring. "This belongs to Raven, doesn't it?"

The peacock dangled in the air, mocking him. The warmth drained from his face. "I have no idea how that got there."

"Raven didn't wear these to the funeral. I would have noticed, especially after she bumped into me and knocked my coffee all over my fingers."

Blake removed his cap and scratched his head. "I didn't know she did that."

"Are you and Raven dating?" Karly stared out the window, not looking at him.

Would you care if we were? "Absolutely not."

She whipped the jewelry out the window as they drove away. "Then whose earring was that?"

Blake placed his cap back on his head and looked straight ahead, concentrating on the highway traffic. "I have no idea. It's a used vehicle. Maybe it's from the previous owners. I bought it privately on-line, so it wasn't detailed. I got it as is."

Blake heard the stammer in his own voice. Wait a minute. Why did he feel guilty? He glanced over at her. "Look, Karly, I'm setting the record straight. I have no idea whose earring that is and nothing is going on with Raven and me ... at least not on my end."

Karly folded her arms across her chest. "Just take me home."

CHAPTER THIRTY-THREE

Karly entered the conference room Monday morning and stopped to watch Harrison as he flipped through a stack of papers. He looked up at her and smiled. "Good morning, Karly."

"Good morning, Harrison. You sound bright and cheerful today. What are you doing?"

"I'm going over the entries for our canoe race this Saturday. I'm excited about the number of teams, even though we didn't quite reach our goal of two dozen."

"How many do we have?"

"Nineteen."

"Not bad."

"No, it's not. How did your practice with Blake go on Saturday?"

"Good." She cocked her head to one side. "I wasn't aware that you knew we went out. I'm glad we did. I wasn't in as good a shape as I thought I was. I really needed that practice."

"You look good to me." His eyes skittered the length of her body and back.

She gave his shoulder a playful shove. "You're a flirt. Has anyone ever told you that?"

"Just you."

"By the way, I think I owe you a big thank you."

He stapled a few forms together before looking up. "For what?"

"Paying my debt."

"How did you know it was me?" Harrison's lips twitched.

"Just a guess. It was extremely generous of you, but I can't accept a gift like that. I'm paying you back."

"That's not necessary." Grabbing the forms, he headed to the filing cabinet.

"That wasn't your debt to be paying. I'm the one who smashed the display with my clumsiness. I need to face up to my responsibilities."

He slid the drawer closed and walked back over to her, resting his hands on her shoulders. "I'd do anything for you, Karly."

"But ..."

"It's a gift. That's the end of it."

"No, it's not the end. I'm paying you back as soon as I raise the money."

Harrison let go of her and waved a hand dismissively. "No, please don't. I have plenty. It wasn't a burden to me."

"Well, thank you." Karly slid her bag off her shoulder and set it on his desk "Who's your partner for the canoe race?"

"Heather."

"Have you had a chance to practice yet?"

"Yes. We went out on Saturday too. We were behind you all the way."

"You were? That's odd that we never saw you."

"You both seemed a little ... pre-occupied with each other."

Karly parked her hands on her hips. "Were you spying on me? That's kind of creepy. Especially since I didn't see you. Surely, we would have noticed you when you turned back. You would have been ahead of us then."

"No, I wasn't spying, and sorry to creep you out. You didn't notice us because we didn't go nearly as far as you did. We were only out until about three p.m. Really, it was a much-needed practice." Harrison went over to his desk and tossed the stapler into a drawer. "As far as Heather goes for a partner, she's much stronger than she looks. Besides, there is more to winning a marathon canoe race than just muscles. Navigation errors have cost many strong teams to lose to a weaker. She knows this wilderness area well, having been employed here for almost twenty years."

Karly stared at him blankly. That was a long answer to a question she didn't ask. Why did Harrison feel the need to justify his choice in Heather as a partner? Interesting.

"And I kind of felt sorry for her. She really wanted to enter and since both of us were lacking a teammate, I thought we may as well give it a shot. Besides, I lost the partner I wanted to the competition. So, I decided I might as well make you jealous and go with Heather."

"Is that what I am?" The shaky voice came from behind Karly. She turned and saw the tall, broad-shouldered woman standing in the doorway, her hands on both sides of the doorframe as if she needed the support. "Am I just a pawn in some romantic game between the two of you?" Heather's eyes darkened as she stomped into the centre of the room. "After all this time working together ..." she scowled, "I deserve more from you than that."

Harrison's face lost all colour. "No, Heather. You misunderstood me." But despite his back-pedaling, Heather ran from the conference room, knocking over a stand of National Geographic Magazines in the process.

"Are you just going to stand there?" Karly pointed. "Go after her and tell her she's wrong."

"I can't do that." Harrison walked toward the fallen bookstand, bent down and picked it up.

"Why not?"

"Because she isn't wrong."

Poor Heather.

Karly bent down, grabbed a few magazines, and placed them back on the stand. "Blake signed us up before I knew what was happening. I didn't choose him over you. It's just the way things unfolded."

"Is that the truth?" Harrison let a magazine dangle at his side.

"That's exactly how it happened."

"But if you had the choice, which one of us would you have chosen?"

"I honestly don't know anymore. Especially after what I just heard." Karly hurried from the room, dodging a few scattered magazines still lying on the floor. And she didn't look back.

CHAPTER THIRTY-FOUR

The campground was bustling with activity. As well as the usual summer campers, many racing participants had arrived early in the week to familiarize themselves with the course. Every day, at least a dozen teams congregated on the waterways of No Trace, pushing and exerting themselves to the limit, hoping to win the grand prize ... their choice of any canoe from Wagami Outfitters in Aspen Ridge and a free month's stay in the campground. As a result, the staff was busier than usual.

Karly did her best to physically prepare for the canoe race. Bright and early every morning, before she headed off to work, she jogged around the campground. Add that to her normal duties and by nightfall she dropped into bed exhausted.

Although Blake attempted to contact her, she ignored his messages. His latest text 'we need to talk' was getting to her. Perhaps she should give him a chance to explain about the earring. But what else could he possibly say? He'd denied it was Raven's. Why didn't she believe him?

Come to think of it, why was she giving Blake such a tough time about that earring? To be honest, she really didn't think it *was* Raven's. Or care.

Her thoughts flew to the day she spent with Blake, canoeing and portaging. Something troubled her about that day, but she couldn't put her finger on it. It had been such a wonderful day until ...

Bingo!

Why hadn't Blake kissed her?

Sure, the pelican plastered her with a warm, messy, pile of poop and put a damper on the moment, but after Blake's maniacal laughing subsided and she cleaned herself up, why not then?

Now, she understood the reason for her accusing distrust. It had absolutely nothing to do with Raven or a peacock-feathered earring.

With her thoughts in turmoil, she grabbed her water bottle and left the cabin to clear her head. It was Wednesday evening. The race was only three days away and if she didn't come to grips with her emotions by then, it could hinder the outcome. It would be difficult to spend two days with Blake under intense pressure from the race, considering the circumstances.

Karly strolled toward Beaver Pond Trail, which was only a short distance away. No jogging tonight. She was terribly exhausted and just needed some fresh air. Besides, the empty cabin reminded her of how much she missed Madison. Maybe she'd be fortunate and see a beaver or two.

As she stood on the boardwalk over the creek, searching for her beloved beavers, her mind wandered back to the night Blake had hesitated about sleeping on her couch. Why had he been so worried about protecting her reputation, if he was carrying on with Raven? Wasn't that hypocritical? It just didn't jive, given all they had shared under the branches of the birch tree—especially their incredible God moments.

A heavy weight sat on her chest, reminding her of her clumsy accident with the wooden moose head. As embarrassing as that incident was, she'd relive it again in a heartbeat instead of the real source of her pain. What should she do about Blake?

An eerie sensation came over her as dusk settled in. Odd. It was as if an evil force operated a dimmer switch. It seemed to happen so quickly. How long had she been pacing the boardwalk? Foolish of her to be caught out on a trail in the wilderness of No Trace in the dark, without a flashlight.

As nocturnal calls of the forest sounded, she scanned the dense woods. Prickles of fear tiptoed up and down her spine, unleashing a gaggle of goosebumps over her entire body. Suddenly chilled, she hugged herself tightly. The forest had never bothered her before. Why was she so creeped out now?

Run, Karly, run!

Karly wasn't sure where the warning came from, but the urge to bolt at lightning speed catapulted her from her spot on the wooden walkway. She raced across the boardwalk and hit the dirt trail. She'd only taken a few steps when the bushes rustled beside her and a large, dark figure jumped out and grabbed her arm. The cloaked being was covered from head to toe in black and glared at her with a set of angry eyes bulging from the black balaclava.

Karly kicked at her assailant, who managed to somehow avoid her erratically-flailing legs. She swung her one free arm—the one holding her water bottle. When the almost-full, durable plastic, one-litre bottle connected with the side of the perpetrator's skull, the jolt reverberated up her arm. The force of the impact not only knocked the bottle from her hand, it caused her attacker to moan loudly and release the grip on her arm. Karly seized her opportunity and took off running. Fueled by adrenalin, she fled as fast as her legs could carry her.

She desperately wanted to know if that horrifying hooded nightmare was behind her, but didn't want to lose precious time by turning to look. She rounded the last bend in the trail and spied her cabin.

She had to stop. For just a moment. To catch her breath.

Karly bent over, grabbed her knees, and gasped for air. Since she was stopped anyway, she threw a harried glance behind her. Nothing. Good. Her sides ached, and her throat burned. She hadn't pushed herself that hard—probably ever.

Don't stop now, Karly. You're almost there.

Karly summoned the last bit of energy she could find, stumbled toward the door, unlocked it, and hurried inside to safety. Her hands trembled so badly she could barely slip the deadbolt into place. Adrenalin waning, her legs gave out beneath her and she sank to the floor.

Flat on her back, her chest heaved wildly. What had just happened? If Josh was the killer, who had tried to attack her just now?

In disbelief, her mind replayed the horrifying events of the last few minutes. It was the strangest thing. She had felt the evil just before her attack. Had God warned her to run? It wasn't audible, but the urgent plea had come from deep inside somewhere. Hands still trembling, she sat up and reached for her cell. Before her mind could even think rationally, she punched the phone icon and called Blake.

He answered on the first ring.

"Can you please come over? Someone tried to attack me. I need you."

"I'm on my way."

He wasn't kidding. When someone banged loudly on the door two minutes later, she jumped. "It's me, Karly."

Karly's legs felt like sloppy pasta as she wobbled to the door and slid the deadbolt across. She must have looked a sight because Blake immediately opened his arms and she collapsed against his chest. His arms wrapped around her tenderly.

"What happened?" he whispered into her hair.

But Karly couldn't summon up the energy for words. Being locked in Blake's safe embrace was all she needed or wanted. Blake closed the door, locked it, and led her to the couch. "Sit down and tell me what happened." He pulled her against his side.

Karly ran a tongue over her parched lips and remembered her water bottle was somewhere out there on the trail. "I need some water first."

Blake hurried to the kitchen and returned with a full glass. After Karly downed it, she wiped her lips and began.

When she'd unloaded the brief but horrifying episode, Blake's eyes filled with concern. "Have you notified the police?"

Karly shook her head. "Not yet. You were the first person I called."

Blake took out his phone and dialed 911, while Karly leaned her head against the couch cushions, totally spent.

"The police will be here soon. They're tied up momentarily with a motor vehicle accident involving a deer."

Blake reached for her again and tucked her head against his shoulder, wrapping her securely in his arms. His voice grew husky. "I'm so glad you're okay. It could have been way worse. I don't know what I would have done if anything happened to you." He tucked a strand of hair behind her ear.

Blake's heartfelt admission surprised and delighted her at the same time. She gazed up into his warm, tender eyes. Blake leaned down and placed a gentle kiss on her forehead.

The disturbing events of the last few moments fled like clouds on a windy day. She closed her eyes as his lips covered first one eyelid then the other. Her head swam with the intoxication of his touch and her stomach somersaulted like a kid on a gymnastic mat. The desperate longing for his kiss made her insides tremble. When it didn't happen, she opened her eyes in confusion.

Blake released her and sank back against the couch, covering his face with his hands. "I'm scared out of my mind."

"Why?"

"I had my doubts that Josh was Madison's killer and what happened to you tonight confirms it." The tormented look on his face worried her.

"Why don't you think Josh did it? If he isn't the killer, why did he try to kill me at the top of Lookout Trail? It doesn't make sense."

"I don't have any answers, just a gut feeling."

"Who do you think killed Madison?"

His features contorted. He opened his mouth as if to speak and then shut it again.

She stiffened. "You think it's Harrison."

Silence.

"For what it's worth, I think you're wrong. Harrison is not a killer." The words came out harsher than she'd intended.

"I hope you're right, Karly. I really hope you're right." When he reached for her hand and squeezed tightly, the anger whooshed out of her. "But if it isn't Josh or Harrison, who do you think attacked you tonight?"

"I don't know. But how did you get here so fast? For all I know, you could have been my attacker."

Blake's eyes narrowed. "Now Karly, why would I have to hide in the bush all decked in black waiting for you. If I wanted to attack you, I could get you any time I wanted to. I know where you live." His voice grew spooky and high-pitched as he pointed a crooked finger at her and scrunched up his face. "I'll get you my pretty, and your little dog too."

Despite the stress of the traumatic attack, Karly laughed at Blake's impression of the wicked witch from the Wizard of Oz. "For all I know, you staged the whole thing, so I would call you in a panic and throw myself into your arms. Or at least finally talk to you after the earring episode."

A deep belly laugh sounded in the cabin. "Your mind works in sick and twisted ways. You obviously don't know me very well." He leaned forward and dipped his head in front of her face.

"What are you doing?"

"Exposing the lack of evidence."

"Huh? I'm not following you."

"If I was your attacker, wouldn't I have a goose egg or cut on the side of my head?" He grabbed her hand and pressed her fingers to several spots on his scalp.

The musky scent of his shampoo and aftershave wafted up her nostrils. Although she could have left her hand in his hair a lot longer, she withdrew it. "Don't be silly. Of course, I don't think it was you. But, I still don't understand how you got here so fast."

Blake placed a finger under her chin and tipped her face to look at him. "I'll tell you how I got here so fast. I was on my way to force you to listen to me. I'm sick of the silent treatment. I want to clear the air."

Karly averted her eyes—she couldn't meet his scrutinizing gaze. And the seriousness in his voice shook her. The tension in the room was thicker than the woods at No Trace Campground.

"Karly, look at me." He waited until she complied. "You need to trust me. There's nothing going on with Raven and me. To be honest, at one time, I considered asking Raven out, but I'm glad I didn't."

"You are?" Karly sat up a little straighter.

"Yes."

Hope surged through her as she waited for him to go on. She longed to hear those three words. That he loved her. And she was the reason. But he didn't say anything more. Her shoulders slumped. "So, does Raven know that you're not interested in her?"

"No, well, I've tried dropping several hints, but she doesn't seem to have gotten the message." Blake combed his hair with his fingers.

"Why don't you just tell her? What are you waiting for?"

"I will. Soon. It's not that easy. I don't want to hurt her."

"Like you hurt me?" The words flew from Karly's mouth before she could stop them.

"*I* hurt *you*?" Blake flew to his feet, glaring down at her. "Need I remind you, you were the one who jumped to the wrong conclusion about us three years ago, and took off running. Literally. But not before you dumped me in the frigid lake water, suit and all."

Karly's eyes unexpectedly filled with tears. "All true. But ..."

"But what?" Blake's voice rose.

"I had a very good reason to jump to the wrong conclusion."

"Really." Blake paced in front of her couch. "Like what?"

A few tears trickled down her cheeks and she swiped at them. She couldn't voice the words—couldn't tell him what she longed to hear. Otherwise it was meaningless.

"Hello? Are you going to enlighten me? How is that fair? I'm supposed to guess why you assumed I wanted out of the relationship, when I didn't? That makes about as much sense as me being your attacker out there in the woods, just now." Blake flung his arm in the direction of the trail.

She cupped a hand over her mouth to hold back a sob, as tears cascaded over her cheeks like a breeched dam.

"Fine, I'm out of here." Blake stormed toward the door, whipped it open, and was gone.

Karly covered her face with her hands and sobbed uncontrollably. Could life get any worse?

CHAPTER THIRTY-FIVE

Thursday morning, after their nine o'clock employee meeting, Harrison motioned for her to stay and talk to him. Karly made her way through the crowd of employees filtering out of the room, ready to resume their daily tasks, and stopped in front of his desk. "Why the long face?"

Harrison's eyes darkened. "Have you heard the local news this morning?"

"No, why?"

"The police released the identity of the body discovered at Potter's Lake."

Her eyes widened. "And?"

"It was Jessica Wakely."

A hand flew to her mouth. "Oh my." She walked around his desk and placed a consoling hand on his arm. "Are you okay?"

Harrison sank onto his chair and dropped his face into his hands. Then he looked up at her and sighed. "My emotions are all over the place. I'm glad they've finally located her body after two whole years, but …"

"You're upset, of course. Have they released the cause of death?"

"No, but they did say they suspect foul play." His eyes were heavy with grief. "She was murdered, Karly. Murdered. I can't wrap my head around that. How could someone have done that to her? I mean, I suspected it, but it's still a blow to have it confirmed."

Karly shook her head. "That's horrible."

"Tell me about it." Harrison placed both hands on the top of his head, as though his skull could barely contain such awful information.

"Do they have any suspects?"

"If so, they haven't said. The police chief did say a homicide investigation had begun. I'm a mess just thinking about it. I have a feeling I'll be hauled in and raked over the coals. I don't think I can do this again, Karly. It's horrendous to be suspected of such a crime when you had absolutely nothing to do with it."

It wasn't difficult to perceive the turmoil Harrison was experiencing. She reached for his hand and squeezed tightly. Even though she had seen a different side of Harrison the other day, when he admitted to using Heather to make her jealous, she wouldn't wish this on anyone.

The room was empty and deathly silent. The last employees, two female summer students, had just left, giggling at something on their phones and completely oblivious to the bleak conversation behind them.

Karly's mind swirled with her philosophical question from last night. The one about whether life could get any worse. Well, it just had. At least for Harrison and the family of Jessica Wakely.

Things were getting awkward. Harrison wasn't saying a word. Unusual for him but, considering the circumstances, understandable. She really didn't know how to help him. "Maybe I'll leave you alone with your thoughts."

But Harrison reached for her, his fingers pressing painfully into the flesh of her forearm. "No, please don't go. I need you, Karly. You're probably the only one who understands what I've gone through since Jessica went missing. It's not something I've ever talked about with anyone. Not even my mother."

Before she knew what was happening, Harrison yanked her towards him, and she tumbled awkwardly into his lap. The shock factor stymied her briefly.

Get up, Karly.

"This is all wrong, Harrison." When Karly's eyes connected with his turbulent, stormy ones, an uneasiness surged through her. "Let me go."

Karly fought to free herself from his grip, but the pressure around her tightened. He grabbed the back of her head and pulled her toward him. "I need you, Karly." His lips slammed against hers, the kiss painful and demanding.

Karly shoved both palms against his chest and stumbled from his lap, landing on her butt on the floor. She clambered to her feet, raised a trembling hand, and slapped him across the face. "How dare you!"

Harrison covered the side of his face with his hand, where red fingerprints had already begun to rise.

"You had no right to kiss me." She shook with fear and anger.

Harrison looked down at the floor.

Karly took a step backward. A shaking hand flew to her lips. "I understand you received upsetting news today, but ... this was not the way to handle it. From now on, just stay away from me." She spun on her heel and sprinted toward the exit

She ran full speed through the campground. She didn't care where she went, just far from Harrison. Maybe if she kept running, she could out-run the problems that seemed to keep piling up like dirty dishes in her sink.

Her energy spent, she flopped to the sand on the far end of the beach at Samson Lake and sprawled out flat on her back. Karly stared at clouds flitting by and imagined shapes, trying to distract herself, a favourite habit from childhood. Her eyes drifted shut for a few minutes, until she heard splashing water and propped herself up on her elbows.

A young family with two small children played in the lake a short distance away. Karly's thoughts flitted to her happy childhood. What she wouldn't give to trade all her adult problems for the carefree life of a kid again. Her childhood had certainly been happy ... until her mother died.

Karly dropped onto her back again and watched a seagull soar on wind currents. Maybe she should have been born a bird. To soar. And fish. And never have to face the things she was facing in her life now.

Her lips hurt. Blake's irritating warning popped into her brain, the one about spending too much time with Harrison alone. *If you play with fire, Karly, you're going to get burned.* Is that what she had been doing? Playing with fire? Madison had warned her that tongues were wagging—that everyone thought that she and Harrison were an item.

Great! Karly smacked the palm of her hand against her forehead. More guilt. Had she been sending the wrong signals to Harrison all along? She didn't mean to. But, no worries there anymore. It would be strictly business between the two of them from now on.

Still, her heart ached at his betrayal. He'd told her he had feelings for her, that he'd wait forever if it took that long. Karly snorted. How long had he waited? Two days? He must never have cared about her, not really, or he wouldn't have treated her so badly today. Had Blake? Or when it came right down to it, was there something inherently unlovable about her?

Pull yourself together Karly, and get back to work. Weeds were attempting to take over the parking lot and they weren't going to pull themselves. Karly got to her feet and brushed sand from her tan-coloured shorts.

As she trudged along the shoreline, she found herself praying to a God she really wasn't even sure existed. But somewhere deep inside, she hoped he did, because if there wasn't something greater than her out there, greater than any problems she might be facing, life didn't have much to offer. And she didn't know where else to turn. Funny how, in her younger years, she'd thought herself strong, capable of handling anything and everything. Except for the death of her mother.

God, I can't go on much longer like this. She missed Madison, Harrison was not the friend she'd thought he was, and Blake, well, Blake confused her even more than he had when they were dating. She had never felt so depressed in all her life. If something didn't change soon, she ....

She'd what? Run away? Like she had last time? *How did that fix things, Karly?* Not very well, apparently.

God, if you're real, I need you. Oh, I need you.

CHAPTER THIRTY-SIX

It was barely dawn, and the sun hadn't made an appearance yet. Lingering pockets of mist hovered over the tranquil lake. The dark woods that surrounded the water were coming alive as wildlife yawned and stretched.

Early that morning, Blake had flown two American doctors into Shadow Lake for a wilderness adventure with Henry. One of the men, a cardiac surgeon from Minneapolis, Minnesota had gotten an emergency call concerning a patient as soon as they landed, and stepped out onto the dock to accept it. Cell service was intermittent in the wilds of No Trace, but Shadow Lake seemed the exception, receiving transmission from a cell tower in the state of Minnesota, which bordered the wilderness on the south.

The call seemed to be taking a long time, so as they waited for the doctor, Blake and Henry ambled slowly along the edge of the lake. "Penny for your thoughts, my friend?" Henry tilted his head towards him.

"Oh, it's nothing you'd want to hear about." Blake avoided eye contact with Henry as he stuck his hands into the pockets of his jeans.

"Matters of the heart are my specialty." Henry pointed proudly at his chest. "I've been happily married for twenty years. I know something's bothering you and it's female related, if I'm on my game."

A patch of mist evaporated on the other side of the lake, and a deer appeared on the far shore. "How did you know?"

"I sense that things are not going well with your future Mrs. White Pelican?"

"Her name is Karly. And no, things aren't going well at all. I don't think there will ever be a future with Karly." Did his voice sound as 'Eeyore-ish' to Henry as it did to him?

"I'm a good listener."

Blake exhaled. "She wants me to figure out why our relationship fell apart three years ago. Honestly, I have no idea. She was the one who jumped to the wrong conclusion on the dock and disappeared from my life." He couldn't believe he was so quickly unloading his baggage, but Henry was right, he was a good listener.

His friend halted beside him and gripped his shoulder. "Wait one minute. I'm not following you." Henry's eyes clouded in confusion. "You and Karly used to date?"

Blake sighed and kicked at a small rock, sending it airborne into the lake. Mesmerized by the ripples his action created, his mind wandered back to that time. A heaviness settled on his chest. "Yes. Sorry. I forgot you didn't know. We met at Williwaw Lake Campground and dated long distance for nine months, since Karly lived in Kitchener and I was in North Beaver Falls. It ended abruptly at our friends' wedding." Blake's stomach tossed as he remembered that awkward, and still incredibly raw, scene on the dock. "All over a misunderstanding."

"A misunderstanding? Do you wish to enlighten me?"

By now, they had reached a small wooden bridge that crossed a marshy section of Shadow Lake. A pair of red-breasted mergansers drifted underneath. Probably a happy waterfowl couple, spending time together. Blake propped his elbows on the railing and stared out over the water.

"I was trying to figure out how to tell Karly that I'd been accepted into flight school and would have to move even farther away, to Thunder Bay, to obtain my licensing. I was troubled about the move, not sure how it would affect our relationship, and worried that Karly may just want out. We already struggled because of the distance. Then, before I could even get a word out, she ... jumped to the wrong conclusion." Blake closed a fist and hammered the railing loudly, surprising even himself at the anger and frustration he harboured inside.

His impulsive act startled the mergansers. A flurried frenzy of flapping and they were airborne. He watched as they disappeared over the top of a row of pines. Henry crossed his arms and stared at him. His friend's hooded gaze made him squirm. Blake was normally more in control of his emotions than this, but Karly could always drive him crazy. Even when she wasn't present.

A little embarrassed at his outburst, Blake dropped his arms to his sides, the dejected action a truer indicator of how he really felt. "She took my nervousness about sharing my news all wrong. She thought I wanted out of the relationship. To say she over-reacted was an understatement. She wouldn't even let me explain, just shoved me off the dock into the water before racing down the boardwalk and disappearing from my life. Literally. The next time I saw Karly was the night Harrison called me and had me fly her to the Aspen Ridge emergency because she had heat stroke."

"Hmm." Henry rubbed his chin. "Karly's right. You are the entire reason for all this tension between you two."

Blake recoiled as though he'd just been slapped. "Me? That's outrageous. You've got to be kidding."

Henry poked a thick finger into his chest. "Yes, you. You need to figure out why she so quickly jumped to the wrong conclusion."

"Because she's impulsive and flighty and ..."

The smug look on Henry's face rattled him.

Blake threw his hands in the air. "What? You can't leave me hanging like that. I need to know why you think I'm the reason. How did you possibly jump to that conclusion?"

"Only you can figure that out, my friend. Search deep inside and you will find it. And while you're at it, pray. God will reveal it to your spirit. He tells us that if we lack wisdom, he will give it to us, if we ask."

"You're a Christian, Henry?" Blake's eyes widened.

"Yes, I am, brother." Henry's smile reached from ear to ear.

Excitement charged through Blake. Something had drawn him to this man from the first day he had met him. Now, he understood. "Me too."

"I knew you were."

"But how? It's only a very recent decision."

Again, Henry pointed to his chest. "I felt it deep in here. Can I tell you my story? Every time I think about it, I'm humbled and awed. And I get excited about every opportunity to share it."

Blake nodded, as his mind transported him briefly to that miraculous day in the hospital waiting room when *he* first believed. But when Henry began, he listened with rapt attention.

"Several years ago, I was a wilderness guide for a grumpy old man. The man was as miserable as a night heron with arthritis."

Blake was instantly drawn to Henry's story and couldn't help but smile at the metaphor, or was it a simile? He never was very good in English.

"One day as we canoed together, a freak storm came up, slammed us against some rocks, and tossed us both into the rough waters of a remote inland lake. As a result, a hole was gouged in the side of the canoe and, unfortunately, in my head." He reached up and rubbed his scalp. "I thought I would bleed out. If not for that cantankerous old man, I probably would have. Stanley dragged me from the choppy lake and saved my life. We were stranded for a few days, just the two of us. Back then, we didn't own cell phones. As the hours wore on, I came to realize that he wasn't as miserable as I had perceived. Once I got to know him, it was a whole different story. And he had gifts."

"Gifts?" Blake asked.

"First, he prayed for my head and a miracle happened. The bleeding stopped, and the headache was gone. Then the old man and the handsome guide," he pressed a hand to his chest and smiled, "brought our talents together and repaired the hole in the canoe the good old-fashioned, Canadian way."

"Canadian way?"

"Stanley had a large roll of duct tape." Henry guffawed loudly and slapped his knee.

Blake shook his head and laughed.

"If it wasn't for that almost-deadly accident, I never would have heard about Jesus and his ultimate sacrifice. That turned out to be the best gift of all. Since then I've learned an important lesson, to never judge a man by the outside; he could possess the most valuable jewel in the entire world. Now, the name of my community is very precious to me."

"Shadow Lake? What do you mean?"

"Every so often, it's reported in the village that the shadow of a cross appears on the water. Logically, there is no explanation for it. And there is no predicting who will see it or when. It reminds me of the suffering my Saviour experienced for me. Living here, I will never forget. Even though I have not seen the cross myself, I keep hoping one day that I will."

"Is that how the village got its name?"

Henry nodded. "Yes, it is. And this name has been around for a few centuries, so the shadow of the cross is not something new here."

"That's incredible, Henry. Thanks for telling me. Now, I, too, will always think of that when I land." Blake scanned the surface of the water, just as the sun's brilliant orange rays broke through an opening in the bush, scattering the mist in its path.

Henry waved toward Blake's Cessna. Blake followed his motion. The doctors stood by the canoe, one of them indicating with an upraised arm that they were ready to go. "Time to head back."

As the friends walked toward the dock, Henry offered advice. "Now you need to pray for a divine answer to your future wife dilemma."

"I'll pray, but really, I still don't understand how I could be the reason for the problems between Karly and me. I think you're wrong, Henry."

Henry clapped him hard on the back, so hard his teeth rattled in his mouth. "Just pray. And you better make it a top priority. The next full moon is coming soon."

Blake coughed.

"What wrong? You don't like my timeline?"

"No, you smacked me a little hard there, Henry. You don't know how strong you are. I may have to check to see if you loosened any teeth."

"Now, who's the funny man? Toughen up, white pelican."

Blake ignored the remark as they arrived in front of the men. "Everything okay?"

The cardiologist nodded. "I was able to get a colleague to take the case. I should be good now for the week."

"Great." Blake watched as Henry helped the eager fishermen load supplies into their canoe. Then Blake waved as the trio glided away for their wilderness adventure. Henry would be gone for the next week, doing what he did best. Exploring God's creation with those who were excited to view it. Blake climbed in his Cessna, closed the door and did his pre-flight check. Anything to distract him from Henry's unsettling remarks. To be honest, he was as rattled as his teeth.

Was there any chance that what had happened between Karly and him was his fault? He'd take Henry's advice and pray that God would show him if he was responsible for what had happened, but he highly doubted he'd get a response. Not because God didn't answer prayer, but because the problem didn't lie with him.

Nope.

Henry was wrong.

Dead wrong.

It was all Karly's fault.

Wasn't it?

And that full moon bride thing scared the life out of him, since Henry seemed to know him better than he knew himself.

With his thoughts in turmoil, Blake landed his floatplane, scaring a family of white egrets from the water. He headed around to the front of his business. When he noticed a cruiser parked in his lot, his nerves tensed. Now what was wrong?

Officer Neilson stepped from the vehicle. "Do you have a minute, Mr. Fenton?"

"Sure. What seems to be the problem?" Blake stopped beside the police vehicle.

"I just wanted to give you some information in case you haven't heard. Perhaps you're already aware, since it's blasted all over social media."

"Whatever it is, I doubt it. I haven't had time to go on my phone this morning."

The officer nodded. "The body you discovered at Potter's Lake is indeed that of Jessica Wakely, the park naturalist who was reported missing two years ago."

Blake blew out a breath. Not that he was thrilled with the news, but at least it didn't involve his sister, parents, or Karly. "Was she murdered?"

"Foul play is definitely suspected, and a homicide investigation has begun. It will be difficult to identify her killer for several reasons: the absence of a murder weapon, a lack of evidence, the time frame involved, and the fact that the body has been submerged in water for two years."

"I see. Well, thank you for coming by to tell me; I appreciate it." Blake extended a hand, but the officer ignored it.

"Is there anything else?" Blake let his hand drop to his side, his fist clenched.

After a long, awkward moment of silence, Officer Neilson cleared his throat. "I discovered some very interesting information yesterday, while I was probing through campground records from two years ago. Josh Rutherford was a registered camper at No Trace the week that Miss Wakely went missing."

"Are you serious?" Blake blinked. "What are the odds of that? And how old would he have been at the time?"

"Nineteen. Old enough to have committed a murder. And after what happened up on Lookout Trail, the odds of him not being the killer seem pretty slim."

Blake removed his cap and wiped beads of sweat off his forehead with the back of his sleeve. "To be honest, I was hoping it was Josh. If it wasn't him, that would mean the killer is still at large. But one thing has me puzzled. Who attacked Karly the other night on the trail?"

"The two events are probably not linked." The officer's cocky glare annoyed Blake.

"A random attack?" Blake replaced his cap. "I don't know if I believe that."

Officer Neilson opened his car door and slipped inside. "I guess it doesn't really matter what you believe. Just leave the detective work to us."

Blake didn't appreciate the guy's attitude. Not one bit. He clasped his hands behind his back to keep from saluting him in a mocking sort of gesture.

He would respect the uniform, but that didn't mean he had to like the man who was wearing it.

CHAPTER THIRTY-SEVEN

Karly scanned the throng of contestants milling about in the dim light of early dawn. When she located Blake, conversing with Harrison and Heather, she turned away, busying herself preparing for the task ahead. Wonderful. The two men she despised most right now.

"Let me help you with that," Harrison offered a few minutes later.

At the sound of his voice behind her, a knot formed in her belly. In stark defiance, she kept her back to the man. "I don't want or need anything from you, now or ever again."

"Look, Karly, I don't blame you for being angry."

She whirled to face him. "Move!" she snapped. "You're blocking my way. I need to get to the rest of my supplies."

When he refused to budge, her fury escalated.

"I came to apologize. I was way out of line the other day. I wasn't thinking clearly. I was distraught."

Her hands flew to her hips. "Is that what you call it? I have a more fitting description for your behavior and it involves the words despicable and appalling. Not to mention illegal."

"Calm down, Karly."

If there was anything that kept Karly from calming down when she was upset, it was being told to calm down. She gritted her teeth. "Get out of my way."

"Keep your voice down. You're creating a scene."

By now, Blake and Heather had wandered over. Judging by the confusion on their faces, they were unsure of the reason for the heated exchange.

"Is everything okay here, Karly?" Blake asked.

"Far from it. Would you tell this man to get out of my way?"

Harrison threw his hands in the air in surrender mode. "No need." He skulked away with Heather following close behind.

Blake watched them go before turning to her. "What was that about?"

"None of your business."

He frowned. "Someone got up on the wrong side of the bed this morning."

Karly pressed her lips firmly together. "Look. I'm here today because I made a commitment and for that reason only. So, let's get down to business. Start loading your supplies."

"Aye, aye, Cruella." His hand flew to his forehead in a mock salute. Then he dropped his backpack in the canoe.

"Men. I hate the lot of you."

"Can I have your attention please?" Harrison's voice, all business-like and official, boomed over the loud speaker. "For starters, I'd like to welcome everyone to our annual No Trace Marathon canoe race."

Hoots, howls, and clapping punctured the early morning tranquility. Karly wished she could feel a little bit of their enthusiasm. Maybe it would wear off.

"Rock cliffs, boulder-strewn shorelines, dense wilderness, incredible wildlife, and man-eating mosquitoes are just a small part of the No Trace wilderness that has been navigated by First Nations Indigenous peoples, The Voyageurs, and many others through the centuries. And it will be a major part of your adventure over the next few days".

"This race is 95 kilometers each way, starting at Samson Lake and going to Grassy Portage at Muskie Lake and back again. It will be a difficult, grueling task controlled as much by the elements as by you. I am delighted to inform you that we are a crew of nineteen entries ranging from novices to world-class pros.

"I know it's early, but a six o'clock start was necessary to maximize daylight hours. This will hopefully avoid anyone finishing in the dark. If it appears that a team will not finish in daylight, they will be pulled at the second checkpoint at the north end of Lake Taluski.

Tents, sleeping bags, and food have been dropped off at the halfway point, courtesy of Blake Fenton of Wilderness Bush Adventures."

Again, a cheer went up. To her surprise, several looked Blake's direction. He removed his cap and took a bow, inciting more raucous cheers. Karly didn't realize Blake was so well-known already ... and apparently well-liked.

Harrison lifted a hand and the crowd settled. "Cell phones are allowed, but as most of you already know, reception is poor. GPS are discouraged even if they should work. Basically, cell phones should only be used in case of emergency. In order not to be disqualified, you will need to rely on your maps and stick to the route outlined. The weather forecast says a sixty percent chance of thunderstorms for today and tomorrow. Let's hope we remain in the forty percent. Good luck. May the best team win. Now, I'd like to invite long-time, local racing contest, David Boumeister to share some inspiration for the race before we get started."

Karly endured the fifty-something man's humorous poem. Any other time, she would have laughed along with the rest of the crowd. Today she wasn't in the mood. Blake glanced her direction, but when their eyes connected, he looked away.

"Contestants, take your positions."

A shot rang out signaling the official start of the race. Everyone dashed from the beach into the calm brown waters of Samson Lake.

Blake stepped to the bow and she let him. Even though she hated to admit it, he was stronger than she was. And they needed a powerful start to get ahead right at the beginning.

Neither of them spoke.

In no time at all, it was easy to discern who the stronger teams were. Six canoes, including hers and Blake's, had taken an easy lead across Samson Lake. Maybe her anger was a good thing, the driving fuel for her energy. Was Blake exerting the same frenetic force? Perhaps their annoyance with each other could work to their advantage.

A quick look to her left sent disappointment coursing through her. Harrison and Heather glided into view about thirty feet away. So, they were a force to be reckoned with as well. Somehow, she wasn't surprised.

The skies remained dismally grey and overcast, and the air thick with humidity, but the threat of severe weather hadn't materialized yet. The six canoes stayed together across Tubby and Gore Lakes. The shallow waters of Trillium River kept everyone jammed together until they all arrived at the first checkpoint.

The stop gave her a chance to meet some of the other contestants. A blonde, clean-cut man in his early thirties seemed to be the jokester in the crowd, yelling good-natured taunts at some of his fellow rivals. He meandered in her direction and stuck out his hand. "Hi, Angel, I'm Danny. Did it hurt when you fell from heaven?"

"Good grief." Karly rolled her eyes. "Can't you come up with something more original than that?" Although a bit short by her standards, he was kind of cute with his closely-cropped hair, muscular build, and adorable dimples. Good thing Karly was done with men.

"That bad, eh?" he countered. "What about this? I'd paddle the lengths of No Trace and back again blindfolded, just to get you to laugh at one of my dumb pick-up lines."

Despite herself, Karly's mouth hitched up at one corner. "That's a little far-fetched, and probably impossible, but it beats the angel line hands down."

"Thanks. Who's your partner for the race?"

"Blake Fenton, and I'll thank you to stop flirting with my teammate." Blake came up behind Karly and rested a hand on her back. "She doesn't need the distraction. Besides, getting a date with her will be just as impossible as that challenge of yours, so you may as well stop while you're ahead."

Karly pursed her lips. How dare he!

She glared at him. "Back off, partner. My dating life is not up for discussion, especially by you. You had your chance once."

Hurt flashed across his face as he dropped his hand. For a brief second guilt flooded through her. Why had she brought up the past and humiliated him in front of several contestants?

Harrison was at her side suddenly, the wide smile on his face showing that he was pleased she had put Blake in his place. He touched Karly's arm as he directed a comment to the flirtatious contestant.

"This one's a force to be reckoned with. I wouldn't be surprised if she wins it."

Karly yanked her arm away. If he was trying to get on her good side with flattery, it wasn't working.

Clearly oblivious to the undercurrents of tension zipping between the three of them, Danny flashed them a grin. "Since there seems to be no shortage of suitors vying for your attention, I have a suggestion. The contestant that finishes first among the three of us will win a date with you."

"Wait one minute. Don't I get a say in this? There's only one of you that I'd even consider going out on a date with." Karly folded her arms over her chest.

"And I suppose you're not going to let us in on who that someone might be?" Danny smirked.

Karly's lips twisted in a sideways smile. "A woman never tells."

"I'll take you on. Harrison held out his hand and Danny shook it.

When she looked at Blake, he had turned his back to her and was staring out over the lake.

Soon they were on the water again, back in full-fledged racing mode, the outrageous challenge forgotten for the time being. Or so she thought.

"Don't be encouraging those types of guys. You could be inviting trouble." Blake's voice was low, and she had to strain to hear it.

"If you're referring to the cute one named Danny, I think you're completely wrong. His type is harmless."

"You think he's cute?"

"Jealous, are we? And what was that back there? I didn't need your intervention, or your sarcastic comment about how hard it would be to get a date with me."

"I was trying to protect you. Don't flatter yourself. It wasn't jealousy. And, thanks for embarrassing me."

Karly's chest tightened. Blake was right. She felt sick at what she'd done. But her pride stopped her from asking forgiveness. His words were not very nice, either.

The remainder of the day there was silence between them. Karly had never imagined it would be possible to complete that many hours of a punishing and arduous marathon without talking to her partner, but she'd clearly underestimated how mad he was. Or hurt.

Darkness loomed just as the tired pair drew up to Grassy Portage. For the last few hours, they hadn't seen another canoe, so they had no idea what their status was in the race. They were pleasantly surprised to discover they were team number two, directly behind Danny and Marcus. Only fifteen minutes separated their times. Maybe that was the encouragement they needed to begin talking to each other again.

Exhaustion didn't justly describe how she felt. Every muscle in her body ached and then some. As she attempted to climb from the canoe, she stumbled. Blake grabbed her arm, preventing her from landing in the lake.

"Thanks." She looked up into his eyes and tried to read what was there. If eyes were the windows to the soul, maybe she could peer through and understand him better. But, she couldn't read him today.

"Are you okay?"

"I'll be fine. I just tripped." Admitting she was near the point of collapsing was out of the question.

An official greeted them and pointed out the food tent and where they could drop their supplies. It turned out their sleeping quarters were at the far edge of the clearing, near the bush. They deposited their equipment in the communal area and headed for some much-needed sustenance.

Karly filled a plate and ducked out the doorway of the dining tent. It didn't matter if she appeared anti-social, she needed space, so she plunked herself on a large piece of driftwood far from the others. Before she managed her first bite of hotdog, Danny joined her.

"Hey, beautiful, you weren't very far behind us. Something tells me you're going to be our biggest contender after all."

She was so tired, it was draining to find words. So, she sat silently and stared at her food.

"Did you know Marcus and I took first last year?"

"Really." She managed to lift the food to her mouth and take a bite. Even chewing was exhausting.

"So, to be right behind us is phenomenal."

Karly frowned. "You think rather highly of yourself."

"On the contrary, you misunderstand. I'm giving encouragement here."

"Oh, is that what you call it." Karly stood up. She really didn't want to be rude, but she was too tired to eat, and she couldn't abide small talk with Danny. Between Harrison and Blake, she'd had entirely enough of the male species for the time being. "I need some sleep. I'll see you tomorrow." After dumping her plate and most of her dinner into a garbage can set up by the shore, she stalked toward her tent.

She wished everyone would just go away and leave her alone.

CHAPTER THIRTY-EIGHT

Blake watched her storm toward the sleeping area before turning his attention to Danny. "Don't I know you?" He dropped onto the log beside the blonde contestant. He didn't like that Danny appeared to be making moves on his old girlfriend, even if she clearly hadn't reciprocated them. "You look familiar. I mean, besides meeting you back at the first rest point."

"You might have met me," Danny replied. "I'm from Aspen Ridge, born and raised there."

"But I'm new in the area."

"You could have seen me around town. I run the local Outfitter's."

"That's it." Blake nodded. "I think you sold me some fishing line."

Danny smiled, a broad smile, exposing a mouthful of gleaming white teeth. Maybe Karly was right. Their main competitor had a lot going for him. Perhaps Blake had misjudged him. He seemed pleasant enough.

"Is that the day you discovered Jessica Wakely's body?"

Blake nearly choked on the sip of water he'd just taken. "Yeah, I guess it was."

"That must have been tough." Danny's eyes followed Karly's retreating form, causing Blake to swallow a nervous, jealous lump in his throat. It was obvious this guy was very attracted to Karly. "Did Karly know the victim?"

"No, she didn't, but she did lose her good friend, Madison, a little over a week ago."

Danny rubbed his chin. "I remember reading about that in the newspaper." He stood and took a step in the direction Karly had disappeared. "I think maybe she needs some consoling."

Blake jumped to his feet, knocking his bottle of water onto the ground. "I'd leave her be if I were you. She needs time to herself."

"That's the way you might handle things, and I respect that, but it's not my way."

Blake watched the man practically jog toward Karly's tent. Should he intervene or let things be? *Help me, God. I know I came to a decision last night but ... this isn't easy.* A blinding flash of light streaked across the sky and Blake cast a quick glance upward. Great! All they needed now was a severe storm to deal with.

A deep booming voice caused him to turn his head. Harrison was barking orders at Heather as they arrived on shore. Lately, he'd seen another side of the man. Mr. Nice Guy must be on vacation. Who should he be more concerned about, Harrison or Danny?

He blew out an exasperated breath. He'd taken Henry's advice and prayed fervently for an answer as to whether he was the problem in his and Karly's relationship. And God had given him that answer. Now he just had to figure out what to do about it.

This is so hard, God.

The combination of humidity and the encroaching dusk lured every mosquito in North America to the wilderness of No Trace. At least it felt that way. Unable to stand the barbarous barrage on his being any longer, Blake sprinted toward his tent, then stopped abruptly. Wait a minute. He'd asked for two tents, but this one had a sign saying, Blake and Karly. Blake removed his cap and ran a hand through his hair. What should he do about that?

He did a quick check and all the remaining tents had been assigned to different teammates. He knew that most teams hunkered down together, but he really didn't want anyone to get the wrong idea about him and Karly.

Ouch! He slapped the back of his sweaty neck. Those man-eating mosquitoes had larger- than-average stingers. He hurried inside his tent and hunkered down inside the bug-free zone.

Had Danny caught up with Karly? How long would the two of them be together? Blake didn't like the jealousy that surged through him. Karly didn't belong to him, and she'd made it very clear this afternoon that she didn't appreciate him acting like she did. He had to let it go. Still, he was thrilled when he heard the zipper a few minutes later. Karly ducked inside the tent, rubbing her arms. "That was torture. I think I have about a hundred bites on my arms and legs alone. I thought the mosquitoes were bad in the campground, but this is horrendous by comparison."

Blake reached in his bag and pulled out his bug repellant. "Here, use some of this."

"I'm already swimming in the stuff. It doesn't seem to work. I think I'll hibernate inside the rest of the night. Plus, I'm drop-dead exhausted."

"I'm sorry about this." Blake waved a hand around the tent.

"What do you mean?"

"You and I sleeping in the same tent? I asked for separate sleeping quarters, but somehow it didn't happen."

"Honestly, I don't care."

Blake stared at her. "I do. I guess I could sleep outside."

"Are you crazy? There will be nothing left of you by morning. Let's face it, under the circumstances we have no other option."

"I suppose you're right." Blake got up and busied himself with rearranging the backpacks and sleeping bags.

"What are you doing?"

"This is your half and that is mine and neither the two shall meet."

"You are ridiculous. And childish. But if it makes you feel better, knock yourself out." Lightning lit up the tent, followed by a distant boom of thunder.

"Do you think that storm is moving in?" Karly continued to rub her arms.

Was that still because of the mosquitoes, or was she nervous about the weather? He wondered if she carried lingering fear after an intense storm caused a large tree to fall only a few feet from her tent in Lake Williwaw Campground three years ago—the camping trip where he first met Karly. "I hope not, but time will tell."

"Um, I'd like to get out of these clothes. How will I ..."

As quick as a bolt of lightning, Blake dove for the tent's opening. "I'll wait outside. Just don't be too long or I'll be so poked full of holes,

I may bleed out and need to be transfused. Do you still remember how to cross-match blood?

CHAPTER THIRTY-NINE

Karly gave him a playful shove out the door. Of course, she remembered how to cross-match a unit of blood, but out here in the wilds of No Trace? She couldn't be sure why she found it so funny. Maybe she was over-tired and giddy. Either way, it really felt good to laugh.

"Are you ready yet?" Blake's voice was a little tense.

"Not quite."

"Could you please hurry? These suckers hurt like crazy. Do you still carry needles around from your years as a medical lab technologist? Because I think they might have found them."

She laughed, the sensation not only pleasant, but a stress-reliever.

"Okay, I'm ready." She grabbed her pillow and crouched to one side of the tent's opening. She didn't know what had come over her, but she was tired of being angry.

"It's so dark in here. I can't see a thing." Blake zipped the door closed and paused just inside the tent.

Wham after wham, blows from her pillow landed on his head with such force that he stumbled into the middle of the tent, tripping over backpacks and sleeping bags.

"You are in big trouble, Blondie." It didn't take him long to recover. In a flash, he regained his balance, snatched the weapon from her hands, and retaliated violently.

"Stop!" she screamed between fits of laughter. Desperately, she crawled around the tent on her hands and knees, trying to escape the incessant fluffy attack on her being. Suddenly the onslaught ceased, followed by silence. "Where are you?" She asked nervously. "I can't see you."

"All the better for me," he roared, landing another punishing pelt. This one knocked her flat on her stomach.

"Ouch!" Karly wailed.

"What's going on in there? Are you okay, Karly?" Harrison's concerned voice pierced the night air.

She didn't realize Blake was so close until she felt his breath on the side of her face.

"Let's run with it." His voice tickled her ear.

"What's your plan?" she whispered, her heart racing at his nearness.

"Follow my lead."

"Okay."

"Karly? Are you okay?" Her supervisor asked again.

"Is that you, Harrison?" Blake sounded as though he was on the edge of panic, and Karly slapped a hand over her mouth to keep from laughing.

"Yes, is everything okay?"

"Not really. We've got ourselves a nasty intruder. Somehow a skunk made its way into our tent and is holding us hostage."

"That's terrible. What can I do?"

"Karly is near the entrance and she's going to try and get out. Be prepared."

"Okay." Harrison was clearly trying to keep his voice as soft and soothing as possible. "Don't make any sudden moves."

Blake shoved the can of bug spray into her hands. "You know what to do," he whispered.

It took a herculean effort to squelch her mounting giggles.

Karly crawled to the entrance, toting the spray can. "Are you there, Harrison?"

"I am," he responded. "As soon as I see you, I'll yank you free."

"Thanks."

Slowly, she inched open the zipper, caught a glimpse of Harrison's silhouette bending towards her, and let loose, keeping the nozzle pointed at the ground so it wouldn't hit him in the face. The spray caught him on the arms and he gasped.

"Great!" he shrieked, jumping back into the darkness. "It got me. Karly, are you okay?"

Unable to control herself any longer, she broke into hysterical laughter. Blake joined her. "I'm sorry, Harrison. It was bug spray." Karly held up the can just as another flash of lightning lit up the night. And Harrison's angry face.

"That's really funny." Harrison pushed to his feet. "I'm surprised you have the energy to be playing pranks on people." His footsteps disappeared into the night.

"That felt so good." Karly held her stomach as she laughed. Finally, she flopped back from exhaustion and found herself pressed up against Blake. "You don't know how badly I needed to get back at him."

Before she knew it, his arm came around her and she nestled into his shoulder, a natural fit. Why had she been upset with him again?

"What do you mean?" His voice was husky as he stroked her hair. "Does this have something to do with your anger at him this morning?"

"It doesn't matter now. That was so much fun. I needed a good laugh."

"I needed it too. More importantly, I need you, Karly."

His bold and surprising statement came out of nowhere. She was unprepared for the shock it rendered, and without thinking about it, tipped back her head to look at him. Before she could think rationally, his lips found hers—the effect almost her undoing. His sweet and gentle touch made her want to melt with joy. How long she had waited for this kiss.

She snuggled deeper into his chest and sighed.

"Karly?"

"What?"

"You need to get on your own side of the tent—now." His request sounded pathetically weak.

"Do I have too? What if we just snuggled and talked?"

His hand ran up and down her arm. "I don't know if that's possible with you in my arms. But before you go, I need to tell you something."

"That sounds serious."

His arm tightened around her shoulders. "It is. Do you remember that big fight we had the other night when you told me I was the reason we broke up.?"

"Yes."

"I've done a lot of thinking, praying, and soul-searching since then. And I've discovered something profound."

"You have?" Her hand reached up and touched the prickly whisker stubble on his face. Even though she couldn't see his deep blue eyes, she could picture them clearly in her mind.

"You were absolutely right. At first, I thought you were crazy, accusing me of being the reason for our break-up. Then I asked myself why you would automatically assume that I was going to dump you. It was like a light bulb went off in my brain. Because she's insecure, nincompoop."

Karly would have laughed at Blake's use of that silly word, had the topic not been so terribly painful.

"And just why do you think she's insecure, Blake, I asked myself." Blake drew in a shuddering breath. "Because you never, ever," his voice cracked with emotion, "told her you loved her."

His heart-wrenching admission reached deep inside and massaged the tender, aching chords of her heart, causing tears to fill her eyes and spill down her cheeks.

"I love you, Karly Foster. I loved you then. And I love you now. There's never been anyone else for me. I'm so sorry it took me this long to tell you." He claimed her lips again and his kiss was sweeter than anything she could have ever dreamed of or imagined.

He pulled back and wiped her tears away with his thumb. "Our break-up was all my fault. If only I could have told you I was in love with you then. But I was so afraid of pouring out my deepest feelings and having them rejected and my heart shattered. I didn't know how to ... trust."

"It's okay, Blake. It's all in the past. The main thing is that we're together now." Karly rested a hand on his chest. "I love you too, Blake Fenton. I've never loved anyone else. You really set the bar high."

"Who me? The nincompoop?"

Karly giggled. "Yes, you, the nincompoop." She swallowed. "I have something I need to ask you too."

"Raven and I are not together. Never have been and never will be."

Karly shook her head. "That's not what I wanted to ask. How do I become a believer? I'm totally convinced that God loves me. He whispered it at the top of Lookout Trail, then he saved me from being thrown over the cliff. And he gave me you to love. And the new Blake is even more attractive than the old one. It's like you glow or something."

"Aw, Karly. I blow it so often. If I glow, it's only God's presence in me that you see. But I will tell you how to believe. Have you heard of Roman's road?"

"No, what's that?"

"It's several verses in the book of Romans in the Bible. I can show them to you sometime. It basically tells us that we were all born sinners, that none of us is righteous, and the payment for our sins is death and eternal separation from God. But then it goes on to say, that while we were still in our sin, Christ took the punishment for our sins upon himself and he died for us. It's God's gift to us so that those that believe will spend eternity with God in heaven one day."

Everything Karly had heard over her lifetime about Jesus and His sacrifice on the cross, whether through Kerrick, Maya, and now Blake, suddenly all came together and made sense.

Remorse for the life she had lived apart from God weighed heavily upon her. But when Blake spoke again, hope surged through her being.

"Jesus is the Way, the Truth and the Life. If you confess with your mouth that Jesus is Lord and believe in your heart that God raised Jesus from the dead, you will be saved, Karly—saved from spending eternity apart from God. Do you believe all these things in your heart?"

"I do," Karly proclaimed boldly.

"Then you are a new creation in God. The old is gone and the new has come. His Holy Spirit now lives inside you."

Overwhelmed, Karly closed her eyes. "Thank you, Jesus, for dying for my sins and making a way for me to be with you one day. Thank you for loving me so much."

A holy silence filled the tent for the next several moments. Calmness settled over her as she basked in her newfound faith. It filled the deep recesses of her entire body. Words escaped her. How had it taken her thirty-one years to find this?

Blake finally broke the silence. "Karly Foster, will you marry me?"

Between her newfound faith and Blake's admission of love and desire to marry her, Karly thought she might burst with joy. "Yes, I will marry you. I love you Blake Fenton, with all my heart."

When he kissed her again, this kiss carried the sweet promise of a life together, forever, with the man she loved.

Even the wall of pillows and bags he built between them before they both settled into their sleeping bags for the night didn't make her feel any less close to him.

And now she knew nothing ever would.

CHAPTER FORTY

"I can't believe it." Blake's voice was panicky.

Karly tried to move. Her neck ached. Her back ached. Her shoulders and arms ached. She groaned. Was there a muscle in her body that didn't scream in pain? Was she coming down with a flu bug? Still lying flat on her back, she opened her eyes and a blurry tent ceiling came into focus. The grueling marathon canoe race. That's why she hurt everywhere.

But then, as memories of her newfound faith and Blake's marriage proposal came flooding back in, she pushed through the pain to a sitting position and stared across the tent at Blake, whose head she could barely see above the wall of backpacks and camping supplies.

"What's wrong, my future husband?"

A smile came over his face briefly before he scrambled from his sleeping bag. "We overslept. We're in a race or did you forget?"

"Oh, my goodness, what time is it?" Karly whipped back her sleeping bag.

"It's six thirty. I imagine everyone left at six but us. Let's get moving."

Within ten minutes, the pair had sprinted to the beach and found their lone canoe. Other than a few volunteers dismantling the food tent, the overnight checkpoint was all but vacant.

"How far behind everyone are we?" Blake yelled to one of the men.

"The last team left about five minutes ago," an older man answered.

"Thanks." Blake held the canoe while she jumped in.

The pair paddled frantically.

"This is terrible," Blake complained. "We've dropped from second place to bottom."

"That's assuming all teams made it in last night. Besides, there are more important things in life. If we don't win, it's not that big a deal." Karly surprised herself when those words came out of her mouth.

"Is this the competitive Karly I know and love? Where's your fighting spirit?" Blake goaded her.

"Oh that? It got lost in your arms last night." Karly flipped her gaze back over her shoulder and smirked.

Blake's dashingly handsome grin caused her breath to catch in her throat and her heart to flutter erratically. Karly turned back and dug in her paddle.

Just concentrate on the race, Karly.

By now, they'd crossed Muskie Lake and reached their first portage. Although her arms screamed in agony as she lifted the canoe, she pushed herself for Blake's sake. It seemed important to him that they win, so she'd give it everything she had. Funny how her priorities had changed overnight, and she couldn't care less about the race anymore.

After they lowered the heavy beast to the ground, he surprised her and pulled her into his arms. "Have I told you lately that I love you?"

Karly giggled. "Yes. But you can tell me again." An all-encompassing joy settled over her as she snuggled into his chest. All five senses reeled, and her mind wandered into the land of her most favourite things. Loving Blake was even better than the sweetness of gooey cinnamon buns, the freshness of a spring rain, the whoosh of wind whistling through pines, a brilliant sunset and the delicious warmth of a blazing campfire. Karly sighed and snuggled deeper into his warm embrace. After years of running, it felt like she'd finally come home.

"Shouldn't we resume racing?" he asked, as he stroked the back of her head.

"You started this when you pulled me into your arms." Karly tilted her head up and planted a kiss on his nose.

Blake's eyebrows lifted. "Not that I'm objecting, but why did you kiss my nose?"

"Because I love your nose." Karly ran a finger down it.

Blake grabbed her finger and squeezed it. "You mean my big yellow beak?"

"It's not big. It's not yellow. And it doesn't resemble a beak. My kiss is setting that straight, once and for all."

Blake stared down at her, his gaze so intense she thought she might catch fire. "Thank you for helping me set aside my insecurities. Come to think of it, I was never anxious about my nose until Henry's comment, comparing me to a white pelican."

Karly frowned. "You and I seem to have trouble with those birds, don't we?"

"Yes, we do, oh poop queen." Blake's finger traced the edge of her jawline, before he cupped her face with his hands and planted a light feathery kiss on *her* nose. "We'd better get moving."

"Do we have to?" She took a step back, but held on to his sides.

"If we want to have any chance of finishing the race at all."

"All right, if we must."

Blake and Karly climbed back into the canoe and soon were dodging rocks and tree branches in a swift-moving river. Once ashore again, Blake paused, hands on his hips, and stared straight ahead.

"What's wrong?"

"We have a problem." Blake pointed toward the trail where an enormous tree sprawled on the ground in all directions, effectively blocking access. "It appears to be a fairly fresh lightning strike, probably from the storm last night."

"So, what do we do now?"

Blake pulled out his map and studied it. "Wait one minute. I'm confused." He pointed to a spot. "Is this where we are?"

Karly's mouth went drier than burnt toast. "Yes." When her answer came out in a strangled squawk, Blake looked up from the map.

"What did you do? I'm almost afraid to ask."

Guilt galloped through her like a herd of wild horses. "Um, I ..."

Blake let the map dangle at his side. His gaze drilled her. "I'm waiting."

Karly wrung her hands and stared down at her hiking boots.

Blake let the map fall to the dirt and folded his arms across his chest. He didn't say another word. The silence was killing her. And his gaze was so intense it felt like a truth-seeking laser aimed at her heart. The pressure to spill her guts was excruciating.

"Because we slept in, I sort of ... kind of ... took a shortcut. I figured no one would know." She lifted her head and, with difficulty, met his gaze. Guilt dug at her insides, like the time she was a kid and took a dollar from her mother's money jar. To this day, she didn't know how her mother knew, since she lied and said she had found it outside.

"Karly Foster, I'm ashamed of you. I trusted you with the directions. We'll need to confess when we reach the finish line. I imagine we'll be disqualified."

Karly kicked at a twig on the shoreline. "I did it for you. I thought you wanted to win badly."

"Not at the expense of cheating." Blake's words were firm, but his eyes were tender.

Karly shrugged. "I'm sorry. Do you forgive me? We've lost the race now. What should we do?"

"I'm not upset. And yes, I forgive you." Blake placed his hands on her shoulders. "Well, future Mrs. White Pelican, let's backtrack and do things the right way. We do need to find our way home sometime if we want to plan our wedding."

Karly stuck a finger in the air. "We don't have much time either. The next full moon is only a week away." She whirled and bolted for the canoe. Karly heard his approaching footsteps. Then suddenly he'd overtaken her.

"Hurry up. What's taking you so long?" Blake stood beside the canoe, a sly grin on his face. And he hadn't even broken a sweat.

❖

As they retraced their path through Muskie Lake and followed the suggested map route, Karly's thoughts raced with ideas for their wedding. Funny, how she could care less about the race anymore. Blake had forgiven her for her attempt to cheat, and all that mattered now was spending her life with Blake.

As they were navigating another shoreline, looking for the safest place to disembark, Blake asked her a question. "Yesterday, you told Danny that there was only one of us three guys that you would ever consider a date with. Who did you mean?"

Karly threw a glance over her shoulder as they steered toward a small beach area on the shoreline. "Don't be so silly. I can't believe you'd ask me that. Isn't the answer obvious?"

"A guy just needs to be reassured, I guess."

"Danny is a stranger and Harrison ... well ... he ..."

"What happened between the two of you? You seemed livid with him before the start of the race."

"If I tell you, do you promise not to go ballistic on me?"

"I won't promise anything of the sort." His voice took on an uneasy edge. "Did he hurt you?"

By now, the canoe had scraped to a stop along the sand. Karly climbed out first and held the canoe steady while Blake disembarked. He parked his tall body in front of hers and took her hands in his. He squeezed them both tightly, waiting for her to continue.

Karly's stomach tossed as if she were navigating turbulent white-water in her canoe.

"Karly." He tipped her chin up and the sincerity in his eyes shook her. "I don't ever want there to be any secrets between us. Tell me exactly what happened."

"I'm trying," she whispered. Karly drew in a deep breath. "Harrison was upset after sharing the news with me over the identity of the body you found. That it was indeed Jessica Wakely's and foul play was involved. He knew the police had reopened the case and was afraid that he'd have to relive that nightmare all over again. He was distraught, to say the least."

Blake's shoulders drooped. "I'm almost afraid to ask what happened next."

Karly let go of his hands, placed her palms against his chest and met his troubled gaze. "He kissed me. Believe me, it wasn't the other way around. Harrison admitted to me a few weeks ago that he had feelings for me. He knew I didn't feel the same way and that I was confused about ... you and me. But he was distressed."

"Is that all that happened?"

"That's all that happened. His kiss was painful. Not at all like yours. And I didn't like it—not even one little bit."

Blake's eyes drooped with heaviness.

"I promise that's all that happened. And if it makes you feel any better, I gave him a good slap across the face."

A hint of a smile played at the corners of his mouth. "I think I need to have a talk with Harrison."

"Don't."

"We'll see. I'm not making any promises."

"Once he discovers we're getting married, he'll back off."

"Are you sure?"

"Positive. And he did try to apologize yesterday morning, but I wouldn't let him. I truly believe he got caught up in the moment and made a mistake. He had no one to confide in all these years and I happened to be the one he unloaded his feelings on."

Blake's eyes narrowed. "Have you ever considered that he could be Jessica Wakely's murderer? And Madison's? I still don't think Josh was their killer."

Despite the chill that ran through her, she shook her head. "And neither is Harrison. Absolutely not."

But as evening approached and they portaged through the bush, an uneasiness settled over her. Now, she was starting to feel like Madison—as if something bad was about to happen. Could Harrison really have committed such horrible crimes? It couldn't have been Josh that attacked her on the Beaver Pond Trail. Was it Harrison? The person *was* large. Karly shook her head to dislodge her fears and instead concentrated on the new life that awaited her with the man she loved.

CHAPTER FORTY-ONE

Blake stared in wonder at the back of the beautiful athletic woman in front of him, as her arms reached repeatedly and gracefully into the water. He felt like pinching himself to make sure all of this was real. He had loved her for so long, but until last night, never thought the two of them getting back together was a possibility.

Although he was certain of his strong feelings for her, he hadn't been sure where she stood. Given the long absence between them and the fact that their personalities often clashed, he didn't think a relationship with Karly stood a chance.

But now, thanks to God's incredible timing, bringing him and Karly back together again after all these years, and the advice of his good friend, Henry, they were getting married. Henry had encouraged him to be a man, face his feelings, and commit the whole situation to prayer. And look where that had led. A huge smile came to his face as he imagined the reaction of his friend when he broke the exciting news to him.

It was getting late, but Blake figured that, barring any wrong turns or mishaps, they would arrive back at the starting point before dark. As far as he knew, they were probably bringing up the rear, but that was okay with him. It was funny how one's priorities in life could change so quickly. They'd have to confess they'd cheated anyway. Blake shook his head and chuckled. Life with Karly would be spicy ... to say the least. Of course, he already knew that about her and it only endeared her to him more.

As the pair crossed Buckle Bay and approached another portage, a large ruckus in the bush ahead of them caused him to stop paddling. He allowed his paddle to drift silently at his side through the water, as did Karly. "Don't get out Karly, if it's a bear, we may just do a quick reverse and wait him out."

No sooner had those words left his mouth, when a scratched and bleeding man stumbled towards them. Blake blinked. Was that who he thought it was?

"Harrison?" Karly seemed as puzzled as he was.

Harrison stumbled over a rock and collapsed onto the shoreline, lying in the fetal position.

What was going on? Blake steered the canoe ashore. When it scraped against the rocky shoreline and came to a halt, they quickly climbed out. Karly started toward her supervisor, but Blake touched her arm to stop her. "Let me deal with this. Something isn't right."

Karly nodded and stayed behind him.

"Harrison, are you okay?" Blake knelt beside the man, who was drawing circles in the sand with his pointer finger. "Where's Heather?"

"Don't know. And don't care." Harrison snickered, then he snorted like a pig.

Blake glanced back at Karly, bemused by the strange sounds emitting from her supervisor.

Karly's eyes were wide.

Harrison's arms began flailing at an unknown assailant. "Get away." he yelled.

"What's wrong with him?" Karly asked. "Is he hallucinating? I've never seen him act like that."

"Judging by his awkward, clumsy mannerisms and slurred speech, I'd wager a guess that he's on drugs or he's drunk."

"That's not like Harrison. He's a straight-shooting kind of guy. I've never known him to abuse drugs or alcohol."

"People do desperate things sometimes, Karly. Maybe he's upset about us. You said he admitted that he was in love with you. This could be his way of coping." Blake sat back on his haunches and studied the man. "We did humiliate him last night with the skunk prank. We should apologize for that, once he's coherent enough to understand. Maybe our stunt was the proverbial straw that broke the camel's back."

"But Harrison wouldn't do this. Not in the middle of a race. He's too competitive. Besides, he organized this whole event. He'd love to win it. No, that doesn't make sense."

"Could someone have drugged him, so he wouldn't have a chance of winning?" Blake kept a close eye on Harrison, who had calmed down and was studying a tall weed.

"I suppose that's a possibility. And where's Heather? She could be stumbling out there in a stoned stupor as well." Karly grabbed his shoulder and he felt the tension in her body. "What if someone drugged Harrison to get to Heather? Maybe the murderer has struck again."

Blake considered her words briefly, then turned back to Harrison "Where is Heather?"

Bloodshot eyes stared back at him. Unexpectedly, Harrison wretched, hurling the contents of his stomach towards them.

Blake jumped back quickly to get out of the way. For some odd reason, Karly reached for Harrison's cap that had fallen into the sand, and held it under his mouth, like a vomit basin.

When the vomiting episode had stopped, Blake stepped to her side and stared incredulously at her hand. "Why did you catch his vomit in his hat? Why not just let it hit the dirt?"

Karly's shoulders lifted. "It seemed like the right thing to do at the time." She held the cap at arm's length away from her and pinched her nose shut with two fingers.

Blake thought he'd be sick from the stench, but was totally amused at Karly's actions. "Maybe you should have gone into nursing. Now what are you going to do with that?"

Karly stared at the overflowing, leaking canvas container for a split second then hurried toward the shoreline and dumped its putrid-smelling contents into the water. She ran his cap through the water, tossed it on shore, and rinsed her hands in the lake.

Blake re-directed his attention to their patient who had either fallen asleep or passed out. "I don't think he's going to be much help now. I hope Heather is okay."

"I have an uneasy feeling in my gut. I think I should have a look around for her."

Blake shook his head. "No. I don't want you wandering out there alone in the bush, especially if your hunch is right and Heather is in danger. You could be next."

"Then come with me."

Blake looked down at Harrison who was now snoring. "I don't know if I should leave him alone in the state he's in. What if he wanders toward the lake and drowns?"

A flash of red caught his eye, and Blake leaned in closer. A large scratch dripped a trail of blood down Harrison's arm. "He's been injured."

Karly retrieved her backpack and pulled out a first-aid kit. Removing some antiseptic and a bandage, she cleaned the gash and applied the adhesive strip.

"You stay with Harrison. I won't go far. I promise."

"No, Karly. Don't go!" Blake jumped up and grabbed her hands.

"Then I'll stay, and you go." No sooner had the words left her mouth when Harrison let out a terrifying yell and his hands flew up to shield his face.

"They're after me, help!"

Karly's face was pinched and worried. Obviously, she was upset.

"I don't feel comfortable leaving you with that man, considering his wild outbursts. You could get hurt." Blake shook his head.

"What if I just went a few hundred yards into the woods and looked around? I'll stay close enough that you could hear me if I yelled. Maybe Heather is injured and needs our help."

Blake paced the shoreline and raked a hand through his hair. "Fine. If you promise to be back in fifteen minutes."

"That's a deal." She placed a kiss on his cheek and disappeared into the bush, leaving Blake staring at a man who was now humming some nonsensical, drug-induced ditty.

CHAPTER FORTY-TWO

Ten minutes had already passed and there was no sign of anyone or anything. Even the wildlife seemed to be in hiding. Repeated calls to Heather had gone unanswered. Karly thought of her promise to Blake. Should she turn back? Just one more minute.

Karly rounded a bend in the narrow, overgrown path; a large rock wall loomed ahead of her on the left. Maybe, if she could climb up, she'd be able to get a better view. After that, she'd head back. Grabbing onto sections of jagged rock, branches of small saplings and protruding roots, she made her way to the top.

A quick scan of the horizon revealed her high elevation. Unbeknownst to her, the trail she'd been following had gently wound upwards. About thirty feet below lay a picturesque gorge with white water flowing rapidly across jagged rock. The wild but serene beauty of this wilderness never ceased to thrill her.

Cupping her hands together, she yelled Heather's name again. Her voice returned to her in an eerie echo, bouncing off a high rock wall on the other side of the gorge.

The hairs on the back of her neck prickled. Sensing a presence behind her, she whirled.

There stood Heather, a peculiar look on her face.

Karly blew out a breath. "You scared the life out of me. I've been looking for you. Something's wrong with Harrison. He appears to be drugged. Do you know anything about that? I thought you might be in trouble, so I came looking for you."

"Harrison will survive. You, however, are more of a concern to me." Heather fixed a cold stare on her.

"Me?" Karly blinked as a chill descended over her.

Heather took a step closer, her eyes dark and menacing. "You just made my job a whole lot easier."

Karly's breath caught in her throat. Made her job easier? What job? What was she talking about?

"Don't look so bewildered. You've been a thorn in my side since the first day you arrived at No Trace."

"I have no idea what you're talking about." Karly's heart pounded in her chest and she broke out in a cold sweat.

"Really." Heather grabbed her arm in a vise-like grip, triggering a flashback of her attempted abduction on the Beaver Pond Trail.

"It was you who attacked me on the trail." Karly struggled to get free.

"Very good. Now you're getting it."

Karly grimaced at the incredibly painful pressure on her arm. Harrison had been correct when he mentioned that Heather was much stronger than she appeared. Her efforts to squirm from the other woman's grip were futile. Panicked, she looked behind her and froze at the sight of the fast-moving river below. Another step or two back and she'd fall to her death on the jagged rocks, or drown in the swift current.

"What do you want with me?"

"I want you—rather, I *need* you—out of the picture. With you around, he won't even look at me."

"Who won't look at you?"

"Who do you think? Now you're really showing your blonde roots." A maniacal chuckle escaped her lips. "Do I have to spell it out for you? You're just as stupid as the others."

"Others?"

A disturbing thought barged into Karly's mind—an idea so inconceivable it made her stomach swirl. "You killed Madison, didn't you?" Karly pressed a hand to her mouth.

Heather smiled.

"But we all thought Josh ..."

Heather's grip tightened. "That was the most amazing thing. At first, I thought I'd been caught when that weird stalker, Josh, happened to be hiding in the bush and saw me shove Madison off the cliff. I chased him until I lost him. Thankfully, it all worked out, since he couldn't remember a thing afterwards. I guess the events were just too traumatic for him. Then for some odd reason, he attacked you. In his confused mind, he must have returned to the scene of the crime, and found you there instead of me. I believe he thought that you were Madison's murderer. Poor crazy Josh; he really must have been in love with Madison."

Karly's mind whirled. So, Blake was right on two accounts. Josh didn't murder Madison, and he had been in love with her colourful roommate after all.

"But everyone thought Madison left the Cedar Canoe with a man that night."

"Nope. That was me. Short hair, wearing a ball cap and having a large build does have its advantages in a case like this." Heather cackled like a lunatic. Had the woman lost her mind completely? And just how in the world, did she lure Madison to the top of the Lookout Trail that night. Her shoulders slumped. I guess it really doesn't matter now.

"And I sure wish Josh had been successful in his attempt on your life. It would have saved me the bother. Between Blake and Harrison, you are a hard chick to get alone."

"You killed Jessica Wakely too, didn't you?" Karly's mind raced. How would she get away from this dangerous killer? The disturbed woman still held her in a grip that showed no signs of weakening.

Heather's silence said it all.

"Why?"

"Those types of women are nothing but trouble. I can't stand them around my man. First it was Jessica. She swore up and down that she didn't have feelings for Harrison, but I knew she did. What kind of woman two-times her boyfriend? She didn't deserve Harrison. Whether he knew it or not, he was better off without her."

"You're in love with Harrison?"

"Bingo!" Heather snarled. "Took you long enough."

"But you allowed Harrison to suffer under suspicion of murder all these years."

"Yeah, well, I felt bad about that, but at least it kept the focus off me, so I was free to be near him."

"Why kill Madison? She wasn't interested in Harrison."

A troubled expression crossed her co-worker's face. "I saw how she acted around him. Those big seductive eyes and the way she dressed. Not to mention the way she danced with him."

Karly's mouth went completely dry. Madison had thought of Harrison as a father figure. And her style in clothing was eccentric but never inappropriate. This woman was clearly mentally ill.

"I'm puzzled about something. Why not Raven?"

Heather lifted a shoulder. "I can show mercy sometimes. Besides, Harrison gave her the old heave-ho and broke off his engagement. She wasn't a threat anymore."

Karly's mind tumbled in confusion. Raven wasn't a threat, but Madison was? She didn't get it. She shook her head. The only thing she could focus on right now was getting away from this madwoman. "Heather, I'm in love with Blake." Karly forced herself to speak calmly, hoping reason would work with the woman. "We were engaged last night and are planning on getting married soon. I won't come between you and Harrison."

"Ha!" She snorted. "I don't believe you. Where's the ring?"

"I don't have one yet; the engagement was a spur-of-the-moment thing. But if you come back with me to talk to Blake, he'll confirm it for you."

"Nice try." Heather sneered. "Besides, even if it's true, as long as you're around Harrison will never look at me." Heather's grip tightened. "I'm so sick of hearing him rave about you. Karly this and Karly that. It makes me want to puke. We were getting close until you arrived and messed up everything. You're too much of a distraction. All distractions must be eliminated."

Karly inhaled sharply. The more she tried to wrestle her arm free, the tighter Heather clamped. If only she could think of a way to distract her. *Keep her talking.* "So, let me get this straight. You drugged Harrison? Why?"

"Because Harrison was rambling on about you again—something about hurting your feelings and wanting to make things right—and I just couldn't take it any longer. I have no idea what he was talking about, but I'd had enough. We both knew you were right behind us, since your voices carried over the water. I came prepared to deal with you; I was hoping for a chance to get you alone and bingo!" Heather's laugh was maniacal. "I drugged his power drink. He couldn't know what my plans were, so he had no idea what hit him. When he became almost incoherent, I steered him in the direction of the trail. I knew if you guys found him, you'd come searching for me, thinking something bad had happened to me. Since you're both of such *noble* character." Heather's chuckle was coarse and deep, almost demonic.

Karly shivered. This was one sick woman.

Heather rambled on. "I was sure Blake wouldn't let you search for me alone. I figured I'd have to kill both of you." Heather let go of her arm, finally, and produced a gun from the waistband of her jeans. "But I was up to the challenge, with help from my little friend here." Heather pointed the weapon at her.

Karly flinched and froze to the spot.

"So, here we are. And now I have the one I wanted in the first place. How convenient of Blake. I may not even have to kill that handsome pilot after all," Heather taunted.

Karly gulped back her fear. "Please, Heather, listen to me. You don't have to do this. Besides, once they find my body," a sickening shudder galloped through her, "they'll put two and two together. You'll spend the rest of your life in prison. How will that work into your plans with Harrison?"

"That's where you're wrong. They'll never connect me to your death. They'll assume it was an accident. I don't plan on shooting you. You're just going to have an unfortunate tumble over the edge of the cliff."

"The truth has a way of coming out. You'll never get away with it. Josh is no longer alive to blame. You may have gotten away with

Jessica's death, but I highly doubt the authorities will fail to connect the pieces. And if I don't come back, Blake will come looking for me."

"Do you think I'm worried?" Heather cackled again and waved the gun in the air high above her head.

Over the top of a fir tree behind her attacker, a large shape appeared. Karly's eyes widened, and Heather turned around to look.

A massive white pelican was joined by about a dozen others flanking his sides and rear. With wing spans of almost ten feet apiece, the approaching flock, flying only a few feet above their heads, was intimidating and very unexpected. And the distraction, was just what Karly needed. As Heather stared upward, Karly shoved her mentally unstable attacker with everything she had. Heather stumbled, and the gun fell from her hand, clanging onto the rock. Karly kicked at it, sending it over the edge, into the gorge below.

"You witch," Heather screamed. She spun away from the cliff leading down to the deep gorge, but off-balance now, teetered on the side of the rock that dropped off several feet into bushes. Arms wind-milling, she disappeared over the edge.

Heart pounding wildly against her ribcage, Karly chanced a look past the edge of the rock. Heather had landed six feet below her, and she was trying to disentangle herself from the brambles.

Run Karly. Now!

Karly made a bee-line down the steep rock face. Skidding and slipping, she let out an anguished cry as her backside landed on something sharp and painful. But raw fear fueled her will to survive and propelled her to her feet and onward, despite waves of discomfort throbbing across her bottom.

With every step, a bolt of fiery pain seared her backside. What had she done to herself in her frantic attempt to escape? Not that it mattered. It was better than the alternative—her body smashed to death on rocks in the gorge.

Karly's mind could barely comprehend what had just happened. Had God come to her rescue once again? The appearance of that low-flying flock was nothing short of miraculous.

She stumbled into the clearing and fell, exhausted, into the welcoming arms of Blake. Deep lines creased his face as he held her out at arms' length. "There you are. I was starting to get worried. You're shaking. What's wrong?"

Karly gasped for breath. "Heather is Jessica and Madison's murderer. And she just tried to kill me."

CHAPTER FORTY-THREE

"What?" Blake gripped her shoulders. "Unbelievable. And she just tried to kill you?" He pulled her against him and buried his face in her hair. "I knew I shouldn't have let you go out there alone. I'm so thankful you're okay. But I don't understand."

"She's in love with Harrison, but the most amazing thing happened. If it wasn't for those white pelicans ..." Karly threw a panicked glance behind her. "She might still be after me. She didn't fall far. And she's tough. And frightening."

Blake scanned the bush and led her away from the trail's opening. Blake pushed her back a bit and stared into her bulging fear-filled eyes. Was she in shock? Her ramblings didn't make any sense. What did white pelicans have to do with anything? Her body trembled as his hand searched through her hair for bumps. "Did you hit your head?"

"No. I know without a doubt that God sent those pelicans at exactly the right time."

Worry charged through Blake. Karly wasn't making any sense. What sort of traumatic experience had she just gone through? He should have never let her go out there alone. She *must* have hit her head. That might explain the crazy nonsense about pelicans. "Are you sure you're not injured?"

Karly looked up at him sheepishly. "I did have a fall."

"I knew it." He felt her head again.

"Not my head. My bottom. And keep your hands to yourself."

Blake's lips twitched. This was the Karly he knew. Blake put his hands on her shoulders and gently turned her around. He inhaled sharply. "No wonder you're hurting."

"What do you mean?"

"This trauma may require ... some sort of surgery."

"What are you talking about?"

"There's a small branch protruding from your ... backside." Blake cleared his throat.

"What? This is no time for jokes."

"I'm not joking."

Karly reached a hand back and her expression appeared flash-frozen to her face. "That can't stay there." A swift motion of her hand and a bloody stub of a branch sailed through the air into the bush.

"What did you just do?" Blake's eyes widened.

"I'm fine, I just removed the ...." Karly's eyes rolled back into her head as the colour drained from her face. Blake caught her just in time. She slumped lifelessly in his arms as he carried her to a sandy spot on the beach only a few feet from Harrison, and laid her gently on her side.

When he noticed a growing splotch of red on her tan shorts, he ran for Karly's backpack and searched for her first-aid kit. Then he cut a large section of gauze and applied pressure on the wound.

Blake shook his head. He could hardly comprehend the events that had unfolded. Heather was a murderer? He'd never in a million years have thought it was her. And she had just attempted to take the life of the woman he loved. He was so thankful that somehow Karly had gotten away, although her crazy account of pelicans had him baffled.

Blake looked toward the trail and tensed. Darkness was falling, and Heather still lurked out there. There was no way they would make it back to the campground now. Would they survive the night? He checked his cell for a signal to place an emergency call for help. Nothing. They needed to be prepared just in case she tried to attack again. Blake's eyes searched the area. He spotted a three-foot section of branch that could possibly work as a weapon. And he did have a utility knife in his backpack. As soon as he could get the bleeding to stop, he'd get his weapons ready.

He looked at Harrison who had fallen asleep shortly after Karly left, and another horrifying thought barged into his brain. Could Harrison be her accomplice? If he was, the odds of them escaping were narrowing.

Thankfully, Karly began to stir. After all she'd been through, he'd have to watch her for signs of shock. Traumatic events such as those she had experienced could do that to a person. He watched her open her oversized azure eyes and blink a few times. "Why is your hand on my butt?"

"Lie still, Karly. I'm trying to get the bleeding to stop."

"You're what?" Her voice carried alarm as she propped herself up on one elbow and stared back at him.

"Don't you remember what happened? You yanked out that stick, fainted, and started to bleed pretty badly."

Karly dropped back to the sand. "It's all coming back to me now. And it's a tad humiliating."

Blake would have laughed had the circumstance not been so grave.

Harrison bolted upright and stared at Blake's hand. He tilted his head. "Why are you holding Karly's backside? Is that blood I see?"

"Yes, it's blood. Karly had an injury."

Harrison scrambled to his feet, made a mad dash toward the water, and bent over with the dry heaves. Blake scratched his head. Could this day get any more bizarre?

Karly reached behind her and snatched the gauze from his hand. "I'll take over from here."

"What were you thinking, pulling that stick out?" Blake cocked one eyebrow.

"It couldn't stay there now, could it? How would I ever sit in the canoe to get back?"

"Good point. Are you in any pain?"

"Just the pain of humiliation."

"It's only a buttock, Karly. I was more concerned about stopping the bleeding. You would have done the same for me if the situation were reversed."

Blake pressed his fingers to her wrist.

"What are you doing?"

"Checking for signs of shock." Blake let out a breath. "Your pulse is strong and steady."

"Of course, it is. Heather will not get the better of me." Karly tried to get up.

Blake placed a hand on her shoulder and smiled. "I admire your determination, but at least take it easy until the bleeding stops fully."

They both turned toward the lake at the sound of splashing. Harrison cupped his hands and threw water on his face. Then he lumbered toward them.

"Can anyone explain what happened to me? I feel as though I'm waking up from a horrendous nightmare."

"You are. You'd better sit back down for a moment, it only gets worse. We have lots to tell you and you're not going to like what you're about to hear. But first, will you grab that large stick and my backpack and bring it over here?" Blake waved a hand toward both objects. Although a bit of colour was returning to Karly's face, he didn't feel comfortable leaving her side, especially with a murderer nearby.

A pale-looking Harrison retrieved the items and plunked onto the sand beside them.

Blake reached in his backpack and retrieved his knife. "While we fill you in on all that's happened, it's imperative you watch the bush for Heather. Our lives could depend on it." He pointed at the stick. "That's your weapon, Harrison." Blake tenderly rubbed Karly's arm, worried about rehashing the horrifying events in his fiancée's mind. "Do you know what type of weapons Heather has on her?"

Karly shuddered. "I kicked her gun over the edge of the gorge, but I really don't know what else she has."

Clearly confused, Harrison stared at the two of them. "I don't understand what's going on."

Blake squeezed Karly's shoulder. "Go ahead. Tell us both what happened."

As Karly relayed the story, Blake watched Harrison's reactions. The man looked as shocked as he and Karly were. Nope, he was not in on Heather's murderous plot. One thing he'd come to realize about Harrison—you could read him like a book. Blake could barely believe the events were real himself. When Karly got to the part about the pelicans Blake was stunned.

"You were serious? A flock of pelicans rescued you from Heather?" Blake's jaw dropped open. "I thought your ramblings were shock-induced due to stress."

"As unreal as it sounds, it's true. At the very least, they appeared exactly when I needed to get away." Karly's body trembled. She wrapped her arms around herself. "I'm cold."

When her teeth began to chatter, Blake became concerned. Was Karly going into shock? The temperature had dropped after the thunderstorms last night. Blake hurried toward his sleeping bag and threw it over Karly, tucking it tightly around her as she continued to apply pressure to her wound.

"Are you sure about all of this? Heather? I would never in a million years have pegged her as a murderer. She killed Jessica? And Madison?" Harrison looked as if he'd been slapped in the face. He ran a shaking hand through his dishevelled hair. "And she drugged me? She's so shy and soft-spoken, almost introverted most of the time; she even blushes when I pay her a compliment."

Karly shot a worried look at the woods. "It's true though. Every word. She told me herself."

Harrison pressed both hands on the sides of his head. "Oh man, I've got the worst headache. But, I'm starting to remember some things. We'd taken a major wrong turn today and gotten ourselves lost—which should be impossible considering both of us know this area very well. Still, it happened. That's how we ended up trailing badly. I figured you guys had probably already won the race. I had no idea you were even behind us until when we heard voices. Even though you were nearby, and we were about to put our canoe in Paul Lake, Heather insisted that we take another break. She even brought me a Gatorade. That was probably where she put the drugs, so she could carry out her murderous plan."

"Those were a lot of details that would have had to play into her hand for this all to work. And amazingly, it almost did." Blake swallowed the lump that had lodged in his throat.

"Heather did admit that she hadn't expected the opportunity to fall into her lap. That we'd made her job easy for her." Karly's voice quivered.

Harrison looked at Karly, his expression tender. "I'm so sorry, Karly. I wish I'd known. Maybe we could have saved Madison, at least." He pushed to his feet and clenched his fists. "Heather forced me to live under suspicion of murder all these years. How could she have done that to me?"

Karly lifted a hand. "She told me she felt badly about that, but it kept the focus off her. And she could stay close to you."

The coos of a mourning dove reached their ears from somewhere nearby. Blake shuddered. Was that a harbinger of things to come? The same uneasy feeling that had come over him the day he observed the gutted buck at Henry's village, hovered over him now, inciting a chill deep in his bones. Perhaps it was the biting cold, strong wind that had suddenly whipped up along with the temperature drop. Or was it the fact that a killer lurked somewhere in the wilderness, possibly observing them even now?

"It's almost dark. There's no way it's safe to go wandering around out there in the wilderness now. And the waterways will be dangerously choppy. Let's do what we can to prepare ourselves in case Heather is still bent on murder." Blake pulled out his cell phone and tried to place a call. Again, no bars.

Having a different service provider, Harrison tried his phone. Also, nothing. He reached into his pocket and pulled out a small but high-powered flashlight and scanned the bush. "I'll keep watch. You take care of Karly."

Harrison ambled along the shoreline, in a close radius, and gathered kindling. "A fire may not be the wisest move, but we need to keep Karly warm. Besides, Heather knows where we are. I doubt she'll attempt anything with two strong men alert and watching, but I'd suggest that at the crack of dawn, we're out of here."

"Excuse me," Karly piped up. "And a strong woman."

Blake forced a smile. "Yes, Karly, you are a force to be reckoned with." He left it at that, but couldn't help worrying that the woman he loved with all his heart could still be deeply affected by the traumatic events she had just experienced, especially since she had suffered the loss of her good friend recently. Strong or not, he'd watch her very closely.

"Will you get me a couple of large bandages from my first aid kit, Blake? The bleeding has stopped."

A moment later Blake held them out, just beyond her reach. "How will you manage to apply these yourself?"

Karly pulled her bottom lip between her teeth. "Oh, I hadn't thought of that." She wiggled her fingers toward him. "I'll manage somehow. You just run along now and help Harrison collect firewood." Karly waved a hand.

Blake smirked before handing them to her. "As you wish, my lady."

As the fire Harrison made crackled, popped, and lit up the area, Blake scanned the bush, alert for Heather's approach. With high winds causing the leaves to rustle and trees to groan, his job was difficult.

"Blake?" Karly whispered. "I'm afraid. Don't leave me."

Blake wrapped his sleeping bag around himself, snuggled beside her and pulled her close. "Don't worry, sweetie. I'm not leaving your side. Close your eyes and get some rest."

Karly yawned. Blake stroked her hair until he could no longer see the firelight flickering in her irises.

Blake cast a glance at Harrison who was huddled near the fire for warmth, wearing only his T-shirt and jeans. "You must be cold. Where are your supplies?"

"Back with our canoe, which is sitting on the shore of Paul Lake. We'd made it that far when ... well ... you know the rest." Their eyes met, and Harrison's shoulders drooped. *He knows something has changed between me and Karly.* They'd have to deal with that later. Now was not the time to enlighten him about their engagement.

All of them surviving the night took top priority.

Blake rested his cheek on the top of Karly's head and prayed like he'd never prayed before. *Please God, keep us all safe and allow Heather to be apprehended before she can hurt anybody else.*

CHAPTER FORTY-FOUR

Blake's eyes shot open at the snapping of a twig. He bolted upright in his sleeping bag and stared at the empty bedroll beside him. Where was Karly? He whipped back his bag and jumped to his feet. In fact, where was Harrison?

When the bushes rustled behind him, his heart slammed against his rib cage. He whirled and let out a breath as Karly limped toward him.

"Where were you? I was worried."

"I'm fine. I needed a little privacy."

"Oh. Where's Harrison?"

Karly shrugged. "I haven't seen him."

Blake raked a hand through his hair and stared at the cold campfire. Harrison hadn't added fuel in a few hours. Perhaps he'd fallen asleep and now needed some morning privacy too. He'd give the man a few minutes before he became concerned.

"We made it through the night. God kept us safe." Karly walked into his open arms.

Blake pulled her close and stroked her hair. "Yes, He did. But now, I really think we need to get out of here. Something doesn't feel right. Let's pack up quickly and canoe out. Now that it's daylight and the wind's died down, it's probably safer to find an alternate route back by water, than to traipse through the bush with a killer on the loose."

"True. But what do we do about Harrison?" Karly rolled up her bag.

Blake jammed his sleeping bag under his arm. "He can join us in the canoe." *If he returns.* Blake kept that thought to himself. No sense worrying Karly further when he wasn't even sure what was going on.

"Uh, Blake?"

"Yes?"

"Our canoe is gone."

Blake turned from stuffing his sleeping bag in the case and stared at the empty shoreline of Buckle Bay. His stomach dropped.

No Harrison. And no canoe.

Had Harrison done the unthinkable? Did he run away and leave them to deal with a mentally unstable woman? What other explanation could there be? What a coward.

"Maybe somehow it came loose in the wind last night." Blake pulled the ties closed, securing his sleeping bag inside. Then he stepped to the water's edge and grabbed her hand. "Let's make a quick search and see if we can spot it."

The pair walked a few minutes in each direction before giving up. Blake squeezed his jaw until his face turned white. Should they take a chance on facing Heather in the bush? All kinds of things could go wrong if they did, but sitting here waiting for something to happen wasn't going to solve anything either. Worry charged through Blake's mind.

As though she could sense it, Karly squeezed his hand tightly and searched his eyes. "It'll all be okay. I've been praying, and I trust that God is listening. He's shown himself faithful to me in such a personal way over the last few weeks. Deep inside, I know he is with us."

Blake's eyes blurred, but he willed his emotions to stay under control. The newfound faith of his fiancée overwhelmed him. Of course, God was with them. Hope and peace spread through his chest as he pulled her close. She snuggled into the crook of his neck. "Thank you, Karly. I needed to hear that. You're right. God is with us. Let's go."

As they stepped onto the trail. Karly carried his knife and he the heavy branch. Just in case. "You go a few steps ahead, so I can watch you while I scan the bush. I don't want you behind me."

Karly stopped when they rounded a bend in the trail and a large rock loomed on their left.

"What's wrong?" Blake whispered in her ear.

"This is the spot where Heather tried to kill me. She fell into the bush right about there." Karly pointed, her hand shaking.

Blake strode over to the rock and stepped into the dense undergrowth. Crushed vegetation verified exactly where Heather had landed. He trudged from the bush, pushing back thorny branches. "I can see where she fell. She's not there now, so let's be careful."

Karly nodded, her eyes wide and fearful.

"Stay by my side for a little while. The path seems wider here."

"You won't get any argument from me."

The two of them saw it at the same time. The sneaker-clad foot protruding from the bush onto the trail. Beside him, Karly sucked in a breath. For a split second they both froze in their tracks.

"That's Harrison." Karly clapped a hand over her mouth. "I recognize his running shoe."

"You keep watch." Blake hurried to Harrison's prone body, which lay in a crimson puddle. He dropped to his knees and searched for a pulse. "He's alive, Karly. I need your first aid kit," Blake said urgently.

Karly slid her bag from her shoulders and produced the kit. Blake whipped off his sweatshirt, balled it up, and applied pressure. Harrison groaned before his eyes slowly opened.

"Thank God." Blake blew out a breath. "Don't move, Harrison. It appears you've been stabbed. Can you tell us what happened?"

"Heather attacked me." His voice came out in a whisper. "When I realized the canoe was missing, I knew she was nearby and had sabotaged our way of escape. I went searching for her at the crack of dawn. I thought I could reason with her." He sucked in a ragged breath. "But she went ballistic when I told her that I didn't have romantic feelings for her. She pulled out a knife and tried to attack me. We wrestled, and I tripped backward over a fallen tree branch. That's when she stabbed me. I got up and tried to give chase but, well, I guess I didn't get very far. She's out there somewhere. And very dangerous. I'm sorry. I may have made things worse."

Harrison tried to get up, but Blake pressed a hand to his chest to force him back down. "You're not going anywhere until we get this bleeding under control. Blake looked up at Karly. "I need something to act as a large pressurized bandage. Any suggestions?"

Karly nodded. "I'll be right back."

After a quick dash into the bush, she returned and held up a wide white piece of elastic-looking fabric. "If you can somehow manage to slide this over Harrison's head and across his chest, it'll act like a tourniquet around his waist."

Blake accepted the proffered piece of clothing. "I have no idea what this is, but it might just work."

"It's a tube top."

He shrugged. "I don't care what it is, as long as it does the job."

In a couple of minutes, after much juggling, the fabric sat snuggly around a thick pile of gauze on Harrison's side.

"How does that feel?" Blake asked.

"I can barely breathe. Is this really necessary?"

"Unless you'd rather bleed out, I'd advise you to keep it on."

Blake tied his sweatshirt around Harrison's waist for extra measure.

Karly reached in her bag and produced a small container of pain relievers and a bottle of water. "Here, Harrison, swallow two of these. They should help with pain."

Karly lifted Harrison's head and helped him swallow.

Blake checked his cell again. No bars. "Where do we go from here? We can't make an emergency call to get you help. I think we've got the bleeding stopped for now. Can you make it back to the campground?"

Harrison winced as he turned slightly onto his good side. "I'll be fine. Let's go."

Blake grabbed one arm and Karly the other and they helped Harrison to his feet. He wobbled a little, but they held onto him tightly. "Steady as she goes," Blake encouraged him.

Harrison took several deep breaths. "If only I could have talked sense into Heather. She was strong, and I tripped and ..."

Blake clasped his shoulder. "Don't blame yourself. What you did was brave. Let's just all keep alert."

After a short walk through the bush, they reached Paul Lake.

"That's our canoe." Harrison pointed. "We had gotten this far yesterday, when Heather insisted we take a break." Harrison grabbed his side and stared at his bloody hand. "And that could only mean one thing. Heather is still here somewhere."

Blake studied Harrison. Given the amount of blood soaking through his sweatshirt, he wouldn't make it to the next portage.

"Harrison, I'm afraid all the jostling from that walk started up the bleeding again. I need you to lie back down, so I can take care of that."

As Blake applied pressure, he kept an eye on Karly who was in protective mode, clutching the large branch in her hand and pacing the shoreline as she scanned the bush for any signs of Heather. As much as he loved her bravery, which shocked him after all she had been through yesterday, he wished she wouldn't stray quite as far as she was. As if she had read his mind, she turned, and her gaze landed on him. He motioned her to return with a flick of his hand and she complied.

"I could really use a drink of water." Harrison licked his lips.

Blake checked his wound. "I think it's finally stopped again. Stay still a few more minutes." He scrambled to his feet, all the while keeping an eye on Karly. "Just going to rinse my hands in the lake and I'll get you that water, Harrison. Hang tight."

"I'm not going anywhere."

Blake stooped down and swished his hands back and forth through the water. He straightened up, shaking lake water free from his hands. He reached for his backpack and pulled out the metal water canteen full of water, thankful that he had packed extra.

He looked toward Karly again and a bolt of fear knifed him in the chest.

"Karly! Behind you!"

Heather charged from the bush, only a few feet behind Karly, knife raised in mid-air.

Karly turned and swung the heavy limb, but only managed a glancing blow to her arm. Heather cursed loudly and continued to advance towards his fiancée. Blake swallowed the terror running rampant through his entire body. Before he could even think rationally, he let loose with the canteen that was in his hand. It sailed through the air and hit Heather smack on the forehead.

While she wobbled unsteadily, Karly took another swing at her with the limb. This time she didn't miss. Heather swayed for the last time, landed on her side on the sand, and didn't move.

Pounding, pumping, sputtering and spitting, his heart felt like it would explode from his chest. Blake ran toward the woman he loved as fast as he ever had his entire life, and pulled her into his arms. "It's over now, honey. It's finally all over."

Despite his weakened state, Harrison stumbled towards them, bent over, holding his side. "You took her out with a canteen of water?" He picked up the dented metal container. "Look at that goose-egg on her forehead." He gaped at Karly. "And you nailed her with that heavy limb. Remind me to never get on either of your bad sides."

"While she's unconscious, I think we'd better bind her wrists and ankles so she's no further threat." Blake let go of Karly, reluctantly. "You lie down, Harrison, or you'll get that wound bleeding again. Karly and I will handle things."

While Harrison complied, Blake retrieved some rope from his backpack and Karly helped him bind Heather's hands and feet.

"Hello there. What's going on? Is everyone okay?"

Blake turned to see racing contestants Danny and Marcus approaching in their canoe.

"Man, are we happy to see you guys. No, everything is not okay." Blake hurried to the shoreline and explained the entire situation to the men as quickly and briefly as possible. "So, as you can see, we're thrilled to get your help. How did you know to come looking for us?"

"When neither of your teams returned last night, we had a suspicion something was wrong. Knowing that all of you are tough contenders, we suspected a problem. Never in a million years would we have guessed this scenario, though."

"Wise thinking. Thanks for coming. If you could take Heather back in your canoe, we'll take Harrison.

Soon both teams were on the water with Danny, Marcus, and a still-unconscious Heather in the lead canoe, while Harrison, Blake, and Karly brought up the rear in Harrison's canoe.

A few hours later, both groups arrived at the main campground building. About an hour out, Blake had been able to raise a signal on his cell phone and alert the authorities, so the Aspen Ridge police were waiting on the shore, along with two ambulances.

As a pale and shaking Harrison was placed onto a stretcher and loaded into the back of the ambulance, Karly rested a hand on his arm. "I'll say a prayer for you."

"Me too." Blake nodded.

"Thanks. I can use some prayer. But I have to say, I feel as though the weight of the world has been lifted off my chest since no one will suspect me of murder now." Harrison's voice cracked, then his eyelids drifted shut.

"Sorry, I'm going to need you to step back." The paramedic reached for the door. "He's lost a lot of blood."

As they watched the ambulance speed away, Blake reached for Karly's hand. "Come on, honey, it's been a tough day. Let's get you to the hospital to get that wound of yours tended to as well."

"I'm fine. I'll make a doctor's appointment in the morning."

"Are you sure?"

"Yes. I really don't even want to be in the same building as her right now." Karly inclined her head toward the second ambulance as it drove off, carrying Heather, who had come around just as they were loading her inside.

"I don't blame you; she's an extremely troubled woman." Blake squeezed her hand. "Let's just pray justice will be served."

CHAPTER FORTY-FIVE

Blake was not looking forward to dealing with her, but it had to be done. He drove to the diner and trudged inside. He stopped at the counter and was about to ask another server if Raven was working today, when he saw her approach.

"Hey there, stranger, I haven't seen you in a while. Your usual booth?"

"I'm not here to eat."

"You seem so serious, silly bear. What's wrong?"

Blake's stomach felt as though a cement block sat in it. And that awful nickname didn't help.

"Can I speak to you privately?" Blake asked.

Raven nodded and led him to a far back corner of the kitchen. "Moe's off today, and our part-time chef, Scott, won't mind if I bring you in here."

The delicious smells would normally tantalize his taste buds, but today his stomach swirled in protest.

"What is it?" Raven looked up at him with her indigo eyes.

"A lot has happened over the last few days. I suppose you've heard that Heather has been charged with the murders of Jessica Wakely and Madison Springfield."

Raven snorted. "It's plastered all over the news. I'd have to be a mole and live underground to have missed that."

Blake took a deep breath. "There's other important news I'd like to share with you. Karly and I became engaged over the weekend. We'll be married soon."

The menu dropped from her hand and her eyes narrowed into dark angry slits.

"I want to apologize if my actions over the last several weeks led you to believe that there was anything between us. You are very attractive Raven, but my heart has never belonged to anyone but Karly."

Her lips were clamped tightly shut and her arms folded across her chest. She didn't say a word.

"We would really like it if you came to the wedding."

"I don't think so." She pointed toward the back exit. "Get out."

CHAPTER FORTY-SIX

Karly pushed the hospital door open and found Harrison whamming his spoon rather forcefully in what appeared to be a bowl of orange Jell-O. Blake scooted in behind her.

"Digging for gold?" Blake quizzed.

"You don't know the half of it."

"We brought you that cup of coffee you were craving, along with a few of your favorite chocolate-glazed donuts." Karly set the coffee down on his tray and held up the bag, letting it sway in front of him.

"How did you know I was craving coffee and donuts?" One of Harrison's eyebrows rose.

"You don't remember? That's all you mumbled about the whole way back in the canoe." Karly smirked.

"I did? Must have been delirious from blood loss. And I hadn't eaten in several hours. So, it makes sense." Harrison reached for the bag. "No matter. You guys are an answer to prayer."

"You've been praying for coffee and donuts?" Blake tilted his head.

Harrison started to laugh, grabbed his side and inhaled sharply. "The food here leaves the taste buds very disappointed." Harrison pointed toward his Jell-O.

"How are you feeling?" Karly placed a hand on his arm.

"The good news is that the blade missed vital organs. I received two units of blood and I'm a little weak but nothing time won't fix."

"We want to thank you again, Harrison, for saving our lives." Karly added.

Harrison waved a hand through the air. "I didn't do anything. You guys are the courageous duo."

Blake stepped to her side. "You bravely went in search of Heather to try and stop her before she got to us."

Harrison's face grew solemn. "I had to. I couldn't let her continue her murderous rampage any longer." He raked a hand through his hair. "How could I have been so totally blind to her actions all these years? I had absolutely no idea that she was in love with me. Or would kill to try and have me."

Karly patted his hand. "You aren't responsible for other people's actions, Harrison. Only your own. And it's all over. All we can do now is hope and pray that justice will be served."

Blake cleared his throat and squeezed her hand. "Harrison, we have something we'd like to share with you. Karly and I got engaged the first night of the canoe race. With all that happened immediately after, being in a race for our lives, we just didn't have the opportunity to tell you."

Harrison looked down at his sheets for a minute and pulled at a loose thread. Then he looked up, extended a hand toward Blake and smiled—a smile that didn't quite reach his eyes.

"Congratulations. I'm happy for the both of you. I sensed something was different between you those two days in the bush that we fought for our lives." Harrison adjusted his blankets. "Thinking back to what you mentioned, Karly, about being responsible for our own actions, I want to apologize again." Harrison shuffled in his bed. "Blake, can you lower my bed a little? Sitting up in this position is pulling on my stitches." Harrison pointed toward the button at the foot of the bed.

After Blake complied, Harrison continued. "I kissed Karly against her wishes. I'd just gotten the news about Jessica's body being found and I wasn't thinking clearly, but still, that's no excuse. I hope both of you can forgive me. My actions were not only unprofessional, but also ungentlemanly."

"Karly told me all about the incident, and under the circumstances, you're forgiven, Harrison." Blake shifted from one foot to the other.

"It's in the past, Harrison. All is forgiven." Karly glanced at Blake, then she pulled her bottom lip between her teeth. "And we're both sorry for that skunk prank we pulled."

"Sure, you are." Harrison's lips twitched. "As far as pranks go, it was funny. I have to give you credit."

"One more thing, then we'll get out of here and let you get your rest. We want to invite you to our wedding—if you've recovered enough to come by then," Blake added.

Harrison's eyebrows rose as he reached into the bag and pulled out a donut. "I'd be honoured to attend; I'm sure I'll be out of the hospital by the date of your wedding. When is it?" He took a large bite.

Blake shot a look at Karly. "This Friday."

Harrison coughed, almost choking on his donut. He reached for his coffee and downed a large gulp. "What? In four days?"

Blake wrapped an arm around Karly's shoulders. "We've wasted the last three years; we don't want to waste another minute. The ceremony will be held under a full moon at Shadow Lake at midnight, followed by a very small reception hosted by Henry and his wife Shawna. We really hope you'll be able to attend."

"I'm supposed to be discharged Wednesday." Harrison popped another bite into his mouth.

Karly hugged him. "Hurry up and get well. You'd better be there or else." She wagged a finger at him.

"Or else what?" Wrinkle lines appeared on Harrison's forehead.

"Believe me, you don't want to be on the receiving end of Karly's wrath." Blake kissed her cheek. "And I mean that in the most loving way."

"Sure, you do." Karly gave him a playful shove.

CHAPTER FORTY-SEVEN

"I'm so thrilled that you and Kerrick came. And you brought baby Noah. He's so cute." Karly hugged her best friend. "I've missed you so much, Maya. Please forgive me for letting all this time pass without being in touch with you."

"Don't give it another thought. I'm so happy I can be here for your wedding. I remember the first day you met Blake. You were so mad at him when he checked us into Williwaw Lake Campground, especially when he ordered you to shut your mouth—or you'd swallow all the blackflies in the park. You squealed your tires and kicked up dust in his face as you gunned the accelerator. I knew right then and there that you guys had a thing for each other."

"How did you know that?" Karly crossed her arms. "That doesn't make sense."

Maya shrugged. "I just knew."

"Did you also know that one day I'd become a Christian?"

A sharp intake of her Matron of Honour's breath was followed by hugs and tears. "I'm so happy."

"You're not allowed to cry. It's my wedding day."

"I'm sorry. Let's go. The full moon has just risen above the tree line." Maya swiped at a tear and gave her a gentle push.

In the blackness of midnight, Karly emerged from the row of thick pines surrounding Shadow Lake. The brilliance of a magnificent full moon, glimmering across the lake, lit up the handsome silhouette of her future husband, standing on the shoreline. Her body trembled in anticipation of the life that awaited her from this moment on.

Despite her nervous jitters, an unbelievable joy settled over her. In just a few short weeks, her life had changed dramatically. The truth about Jesus Christ and his powerful love had become abundantly clear, and oh so very personal. Now she was getting married to the only man she'd ever loved, at a wilderness location.

As the pastor began to recite the wedding vows with a reading light clipped to his notes, Karly practically floated.

"I now pronounce you, Mr. and Mrs. White Pelican." He cleared his throat. "I mean Mr. and Mrs. Blake Fenton. Blake, you may now kiss your bird—I mean bride."

Karly heard Maya giggle beside her and Kerrick's deep laugh on the far side of Blake. She giggled along with them before losing herself in the warm, tender kisses of her husband.

"I told the pastor to say that," Henry bellowed from the front row of guests, after they ended the kiss. "I think I missed my calling in life. I should have been a comedian instead of a wilderness guide."

"Yes, my husband, the funny man. Now, I need your help with the preparations and that is no joke." Shawna pulled him playfully by the ear, inciting more laughter among the small crowd. Henry staggered along beside her, acting as though he was being dragged against his will, all the while grinning widely.

As the wedding guests disappeared inside Henry's home, Karly and Blake, arms wrapped around each other, stared out over the moonlit lake.

"I love you, Mrs. Karly Fenton," Blake whispered in her ear. "I can hardly believe we're together after those three difficult years apart. In all that time, did you know I couldn't date another person? No one came even close."

He kissed her neck and she thought she might just melt into a puddle right there on the shoreline. "I have loved you too, Blake Fenton, ever since that first day at the kiosk. A wise person told me recently that everything happens for a reason. The timing wasn't right before. Now it is. So, no regrets. Let's put the past behind us and start fresh. And you set the bar high too, Mr. Fenton. There was never anyone else for me."

Karly glanced over the shimmering lake and tried to blink away the tears that blurred her vision. She blinked again. "Blake, do you see that?" She pointed over the water.

Blake kissed her cheek. "I don't care how many white pelicans are out there."

Karly touched his chin and turned his face. "Blake, look."

"The cross," Blake whispered. "Henry told me about this. He's never seen it, but apparently, it's been appearing at random to the locals for centuries. I'm blown away. Actually, I'm gob-smacked."

"Hence the name Shadow Lake." Karly stared incredulously at the shadow of the enormous rippling cross in the centre of the moonlit lake.

Blake dropped to his knees suddenly and Karly felt a powerful desire to do the same. Blake wrapped his arm around her waist and pulled her close. "I can't help but think that this is a sign that God is with us, and is blessing our marriage."

"Me too." Karly's heart was filled to overflowing. God's love was deeper and wider than anything she could ever imagine. To think the God of the universe would care so much about them that he would grace them with his presence on their wedding day. She wasn't sure how long they remained, but it seemed only seconds before the cross disappeared when a cloud drifted in front of the moon.

Blake jumped to his feet and pulled her close again. The smell of his woodsy cologne delighted her senses. His next kiss made her knees weak. Then he grabbed her hand and pulled her toward the dock. "Come, my bride, our honeymoon begins now."

"Dare we sneak out early? Won't we insult Henry and his wife?" Karly giggled as she lifted her long dress and ran to keep up with him.

"Nah, he'll understand."

Karly climbed aboard, awkwardly stuffing her wedding dress inside the floatplane. "I feel so naughty. Are you sure we should skip out on our own wedding reception?"

Blake slipped in beside her. "I haven't been surer of anything in my life. Besides, Henry gave his blessing."

"His blessing? You mean to tell me that you pre-arranged this escape?"

His devious laugh ricocheted around the inside of his Cessna. "Just what am I going to do with you, Mr. White Pelican?"
"Love me, my pelican bride. Love me for the rest of my life."

PROLOGUE - STARRY LAKE
A Campground Mystery #3

Blending into the dark row of evergreens, Harrison observed the bride and groom skipping out on their reception. A jealous pang knifed him in the chest. Although he was happy for his friends, the pain was almost unbearable. The wounds were still fresh. He had loved Karly, but had to step aside, as her heart belonged to another. Why was he always too late? Would there ever be anyone for him?

And what was all this religious stuff? Was it for real? He didn't know Blake well, but Karly's newfound faith seemed genuine. Being the level-headed person that she was, he couldn't imagine her making a major decision like that without valid reason.

Harrison sighed. Coming to this wedding was a big mistake. With his body weak from the trauma and his spirits low, he could barely find the energy to stand upright. Harrison tensed when a small hand found its way into his palm.

Raven!

He withdrew his hand as though he'd touched a hot stove. "What are you doing?"

"I thought maybe we could start over and put the past behind us, my puppy dog."

"We've been through this before. It will never work. And, I'm not your puppy dog."

"Don't you find me attractive?" A delicate finger traced a path up his arm.

He snatched his hand away again. "You're attractive Raven, but there's more to a relationship than appearances."

"But we were happy once, weren't we? Until that two-timing, relationship-wrecker came along and stole you from me."

"That's not how it happened, and you shouldn't speak ill of the dead. You and I were having our own problems. Jessica just brought them to the surface."

"We were? What were they?" Raven stepped in front of him, blocking his view of the moonlit lake.

"Raven, I don't have the energy to re-hash things with you. Just trust me on this, we're through. Besides, your spiteful and vindictive actions the last few years have cemented my decision to end our engagement."

"My spiteful actions? You should consider yourself lucky that I want you back after your despicable behaviour," Raven snarled as she poked a finger at his chest.

"My behaviour?" He was aware his voice was raising several decibels, but he didn't care. There was no one around anyway.

"You practically drooled all over Jessica, and then Karly, and the whole community knew it. Now you look like a sad puppy who's lost and can't find his way home."

Harrison's anger suddenly deflated. The truth slammed into him like a ton of bricks—her words hitting home with an intensity he wasn't prepared for. For the next moment he remained silent, reeling from the impact.

"You're right Raven, I'm sad and lost. For the last few years, I've been travelling in circles, getting nowhere, trapped in a life that has done nothing but disappoint me. I don't know the answer for me, but one thing is clear. It isn't you."

"That was harsh," Raven huffed. "Fine, have it your way." She whirled her tiny body around with amazing speed, flew through the line of trees like a nighthawk in flight, and disappeared into the blackness. A blackness that was as dark and abysmal as his soul.

Dropping to his knees, every ounce of him spent, an audible sob left Harrison's mouth and echoed across the water. The despondency in his soul was crippling. He welcomed the stabbing discomfort in his side that his impulsive action had caused. Pain was a welcome distraction from his hellish downward tailspin.

He'd never in his life felt this low. Deeper and deeper he spiralled into the menacing chasm of gloom and desolation. Would the emptiness ever go away?

A searing hand touched his shoulder and a simultaneous bolt of heat sprinted through his body. The sensation was so ethereal that his senses reeled. What had just happened? He looked around. But no one was near.

A flicker of hope stirred deep within his chest. Faint at first, it grew in intensity until it propelled him to his feet. Something wonderful was happening and he couldn't help but embrace it. It was tangible and swallowing him whole.

There was something out there. It was more real than anything he'd ever experienced in his entire life. He twirled in a circle, his hands high in the air. Crazy—but he almost felt like dancing.

He gazed across the moonlit lake and blinked, unable to believe what he was seeing. It had to be a reflection from a structure nearby. But there was nothing around but dense bush. Nothing manmade that could account for its presence. And it hadn't been there a minute ago.

A shiver ran through him as he stared at the silhouette of a cross on the surface of the lake. With it came an inexplicable and bizarre desire to remove his sandals—even though the thought made no sense to him.

Barefoot and gazing at the cross, he couldn't help but feel, even with his infantile knowledge of God, that the place he was standing on was holy ground.

Coming soon:
Starry Lake

He took one last look across tranquil Lake Huron in the moonlight and sighed. For ten months, this truth trek to discover the meaning of life, had gotten him nowhere. If Harrison Somerville didn't have answers soon, he'd come to understand what he had expected all along. There was no God. No truth. No love.

Lily Martin is at her wit's end. Being a single parent of a ten-year old is challenging. But Jasmine is no ordinary child. Gifted with an extremely high IQ, an unquenchable thirst for scientific knowledge, and a penchant for mischief, most days Lily wrings her hands in frustration. But the mother-daughter camping trip soon brings much bigger problems.

For the oddest reason, Lily Martin and her spirited daughter, Jasmine keep dropping in Harrison's path. Literally. Harrison is charmed by the antics and mind-boggling intelligence of the spunky child. Before long, he feels compelled to protect this mother-daughter pair from Lily's belligerent ex and a strange man that begins appearing on trails and her campsite.

And wonder of all wonders, Lily has the answer he's been searching for—so she says.

An imminent weather warning brings his truth trek to a crisis, while his feelings for Lily confuse and overwhelm him.

Then the unimaginable happens.